Hi!

I'm six and my na[...]
am quite precocio[...]
someone my age. I think that she thinks I just talk
way too much. But someone has to pay attention and
ask the questions—even if they are impolite! Otherwise
my two little sisters and I would never know what was
going on around here. Since my daddy died two years
ago things have not always been easy, as my mommy
says.

But things are going to be better now that my uncle
Matt has moved back to Dallas. Because Uncle Matt is
big and strong and he always knows just what to do in
a 'mergency. He knows how to play games like freeze
tag and ring-around-the-rosy, too.

I told Mommy I want Uncle Matt to be our daddy
now. Mommy's cheeks turned all red. She said she
didn't think that was going to be possible. I told
Uncle Matt the same thing. He turned red, too. He
also said he didn't think it would be possible, either.

I don't know why not. Mommy is much happier
whenever Uncle Matt's around. And so are my sisters,
Betsy, who is four, and Nicole, who is almost three. So
what I want to know is…how can we talk them into it?

xxxxx's and ooooo's,

Caroline Donovan

Please address questions and book requests to: Harlequin Reader Service
U.S.: 3010 Walden Ave., P.O. Box 1325, Buffalo, NY 14269
Canadian: P.O. Box 609, Fort Erie, Ont. L2A 5X3

WESTERN *Lovers*™

CATHY GILLEN THACKER

FAMILY AFFAIR

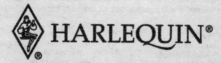

HARLEQUIN®

TORONTO • NEW YORK • LONDON
AMSTERDAM • PARIS • SYDNEY • HAMBURG
STOCKHOLM • ATHENS • TOKYO • MILAN • MADRID
PRAGUE • WARSAW • BUDAPEST • AUCKLAND

HARLEQUIN BOOKS
225 Duncan Mill Road, Don Mills,
Ontario, Canada M3B 3K9

ISBN 0-373-30178-2

FAMILY AFFAIR

Chapter One

"Matt, you know your father and I would never ask you to fly home if it wasn't important but we're really in a quandary right now. Frankly, I don't think we can manage without you."

Matt paused at his mother's low, anxious tone; he knew whatever the problem was had to be of vital consequence, otherwise his folks never would've asked him to get involved. And as for them asking him to fly home...well, he couldn't remember them ever asking him to fly home. He'd done so plenty of times, of course, but never specifically at their request. So whatever was up had to be of grave concern to them—and perhaps to him, as well. "What's the matter, Mom?" he asked with deliberate gentleness, holding himself motionless as he waited for her reply. At times, like now, when he heard the raw yearning in his mother's voice, he wished he lived closer to home. Close enough to drop by. Close enough to see them more than once or twice a year. Close enough to really help out and not just offer token, occasional assistance.

"It's Elyse. She's, well, you know how stubborn she can be."

At the mention of his former sister-in-law's name, Matt's breath stopped midway up his windpipe. "What's she done, Mom?" Matt asked tensely, trying to put a check on emotions that threatened to swiftly spiral out of control.

There was an uneasy silence on the other end of the line.

"Well, this is going to sound like I'm overreacting, and maybe I am, but she wants to put her house on the market," his mother stated finally and with great reservation.

A sigh of relief rippled through his tall frame. Matt flexed his shoulders and relaxed farther back into the custom leather swivel chair behind his desk. "So?" he asked a little too gruffly, turning around and staring out at the smoggy Los Angeles skyline. He sighed and rotated his shoulders in an effort to rid them of their tension. "Maybe it is about time she moved out of the house she and Nick shared." After all, his brother had been dead for over two years now. It was time Elyse got on with her life. Getting rid of that mansion of a house was probably a positive sign, not the negative omen his mother deemed it, all things considered.

"She's also thinking about going back to work. Renting an *apartment*. Putting the children in a day-care center."

"Whoa." Now Elyse *was* moving fast. Too fast for Matt's taste as well as his mother's. "When did all this happen?" He swiveled back around to face his cluttered desk.

"She just told me about it the other day. But I know she's been thinking about it for quite a while. She's been restless and a little on edge."

Feeling his blood pressure rise, Matt forced himself to calm down. Just because his mother was upset was no reason for him to jump the gun and assume the worst about Elyse. True, she had given him plenty of reason to mistrust her in the past. But that had been several years ago.

His mother continued, "I think something's wrong, Matthew. I think you need to talk to her. Get her to confide in you. Heaven knows your father and I have tried."

Matt was silent. "Mom, I understand how you feel, but I don't think I'm the one to interfere. Besides, I hardly think she'd confide in me."

"Why not? The two of you used to be companionable. At least before Nick died." Abigail paused. "Matt, what is it between the two of you? You've acted strangely toward Elyse since the funeral.''

He knew, and he'd tried so hard to behave normally. ''If I've acted…strangely toward Elyse, it's because I wasn't sure how to handle the situation, or her.''

There was a disbelieving silence on the other end of the phone line and then his mother's exasperated voice. ''She's a widow, Matt. All she needs is sympathy and a little tender loving care. Maybe some extra support from us.''

''Right. And you and Dad have given her that the past two years.''

''And you haven't,'' Abigail countered, matching her son's smooth, lawyerly tone. ''So what gives?'' she demanded unrelentingly, after another thought-provoking pause. ''Did the two of you have a quarrel? Maybe sometime after or during the time of the funeral? Did you say something rash or unkind to her? Are you afraid or embarrassed to face her? Is that it?''

Matt didn't want to face Elyse or see her, that was true. But as for the reasons for his distance from his sister-in-law, those Matt wouldn't share. Not with anyone. Not now. Not ever. ''No, we didn't fight,'' Matt answered his mother with more immediate patience than he felt. Although if he'd talked to Elyse for any length of time at all, Matt speculated, they probably would've fought like vicious hellcats, particularly if Elyse tried to defend what she'd done…not just to Nick, but to herself. Damn it, how could she have? he wondered. And how had he been so blind not to have seen? Abruptly he broke off his thoughts and forced himself to calm down. His recollections wouldn't help anyone at this point. He'd long ago decided the best thing he could do for all of them would be to forget what he had stumbled onto. He would forget.…

''Then what is it? Why do you avoid seeing her?'' Abigail persisted.

Matt scrambled for an answer that wouldn't betray any of his thoughts. ''We're just not very close anymore.'' If there was anything he was determined to do, it was to protect his parents from what he had discovered. They had been hurt enough by Nick's death.

"I'm aware of that. You haven't been back to Texas once in the two years since Nick died."

Only because Matt hadn't known how to face Elyse. And because he wasn't sure he could cover up his altered feelings toward her for any length of time. On the other hand, he knew there was nothing to be gained by confronting her now. The past was the past...or at least he was trying to believe that. He was *trying* to forget....

"I just don't understand why there's this distance between the two of you. It's almost as if you resent her sometimes."

Matt knew instinctively that there was only one way to end the conversation with his mother, and that was to lie outright. He hated having to deceive her. He also knew he had no choice and that she would be much happier in the long run if he did so—this once. "I'm sorry if it seems I'm avoiding Elyse. Maybe I have been. Maybe it's the grief, I don't know." He pressed the phone cord between his thumb and index finger.

"You don't resent her then?"

Matt inhaled deeply. He let out the air in a long, controlled breath, then braced himself for another lie. "No, I don't resent her. I just feel awkward around her." There, that much was true. As far as it went anyway.

"Darling, I understand. It's hard being around people who've been hurt, especially when you hurt too. But pretending we weren't all grief-stricken when Nick died won't help any of us. We need to share our feelings of sadness and then move on, start concentrating on the future, and not just our own. We need to help Elyse get on with her life, too."

"Well, it seems like Elyse is doing that," Matt observed gruffly, wishing it were easier for him to control his feelings toward his former sister-in-law.

"I don't think she's really being as prudent as she might. Which is where you come in, Matt—"

"Mom—"

"If not you, then who else? Darling, these are Nick's children we're talking about. Your nieces. Please. Come home and talk to Elyse, get her to slow down, or at least accept some detailed financial advice from you. I know you don't want to interfere and I respect that. But she needs help, Matt. She needs all our help."

Put that way, how could Matt refuse? "All right," he said finally, then gave a heavy sigh. He would do as his mother wished. He only hoped it wouldn't take long and that Elyse wouldn't try and corner him about what he was feeling toward her. Because if she did, it was almost certain he would lose his temper. All the ugliness he'd been withholding and ignoring would come spilling out and he'd expose her for the conniving witch she really was. And then...then where would his family be? Could Matt live with himself if he let that happen? Would Elyse suffer the humiliation stoically or would she flee, her children in tow? If she did, what would his parents think about it all? The facts were clear.... If the truth about Elyse ever came out, it would tear his family apart. And Matt couldn't let that happen. He wouldn't.

A DAY AND A HALF LATER, Matt Donovan stood in the driveway and stared in shocked silence at the sprawling Tudor-style home his brother had bought shortly before he died. The thick green grass was a good six inches high and peppered with clumps of crabgrass and dandelions. All the trees and shrubs of the heavily landscaped grounds were overgrown and in need of a good pruning. Only the windows of the house looked clean and well maintained. The rest of the place was an eyesore when compared to the other very well-tended homes on the shady, tree-lined street. Only a small portion of the cracked and peeling white trim had been painted. True, what trim had been turned a smooth slate gray was appealing. But the overall impression one got of the house was neglect.

How could Elyse have let it go like this, Matt wondered furiously. Hadn't she known how much the house had meant to Nick? Damn her anyway, Matt thought, filling with a fierce, relentless inner anger.

Just then the sound of a car motor rumbled behind him. Matt pivoted sharply to see Elyse pulling into the drive in her late model Suburban. She parked it next to his rented Ford sedan, then gazed at Matt.

For a second their eyes met and held. She paused for a long moment, her hands tightly gripping the wheel, her expression betraying a mixture of surprise and apprehension. Matt, too, stood absolutely still, caught in the living tableau. He'd thought his memories of her—both before and after he knew the truth—were vivid. He was wrong. His memories couldn't compare with the impact of seeing her in person. That she'd once been Nick's wife was temporarily forgotten; she was a woman, a beautiful, vibrant woman just a few years younger than himself. Though at the moment she looked incredibly vulnerable and ill-at-ease, like a woman caught up in the choice between a head-on collision or a fast head-over-heels plunge down a steep ravine. He knew how she felt as their glances held; he too was suffering from a multitude of conflicting feelings. For Matt there was a certain closeness, for the family they'd once been to one another. He also felt respect for the capable nurse and mother he knew Elyse to be. And then there was resentment for the poor wife she'd ultimately been to his older brother.

The truth of the matter was it had been a helluva long time since he'd seen her, been anywhere near her—months longer than he'd intended. And yet even after all the time that had passed, he still hadn't a clue what to say to her, how to react. It was going to be hard as hell keeping his emotions in check, his feelings about her and what she'd done secret, but somehow he would find a way to handle it. He had no choice. It was either that or risk involving his parents in something ugly and hurtful, and that he had no intention of doing.

Aware that she was still watching him curiously, almost testingly, he lifted his hand in an easy wave, forced a smile of good cheer he couldn't begin to experience. Although his first impulse was simply to cut short the small talk and greetings and demand to know what in the devil was going on, he suppressed it. *I won't get anywhere with her if I start off by haranguing her about the condition of the house,* he thought. He had to act civilly, work up to the subject slowly and with great tact.

Elyse collected herself long enough to wave back and jump lithely down from the driver's side of the eight-passenger vehicle. She swiftly circled around the front of the truck and opened the passenger door. Three little girls came tumbling out of the roomy blue interior. They were covered from head to toe with grass stains and smudges of dirt. The smallest had a tear in her overalls, and another a hole in her sneaker. Elyse looked equally worse for wear yet remarkably happy and content.

She was still as beautiful as ever, her aquamarine eyes just as wide and haunting, her dark hair just as thick and curly. The coffee-colored strands flowed to her shoulders in thick softly disheveled waves. She seemed just as single-minded and independent-natured as he remembered.

She'd also apparently recovered from the shock of his presence and was glad to see him. "Well, hello there you big lug," she began the conversation genially, walking over to give him a sisterly hug when he made no further effort to close the gap between them. It was an effort, but somehow his arms managed to close around her. Nonetheless, she seemed to sense his reluctance to be there at all.

Still smiling, she drew back, watching him with wary eyes, a faintly suspicious gaze. "Why didn't you call and let me know you were coming?" she asked softly, without rancor. She acted as if he'd never treated her coldly or turned his back on her after his brother had died. As if family were family regardless.

"The girls and I would've been here to greet you. I would've fixed a big supper, invited your folks; we would have made a real celebration out of it."

Matt had been afraid of that. Any big family scenes with Elyse front and center, he hadn't wanted. He shrugged as he moved back another step. He gestured awkwardly. "I didn't want to put you to any trouble."

She continued to watch him steadily. "It wouldn't have been any trouble."

Oh yes it would've, Matt silently disagreed. Even now he was half afraid to be near her. Afraid he would unexpectedly lose his temper, say something to inadvertently give away his darker thoughts about her. And that he didn't want. His parents had been hurt enough by Nick's death. They didn't need any more traumas in their lives. Which was why he didn't need to be here now. But he was; he'd have to handle it the same way he'd handled his initial attraction to her— by ignoring it, pretending it didn't exist. That had been hard as hell, of course. He'd known the first time Nick had brought Elyse home to meet the family that she was a very special woman. Beautiful, open, feisty, and independent— almost to a fault. But she had been engaged to his older brother Nick. And that had meant hands-off. So Matt had purposefully kept his distance from Elyse, being careful to talk to her only in the most superficial, aloof manner at first. Later she'd become family to him.

He, too, had married. It had been easier then to be around her, but the awareness of her as a woman had lingered. That attraction had angered and annoyed Matt because, although he never would have acted on it or even hinted at it, he still had felt guilty for thinking of Elyse that way...if only subliminally.

And now he was supposed to act like some sort of financial manager and personal advisor to her. He would have to be close to her, physically close. And that he didn't want, because knowing all he did about her now—and he'd been disillusioned plenty before Nick's death—he'd still wanted her. Still he couldn't stop thinking of her as an attractive, sensual, very desirable woman....

She watched him a moment longer, apparently deciding on an equally deceptive everything's-fine course. Then she grinned disarmingly and gestured toward her slightly disheveled state and paint-splattered jeans. "You can probably tell I've been painting the exterior of the house. Just started today as a matter of fact."

It didn't look like she'd gotten very far, Matt criticized unconsciously.

Seeming to read his thoughts, Elyse grinned, unoffended, "The girls had plans for me, too, though. Big plans. We were out at the park, enjoying the spring weather."

"Mommy won't be able to take us so much when she starts back to work," a small voice piped up beside them.

Matt looked into the upturned faces of three healthy, lively little girls. He knew from his parents their ages—three, four, and six. He felt his heart melt a little more as he took in their gentle smiles and cheerful personalities.

"Oh, we'll go to the park, honey, I promise, but just not as often." She turned to Matt and gestured expansively toward the house. "Come on inside. I'll get you something to drink and then after I've gotten the girls settled, we can sit down and catch up on all the news." Matt nodded agreeably. Again, he didn't want to be here but as long as he was, he resolved to make the best of it.

Together they entered the house. To his surprise, after seeing the run-down exterior, the interior of her home was spotless. But then Elyse always had been a good housekeeper, he reflected, reluctantly remembering a few of his former sister-in-law's good points. He supposed the neglect of the exterior was just due to not having a man around the house. So maybe, given the circumstances, it wasn't surprising she would want to sell the house. She obviously couldn't keep up with it and the three lively girls. Girls that looked more like Elyse every day, with their soft dark hair, their creamy skin, and big aquamarine eyes.

"Are you my Uncle Matt?" Caroline asked as soon as her mother had slipped off into the kitchen.

Matt turned to confront Caroline. The oldest of Nick's daughters, she was also remarkably precocious and self-possessed.

Abruptly Matt realized that in the flurry of greeting each other, neither Elyse nor he had reintroduced Matt to her daughters. It had been so long they probably didn't know who he was, except they seemed to have the vague idea he was somehow connected with the family. He found himself smiling, despite the worried direction of his thoughts. "Yes, I'm Uncle Matt," he answered amiably. He got down on bended knee so they would be closer to eye level and solemnly shook her hand. "And you're Caroline," he noted affectionately, remembering the happier times she apparently didn't. Times he had rocked her on his knee. Times he had held and rocked all of Nick's daughters during one of his visits home.

"Yes, I am. I haven't seen you for a long time. Good thing Mommy has pictures of you. How come you never come to see us?"

Out of the mouths of babes, Matt thought, with a wry smile. "Because I live in California," he explained patiently. And it hadn't been wise, not when he felt the way he did about Elyse—so confused and angry…and betrayed somehow…as if by doing what she'd done she'd betrayed not just Nick but all of them, his entire family.

"Don't you miss being here with Grandma and Grandpa?" she asked.

Again, Matt found himself smiling. "Yes, sometimes I do."

"Caroline, I think you've asked Uncle Matt enough questions for now," Elyse cut in, returning with a cold drink for Matt. "And now it's time for baths, everyone." She was answered by a chorus of groans. With the firmness of a marine drill sergeant, Elyse pointed cheerfully to the stairs. "Upstairs, girls, pronto. You can see Uncle Matt again when you're all clean."

The girls took off as directed and Elyse turned to Matt. She leaned forward and impulsively gave him another hug, this one obviously meant to mend fences. "It's good to see you again, Matt," she confessed in a soft honest timbre. "I know we haven't talked much lately but I've missed seeing you."

Matt gave no answer, no similar confession. The truth was he would have preferred to avoid the impromptu embrace altogether, but there was no way he could get around it without raising even more suspicions about his "quirky" behavior of late. Holding her in his arms, he felt a lingering familial affection for her, more common than the newfound distrust. It would be so easy to be with her, he thought, if only he could just forget. But even as the thought came to him, so did the memories, and with that came a dislike and distrust of her that was stronger than any affection he had ever felt for her. Everything he had ever known or thought he knew about her had been a lie. She'd hurt his brother and that he couldn't forgive.

Slowly, carefully he extricated himself from her arms.

He was freed from her touch not a moment too soon; it was all he could do to suppress a grimace. He stepped back as she did and met her eyes, trying with every fiber of his being to make his expression totally blank, totally unreadable.

From the bewildered expression on Elyse's face, he knew he had succeeded. She knew he was put off by her and that she didn't know why. Which was the way he wanted it.

She swallowed hard, the hurt bright and vibrant in her eyes.

She motioned weakly toward the stairs and the sounds of giggling and laughter emanating from the second floor. "I—uh, I've got to go up and get the girls' baths. You make yourself at home, Matt. All right?"

"Sure." He nodded affably but maintained an emotional distance from her.

She gave him a last wary glance before forcing a tremulously bright smile. He thought but couldn't be sure he saw a suspicious moistness shimmering in her eyes; he knew then he had hurt her badly by his continuing coldness. He felt a moment's stab of guilt. After all, what had she ever done to him directly to deserve this icy treatment? *But he had to stop letting her get to him.* She no more deserved a place in their family than any other Judas. He had nothing to feel guilty about.

Elyse started up the stairs. In her absence, Matt made himself at home and looked around a little more. Although the family room was as he remembered, the formal living room and dining room were still unfurnished. Much of the first floor had been repainted, new wallpaper hung. He knew instinctively that the light, sunny colors had been selected by Elyse rather than an interior decorator. Judging by what she'd already told him about her painting the home's exterior, he supposed she'd done much of the work on the interior herself—with excellent results.

Footsteps sounded on the stairs, cutting off his thoughts. Nick turned to see Caroline leading the way into the family room. Elyse followed. She had Betsy and Nicole by the hand. In contrast to their earlier dishabille, all three girls were now scrubbed and clean, their dark hair hanging in wet curls around their heads. They wore soft and snugly flannel nightgowns and smelled of baby shampoo and talcum powder. Aware that Elyse was watching him with all the wariness of a mother bear, Matt said a gentle, personal hello to his two other nieces. He'd missed them and was genuinely anxious to get to know them again. Painstakingly he drew them into softly voiced conversation.

"You look like a picture of Daddy," Betsy said finally, after many efforts on Matt's part to get her to say more than a simple yes or no to him.

"Only bigger," Caroline added self-importantly. Not

about to be outdone by her middle sister, she sidled up to pat Matt's bent knee testingly with her tiny palm.

"You're right. I am bigger than your Daddy. I always was, from seventh grade on," Matt agreed gently. It was an irony that Nick, five years older, never quite got over.

"Mommy said you're a lawyer," Caroline added.

"That's right." Matt met her eyes. "And that's why I'm here. I have something to discuss with your mother." He looked up at Elyse, communicating silently to her that he needed to talk to her alone.

Elyse met Matt's eyes. Although he was still welcome there—because he was family he always would be—she now had her guard up. He was reminded of the few tentative phone calls she'd made to him after Nick's death. He'd talked to her, but he hadn't answered the yearning need for comfort in her voice. He hadn't ever called her back. Sensing the barriers that had sprung up for inexplicable reasons, she'd finally stopped trying to communicate with him at all, except to write an occasional letter about the girls' progress or to send him a picture of Nick's daughters. Obviously she'd felt his arrival there signaled an end to all that; hence her happiness. Now that she knew the truth, that everything was still the same between them—oddly distant on an emotional level—she too was exercising more reserve.

"I'm going to get them some milk, read them a story and then tuck them in," she said quietly, a slight edge to her normally cheerful voice.

Again he felt a stab of guilt. If he hadn't found out the truth about her shortly before Nick died, he never would have treated her badly. A bit aloofly perhaps, but never badly. And regardless of the way he felt about Elyse, he had missed seeing the girls much more than he realized.

He decided his talk with Elyse could wait.

"Mind if I help? It's been so long since I've seen the girls. I'm amazed at the changes in all of them."

Elyse hesitated. "I want them to get to know you."

"I want that, too."

He gave her no chance to change her mind. For the next hour and a half, Elyse and Matt simply played with the girls. They read stories and talked and, together, built a huge block tower. Finally, long minutes later, fatigue overtook the children and Elyse put them to bed.

"You said you wanted to talk to me?" Elyse said quietly when she joined him again.

Matt couldn't help but notice she had freshened up while she'd been upstairs. Earlier, when she'd stepped out of the car in jeans and a white sweatshirt, she'd looked flushed, sandy and exhausted. She still was flushed. But the surface exhaustion had faded and her hair and make-up had been repaired. She looked fresh and glowing and quite capable of handling all her own affairs.

She was a lithe five-seven to his six-foot-one. Her shoulder-length hair, rich and dark, was brushed smoothly away from her face, or as smoothly as the enviably thick, naturally curly strands would permit. Classically beautiful and heart-shaped, her face was blessed with perfectly proportioned features. A full sensual mouth. The straight long nose. The wide aquamarine eyes over her high, pronounced cheek-bones. She had dark eyelashes and even darker brows. She was not only beautiful but hauntingly elegant, refined. It was easy to see how Nick had fallen in love with her. Not so easy to see why she had betrayed him.

Elyse continued to look at him expectantly, waiting for him to begin.

"My mother called me a few days ago. She's concerned about all the changes you're making in your life."

She tucked her hands in the roomy pockets of her pleated jeans. "I know." She didn't appreciate Matt challenging her, too.

Doggedly he continued, "She thinks you're acting rashly."

She pressed her lips together firmly. "I'm not changing my mind about putting the house on the market."

From the definitive way she spoke, it was clear that she'd

already been over the subject with his parents several times. For a moment Matt sympathized with her; he knew how aggravatingly persistent his mother could be when she thought someone in the family was in danger of any kind. "I'm not here to argue that," he said quietly. "It's obvious the house is too much for you to keep up."

"So you have no objections to me selling?" Elyse surveyed Matt testingly.

"None. I do think you ought to reconsider going back to work full-time."

At that, she was quiet for an ominously long moment. She ran a hand restlessly through her dark hair and turned so she wouldn't have to face Matt directly. "I haven't told your parents because I didn't want to worry them, but when it comes to going back to work, I don't have a choice. Not any longer. I've used up as much of the insurance money as I dared, just trying to keep up the payments and make the necessary repairs to the house."

Suddenly everything fell into place for Matt. He knew why the yard was a mess, the house trim only half painted, and why she hadn't hired anyone to maintain either. He could see now how much she'd been struggling. He was irritated with himself for not checking into her financial situation sooner, for not even attempting to discern if she had any problems on that score. Knowing how much money Nick had made at the time of his death, Matt had just assumed she would be fine. "Why didn't you sell the house sooner if money was a problem?" he asked quietly.

"I wanted to sell it immediately but I couldn't, not right away, not without losing a great deal of money on it. Even now, after having lived in it for two more years, I won't stand to make very much of a profit, but at least I won't lose money."

"I see." Matt was quiet, mulling over all she had said. "I thought Nick left you with plenty of insurance money. The last time I talked to him about it, which was several years before he died, he had intended to upgrade the policy he'd gotten right out of medical school and take out at least half a million in insurance, as protection for you and the girls. More if he could swing it.'' And Elyse had intimated to his parents, at least at the time of the funeral, that they needn't worry about her on that score, that she and the girls would be fine. He could only guess she hadn't known then exactly what her circumstances were and once she'd found out, she hadn't wanted to burden anyone else. Not if she could sort out the problems herself. Had that been the real reason she'd called him after Nick's death? he wondered. Had she wanted to talk to him about her financial problems but, because of his reserve, his subtly expressed disinterest, been unable to ask for help? If that were the case... He felt an especially deep stab of guilt.

A fleeting look of sadness and remorse crossed her face as Elyse explained the insurance. "Nick never got around to upgrading his policy. I guess he thought he had plenty of time; I know he always thought himself invulnerable."

Matt was silent, studying the worry he saw in her face, and the pain. No matter what else had happened, she had loved his brother—once anyway. But as for later, how could she have loved him and still have deceived him—apparently with no remorse? If only his feelings toward her weren't so mixed, so filled with anger one minute, so filled with compassion and pity the next. For he, too, had lost a spouse; he knew what a dark, lonely time inevitably followed. He knew how hard it was to adjust, although she'd had her children for comfort. When Holly had died, he'd had no one.

Realizing how much time had elapsed since Nick's death and the probable damage that had been done to his brother's small estate by Elyse's stubborn mishandling of the situation, her desire to go it alone, he became irritated once again. "Why didn't you tell me you needed financial help?" he asked, a bit more gruffly than he'd intended.

She stared at him as if he were a stranger. Recovering, she shrugged noncommittally. "I thought about it. Eventually, I decided not to. I didn't think it was your problem.

And then, too, you were so far away...." Not just in physical distance, her tone implied, but also emotionally.

He felt a moment's guilt at that. He'd deliberately made himself emotionally inaccessible to her since Nick had died—more so than before, even. At the time he'd felt he'd been doing what was best, just keeping quiet, at great cost to himself. But he saw now by not helping her, not even trying, he'd let his brother down in a way he hadn't expected, neglected his familial duty...especially to his nieces.

"Why haven't you explained this to my parents?" he asked quietly. If she had, she would have spared them much worry. And they would have come to him sooner; he could've helped.

"Abigail and Peter are wonderful people and I love them dearly. But you know as well as I do that they have a limited retirement income. If they'd known, they would have insisted on giving me every cent they had. I couldn't allow that. Not when they've already done so much for me at their expense."

Matt knew what Elyse meant. Before Nick had died, his parents had entertained plans to travel extensively. In fact it had been a lifelong dream of theirs. After Nick had died, all that had changed. With the exception of three brief trips out west, to see Matt, they hadn't gone anywhere else. Matt guessed, as apparently did Elyse, that they stayed in the Dallas area to be near their daughter-in-law in case she ever needed help. Or family.

"I'm sorry I wasn't here for you earlier," he admitted grudgingly at last.

She stared at him in bewilderment, taking exception to his tone. Charity was something she would never accept. Ditto for family handouts. "Matt, as I said, it's really not your problem."

There was a time when Matt would've agreed. Not anymore. Now that he'd seen how much she was struggling, he couldn't turn his back on her. He couldn't turn his back on

his brother's children. Like it or not, they were in this together for the duration.

"Yes, it is my problem," he said firmly, ignoring her
contentious look and tone. This trouble was all his!

"Why?" She planted both hands on her hips and faced
him, clearly exasperated with his interference.

Matt refused to answer immediately; he had no intention
of arguing with her. Nor would he plead or cajole. He was
there, he would help, that was it. And the sooner she understood and accepted that the better. "Because I'm making
it my problem," he said levelly, advancing another pur-
poseful step. He would do this for his mother, for his whole
family. "Now, where do you want to start?"

Chapter Two

With the morning light streaming in around her, Elyse stacked boxes to one side of the attic with swift, economical motions, mechanically lifting box after box. Once she had finished, she plugged in the vacuum and switched it on. The low-pitched motor rumbling in the background, she began the arduous chore of picking up the thick gray dust. Over and over, she pushed the vacuum swiftly across the scuffed wooden floor until her heart was racing, her breath coming in erratic pants and sweat was pouring down into her eyes. The physical activity, as intense and almost punishing as it was, felt good to her. It was numbing, even soothing. While she labored physically, she didn't have to think....

Only when every inch of grime was gone did she switch the vacuum off and sit down. By then her legs and arms were trembling with exhaustion. She was inexplicably, unusually close to tears, full of a sense of loss...and long buried memories of Nick. Was it Matt's being there again that had triggered her grief and confusion? She wondered. Was she seeing something similar in the set of their broad shoulders, their quick, ready smiles, their easy grace and low gentle baritones? Or was it simply long suppressed loss coming to the fore, the fact she'd had to be strong for so long?

Like it or not, she wanted to lean on Matt. And at the same time she was unsure of him, of the way he felt toward her—more so than she had ever been or thought she would be.

He'd been back a day and a half now. A simple day and a half! And Elyse still didn't know what to make of him or his unexpected chivalry, although she suspected strongly that Abigail had a lot to do with Matt's sudden appearance in Dallas, his offer to help her, his insistence that she accept. As for the rest? Face it, she told herself, the man was as moody as it was possible for a person to be. One minute he seemed determined to go all out to help her, the next moment he acted as if he couldn't stand the sight of her. But there was no doubting Matt meant it when he said he intended to help her get the house ready to sell and her finances in order. By early Tuesday morning, he had set up appointments with prospective realtors for later in the week, arranged for painters to finish the exterior work on the house, and enlisted his parents to care for Elyse's children at their home while the work was going on. He had hired a crew of professional landscapers to cut the grass and trim the shrubs and trees. Not averse to getting his hands dirty, he then personally took over the chore of cleaning out the garage while Elyse began sorting the clutter in the attic.

Not that his take-charge attitude had been any surprise. Matt had always been a take-charge sort of person. In fact he liked nothing better than getting down to business because it was there his real strength and power and sense of himself emerged. It was fascinating to Elyse, watching Matt skillfully negotiate and give orders and solve problems. And it was frightening, too. It would be far too easy for her to let someone like Matt come into her life and simply take over, remove the burden of being a single parent from her shoulders, for even a while.

The simple truth of the matter was she missed being married. And simultaneously, she never wanted to be married again....

Having regained her breath, Elyse began sorting through a stack of old linens and another box of curtains that were both threadbare and hopelessly out of date. While she worked, she thought about her brother-in-law and the changes the years had wrought. Physically he hadn't changed much. He was still as rugged looking as ever. His eyes were a smoky, smouldering blue. There wasn't a hint of ash or red in his dark brown hair. His hair was cut in a blow-dried, unabashedly sexy style—longish in the back so it fell in one soft straight layer to curl against the bottom of his collar. His bangs brushed down onto his forehead to rest a half an inch above his equally dark brows.

The years had been kind to him physically. Just looking at him, it was easy to drift back in time, to remember. When she had first met Matt he'd been a freewheeling bachelor— quick to laugh or throw a party. His celebrations had been legendary, his list of women long. At first she'd thought he was competing with his older brother who'd had his own share of sexual exploits in his bachelor days. Later she'd decided he was simply enjoying the chase.

Not that he'd been that warm toward her. No, initially he'd been very abrupt—always watching her from a distance, quick with a superficial quip or remark when approached. But when it had come to any real conversation, giving her any true sense of himself, she might as well've been trying to wring friendship out of a split-rail fence. He just didn't give anything in return and eventually she'd given up.

Gradually, as the years went by, that had changed. Or started to. In retrospect it seemed whenever she had begun to get close to Matt, to really get to know him, he had frozen up, withdrawn. And maybe, truth be told, that was just as well. She'd spent entirely too much time trying to understand him. She'd been too interested in what made Matt tick, too intrigued with what lay behind the polished facade. Part of it was sympathy for Matt, pure and simple. As Nick's wife she knew what it was to live in Nick's shadow. Maybe it was because Nick was the oldest, maybe it was the exciting nature of his profession, but Nick had always commanded the most attention from Abigail and Peter. Matt had never seemed to let it bother him; in fact in many ways Elyse knew Matt had idolized his older brother. And yet she sensed beneath his devil-may-care charm that Matt had hungered for some real one-on-one love and attention. Which was what had made his marriage to Holly such a mystery to Elyse. Holly had been beautiful and elusive, the kind of woman men loved to chase and capture. But she'd never struck Elyse as a very giving sort of woman, rather a vulnerable chameleon who could wring whatever she needed and wanted from a man.

And Matt had loved her—loved her intensely. He'd been devastated by her death and, as Elyse had come to expect, remarkably closed-mouthed. The only area in which he'd been continuously warm was in his relationship with his parents and, to some extent, her daughters. That explained, Elyse supposed, why he was getting so involved in her life now.

A powerful and tender man, he had always been there for Nick. So, after Nick's death, she had naturally assumed he would be there for her. It hadn't happened. Instead, in some strange way, Matt had seemed almost angry with Elyse, almost...disillusioned. Full of her own guilt, her own wishes she'd done otherwise, Elyse hadn't questioned Matt very deeply. When he'd said there was nothing wrong, she'd accepted his claim at face value, chalked it up to the depression they all felt. But now she wondered if she had been wrong not to press Matt about his odd attitude toward her. And she wondered if she had, if anything would've changed.

Maybe just being around Nick's widow, his family, was painful to Matt. Or perhaps—although it was a less appealing thought—he'd just lost interest in her and girls. Certainly since Nick's death, he hadn't seemed to care much about Elyse, one way or the other. Thinking back, she realized he'd never written or called to see how she was doing, never inquired directly about the girls, although he *had* kept in regular, close contact with his parents. Undoubtedly he knew all of her news through them without ever talking to Elyse. Still, to have him show up again now, unannounced, ready and eager to help her—it had been a shock. She hadn't known whether to trust him. Did he really want to help or was he being pushed into it?

Since they'd been working on the house, he'd been the model co-worker, not bossing her around directly, not afraid to make suggestions. Basically he did his work and she did hers, and if they met up with one another in the process fine, if they didn't fine. Still, there were times when he looked at her now—when he thought she wasn't looking at him—and he seemed to dislike her intensely, for no reason at all! More puzzling yet, she sensed he was wrestling with something that was bothering him greatly. He wouldn't talk about it; she didn't feel comfortable enough with him anymore to ask what was troubling him. She did wonder about it though. She wondered why he didn't seem to want to touch her anymore, and that, too, was very strange. In the past he'd always been at least accepting of a quick sisterly hug, even though she rarely saw him more than once or twice a year, if that. Now he seemed determined to keep his physical distance. As always, when confronted with the change in his attitude toward her, she felt hurt and bewildered. She wondered what she had done to him.

Of course it was highly possible she hadn't done anything at all, she theorized calmly. Maybe she wasn't bugging him at all! Maybe it was just being back in Dallas again after an absence of two long years that was affecting him. After all the last time he'd been home to see his folks, he'd also had to attend his brother's funeral. Maybe it was hard on him, seeing Nick's old house...without Nick. Seeing the changes. Maybe just being there in the house brought back the trauma of Nick's death to Matt, made him remember how much they had all ached with the loss.

Although Matt hadn't contacted her personally in the ensuing two years, he had always remembered the girls with gifts at Christmas and on their birthdays. Surely that counted for something. Probably she was just imagining the changes in his behavior, making more out of his preoccupation than she should. She did know he had been extraordinarily busy at work, weathering not just a heavy work load but also a scandal of some sort in the L.A. law firm where he worked.

Determinedly pushing her suspicions from her mind, Elyse busied herself sorting belongings into piles destined for charity, for saving, and for the trash.

As long minutes passed, she found boxes of old baby clothes, a bassinet, a carton of white uniforms and nurse's shoes she could use, the flute she hadn't played in years. Nick had dozens of medical books and journals; they were all in the attic along with the files from his office. There was an old rocking chair from the first days of her marriage that neither Nick nor Elyse had ever had the heart to throw out, and a favorite but much worn and washed bathrobe from long ago. Feeling unaccountably sentimental at her find, Elyse cradled the garment in her hands. There were holes in it and it was thick with dust, yet she could still remember the joy he'd expressed that first Christmas when she'd given it to him. Eyes sparkling, he'd jumped up to try it on immediately, then had worn it all morning over his clothes. Later, after they'd made love, he'd worn it again and every night thereafter.

Smiling reminiscently, Elyse sat down on a cushioned footstool, her thoughts turning to the first days of her marriage and to the joy she had felt then being Nick's wife. They had been gloriously happy when he was just beginning his life as a pediatric surgeon at University Hospital. Their schedules had both been hectic, as she'd been a nurse in ICU, but they'd always managed to find time to be together, and they'd cherished every moment they'd had. Eventually, though, their lives had changed. He'd wanted a family; she had, too. And within a year of the time they'd started trying, she became pregnant with their first child.

Although she loved her work, she gladly stopped working when Caroline was born. She'd been content to stay home and take care of her baby. Nick wasn't home much to help but she accepted that.

She had tried her hardest to be a good wife to him.

They had both been deliriously happy when their other two daughters had been born. And yet there had been times in between, she remembered reluctantly, when he hadn't seemed to want to talk to her, times when he had shut her out deliberately. At first, angry and hurt by his alienation of her, it had been easy enough for her to ignore his moodiness. Always his aloofness would pass and they'd go back to being close. She hadn't liked his need for occasional reclusion, but she had accepted it. Later, however, his times of solitude had dragged on, gotten more complex, more soul-shattering. And she'd been helpless to put an end to them.

Had he lived, she might have asked him to seek counseling, to find a better way to deal with the constant life-and-death stress of his work. She'd wanted to strengthen their marriage, to recapture their earlier closeness, to put an end to the sometimes negative, sometimes indifferent feelings he occasionally harbored about her.

But she'd never had the chance, and now all she was left with were questions. Questions about the stress he'd suffered at the end of his life.

It bothered her that he hadn't been able to talk to her in any detail about the illness-invoking pressures he apparently felt. And yet to this day she still didn't know what she could have done to have made his life easier, to have eased the tremendous—but undiscussed—stress he'd been under at the time he died.

Had she been wrong to give Nick the space she felt he needed, when he'd first begun showing signs of extreme overwork that last fateful year? And even more wrong later, when she'd tried, too late, to get involved, to find out what was bothering him so? Tears stung her eyes and she brushed them away.

She had to admit she would probably never know. And that although she'd gotten over the loss of her husband, she would never get over the way she had failed him, the way he had shut her out right up until the very night he died.

Discouragement rounded her shoulders, depression touched her soul. She had loved him and wanted to help; and he had consistently refused to let her. Or to talk to someone else who could. Why? Why had he shut her out? What more could she have done to help? What was she not seeing then and now?

MATT PAUSED at the head of the attic stairs. His gaze trained unerringly on Elyse. He'd been calling her; she hadn't answered. Looking at her, he knew why.

She'd been crying. Obviously still upset and oblivious to his presence, she was sitting on top of an old chest, Nick's old robe draped in her hands. She had a sad yearning look on her face and was still lost in her memories. He understood and empathized with her feelings of loss and grief, her rage at the unfairness of her husband's death. There were times when he still missed his brother acutely and mourned the fact he would never see or speak with Nick again. At least not on this earth.

That alone bonded him to her. The impulse to go to her, to take her in his arms and just comfort her was very strong. But he couldn't do that, not knowing what she'd done to Nick, not knowing how attracted he still was to her. No, whatever she was facing, Matt decided finally, as he turned and retreated silently down the stairs, she'd have to deal with alone.

It wasn't what Nick would've wanted for her. It was the way it had to be.

Two hours later Matt picked up their lunch from a sandwich shop around the corner. Elyse, having recovered from her crying jag—of which she'd judiciously made no mention—decided to sit outside under the live oak trees and admire the freshly painted exterior of the house. Matt, also preferring the outdoors, sat a short distance away from her.

For long moments they ate without speaking. Eventually

Matt followed her glance. "Like what the painters have done so far?" he asked conversationally, keeping his diffident gaze trained on the newly gleaming trim beneath the roofline.

"Oh, yes." Elyse smiled, glancing up at the facade of the house. She didn't have to pretend her pleasure about that. In a few short hours, the professionals Matt had hired had managed to do what it would have taken her weeks to accomplish. Her home now looked newer, more contemporary somehow, and the new slate-gray color of the trim also looked good with the darker black tiles of the roof. "I didn't realize how much that chore was weighing on me," she confessed softly at length. "It's nice to have it done for me, to have you here, helping arrange and supervise everything." She did wish he'd talk to her more freely, help try and recapture some of the almost social affability they'd shared in the past.

His eyes darkened but there was no other discernible change in his expression. "I'm glad I could help," he said in a low, clipped voice.

She wondered what was bothering him and yet she sensed if she asked him what it was he would not only refuse to disclose the nature of his troubling thoughts but would deny their existence as well. "You haven't talked much about California," Elyse commented quietly moments later when Matt had made no move to further their conversation.

Matt shrugged, retaining his implacable calm. Yet when he looked at her it was with weary, brooding eyes. "If I haven't talked much about my life there, it's because there's not much to tell."

She studied him openly, wondering if he was still burying himself in his work as he had after his wife, Holly's, death. "Your work is going well?" Her voice was careful, the question in it gentle but wary.

He nodded, his jaw tightening. "I've got all I can handle."

"Are you still in family law?" she asked.

"Mmmhmm."

Although he was answering her questions readily enough, he made no attempt to be gregarious. She wondered again at his distance, then pushed her uneasiness aside. She was making too much of his moodiness, that was all. Maybe she just needed to draw him out, get him to relax, lose that strangely haunted look.

"Enjoying it?" Because he wasn't watching her, it was easy to keep surveying him—the rugged angular lines of his face, the tousled dark hair, the tiredness she saw around his steely blue eyes. He would always be handsome, she thought dispassionately. Probably had droves of women after him, not that he ever seemed to really notice. No, he'd been a one-woman man and all his love had been bestowed on the sensational-looking film actress he had married.

He turned to her, his penetrating gaze searing straight into her soul. His voice was low, matter of fact, yet so oddly taunting it made the pulse in her throat work overtime. "I enjoy everything about family law—except for the divorces. Some of them get too damn messy for my taste." He finished his sandwich, wadded up the foil and tossed the trash into the white bag they'd reserved for trash.

Her whole body tense, she drew in a slow breath. She could understand his dislike of divorce law. Domestic strife was never easily endured; in cases of divorce it was often known to be unbearable. Not knowing what else to say but wanting the conversation to take a more amiable turn, she moved on, asking the first thing that came into her mind.

"Still playing racquetball and golf?"

He gave his head an affirmative shake, offered nothing more. Yet she plodded on anyway. "Dating anyone special?" *There. If any question was bound to elicit a reaction…a genuine emotional reaction, that was it.*

Matt shot her a narrow sidelong glance, as if he could hardly believe she'd had the temerity to ask such a thing. "No. I'm not seeing anyone seriously," he said dryly, after a long suffering pause. Another second passed. Having had some success goading something out of him, she was about to hit him with another provoking question.

Realizing this, he gave her a deadpan look with just a hint of sarcasm around the edges. ''You know, Elyse, you and my mother ought to get together. You ask a lot of the same questions. You could save yourself some time just comparing answers.''

This was the old Matt, teasing her but giving very little of himself away. ''Very funny,'' she retorted, smiling.

Slowly, his expression sobered. He fingered a blade of grass with unusual concentration. ''What about you?'' he asked casually, his tone dropping to an unexpectedly probing timbre. ''Seeing anyone?''

Again, she tensed. She was conscious suddenly that he had the capacity to hurt her, that she cared what he thought about her—and that on some level he seemed to be disapproving. ''I go out from time to time but there's no one special in my life,'' she admitted honestly after a moment.

Their eyes met, held. Matt had no particular expression on his face. Again he seemed oddly determined to keep her at arm's length. She plucked at the grass in frustration. She didn't like this cat and mouse game they seemed to be playing. It had always been there in the past—but it had never been this acute.

Around them bees buzzed lazily in the soft spring air. The scent of new-mown grass hung in the air. It was a lazy spring afternoon. Why, then, couldn't she relax? Why did she feel so watched, so hunted? As if Matt were secretly on the warpath, after her? Especially when, to this day, they'd never once had words or argued about anything openly?

Inexplicably Elyse felt her frustration with Matt's moody behavior mount to an unbearable level. She needed—wanted—to be close to Matt. She needed to feel closer to all her family and friends. But unless Matt opened up to her more or tried to let them become more intimately acquainted, there was little hope it would happen. No, he'd go back to California. She'd seldom hear from him. And that would be it.

"By the way—" Matt straightened lazily and began cleaning up the clutter from their meal. "—I meant to tell you that a representative from University Hospital called my folks' house last night. They want to talk to us about Nick."

Elyse slowly crumpled her napkin, her mind centering once again on the present. Aware that Matt was staring at her curiously, she asked quietly, "Did they say what it was about?"

Matt shook his head. "They wouldn't tell me anything specific. Only that it's about Nick, his work and concerns our whole family. At any rate they've invited us to dinner. Tomorrow evening, at the Mansion on Turtle Creek. You'll be able to go won't you?" He seemed to expect she would.

Elyse hesitated. She had an idea what the meeting was about, if the rumors about a possible memorial that had been flying around lately were correct, and she didn't like it at all. She was trying to put the past behind her, not immerse herself in remembered grief and the aching sensation of loss once again. A memorial for Nick was a pressure she didn't need. Furthermore, she'd never liked being in the limelight. As Nick's widow she would undoubtedly find herself at center stage. And being scrutinized by the press would be hard on her children; it might even resurrect and deepen their grief. Yet knowing how much being honored would have meant to Nick, she felt she couldn't refuse to help out or, at the very least, listen carefully to the hospital's plans. She owed Nick that much.

She looked up to find Matt watching her. Again she had the sensation of being scrutinized, of being analyzed; she didn't like it. "Of course I'll go," she said quietly, forcing a smile. "I'll see about getting a sitter."

As MATT HAD HOPED, the hospital was planning to honor Nick, not with just a plaque on the wall and a ceremony, as he had first assumed, but in what was beginning to look like a very big way. Matt sat back in his chair, taking it all in, as the director and several high-ranking hospital officials continued to outline plans for press conferences, ground-breaking ceremonies, elaborate fund drives. And all of it would be done in Nick's name, or honor; the board was unanimous on that. Everyone in the family was pleased by the unexpected turn of events except Elyse. And that he hadn't expected. Matt tried hard to keep his disapproval of her to himself. It wasn't an easy task.

"Elyse? Something bothering you?" the director asked when at last he'd finished outlining his lengthy plans.

To Matt's unbridled irritation—he felt she should have been *delighted* over the recent turn of events—Elyse took a deep breath and nodded affirmatively.

"I think the wing is a wonderful idea," she told the director quietly but candidly. "But, as for naming it after Nick...surely there are other candidates, as well?"

"None who have contributed as much as Nick. Look, if you're worried about having to make public appearances on Nick's behalf—" the director guessed, trying to discern the reason for Elyse's unexpected lack of enthusiasm.

She hesitated, avoiding Matt's gaze—deliberately, he was sure.

Swallowing, Elyse said, "I've never been any good at public speaking. And it's not only that, it's a question of time. I'm very busy these days. I have to take care of my three girls. I have a house on the market. I'm going back to work. And I know how much a project like this depends on public support and publicity. I have to be honest with you. I simply won't have the time to put in on the project during the fund-raising stage. And with Matt going back to California in another week—" Elyse's voice trailed off helplessly. It was clear she felt overwhelmed.

"Peter and I could help," Abigail said, clearly hurt Elyse wasn't more enthusiastic but also understanding the pressure the young mother was under. Which was more than Matt could do....,

"And of course the hospital will help," the director said warmly. He reached across the table to link hands with Elyse. "I know this might prove hard for you emotionally, Elyse. It'll take some getting used to. But think of what it will mean for Nick's children, the rest of the family in years to come. We wouldn't ask it of you unless we felt, first of all, that Nick really deserved the honor and, second, that the Donovan family was right for the job."

"He's right, Elyse," Peter said, patting Elyse on the shoulder. "We'll make it work. And this is important—for Nick, for all of us."

For a long moment Elyse was motionless. Finally she nodded. "Of course. I'm sorry I haven't…it was just such a shock." Her voice broke slightly. "I didn't expect quite such an elaborate memorial…."

The hell she didn't, Matt thought furiously, watching her from across the table. Although she hadn't said so directly, he knew she hadn't wanted to come this evening. She didn't want any part of the memorial in Nick's name. Why? Had she really hated or resented his brother that much? He knew Nick had never been much of a husband to Elyse. How could he have been? Gone all the time, at the hospital more nights than he was home. Yet Elyse had known all that when she married him, known it and still….

Damn it, he had promised himself he wasn't going to think about her betrayal to his brother, not once. Unfortunately it was a task easier promised than accomplished.

"THANKS FOR STAYING while I drove the sitter home, Matt," Elyse said cordially as soon as she walked in the front door. In truth she felt anything but grateful to him at the moment. The fact of the matter was he had watched her like a hawk all through dinner and was watching her still.

She knew he was furious she hadn't been more cooperative about the memorial for Nick. She couldn't help it. She was trying to do what was best for all of them. Unhappily she and Matt didn't agree on what that was. Which left her with only one solution, and that was to get rid of him, the sooner the better. They could discuss this another time, when they'd both had time to think about it a little more, to calm down. Who knew? Maybe with time she'd be able to handle the idea, not feel quite so overwhelmed just thinking about it and all the public appearances they were demanding she make on Nick's behalf. But if Matt were to ask her right now, were to press her…she'd be damned if she'd tell him anything but the simple truth, that she didn't want any part of it. She had too many demands on her as it was. And never enough time.…

Ignoring the frank way he was sizing her up, she took a deep breath to steady herself and commented cordially, "I'd offer you a nightcap, but with the realtor coming tomorrow for the first open house—"

"I won't stay long and a brandy isn't necessary," he said simply, loosening his tie with a deliberateness that told her he intended to speak his mind whether she liked it or not. "All I want from you now is a few simple answers."

No, she thought, *he wants me to do things his way. And his way alone!* "Fine." Keeping her voice as pleasant as possible, she prompted with an affability she couldn't begin to feel, "What do you want to know?"

His eyes remained trained unerringly on her face. "What really bothers you about this memorial? And don't bother repeating what you told the director. I know there's more to it than that."

He was right, she hadn't mentioned everything, mainly because she didn't want to upset or worry Abigail and Peter unnecessarily. Unable to keep the aggravation out of her voice, she said emotionally, "You know how those television people are—anything for a tear, anything to up the ratings. The process of raising the money for this memorial could very well turn out to be a brutal experience, not just for me but for us all. Dammit, Matt, I'd think you of all people would understand after the journalist-induced turmoil you went through after Holly died in that accident!"

He jumped as if she'd touched a live wire. "We're not talking about Holly here—"

"Right. We're talking about my kids and I don't want my children hurt by any media circus. I don't want some heartless reporter barging in and asking Caroline what it feels like to have your father, a surgeon, die during surgery, or if it makes them sad they don't have a daddy."

Understanding the reasons behind her anger, he calmed down and tried to pacify her, "I said that I would help—"

She cut him off, irritated because he continued to make everything sound so simple when she knew darn well it never would be, not in a million years. "Let's face facts here, Matt. Your intentions are good, I won't dispute that, but we can't ignore that you're going to be returning to your job on the West Coast in another week. Even with you flying out occasionally to help out, as you suggested you could, the bulk of the interviews will fall to me and, to a lesser degree, your parents."

"You're reluctant to face the cameras?"

"Yes. Aren't you?" He knew how tough it was to be in the public eye. He had experienced a media barrage after Holly had died. Experienced it and suffered badly. She knew therefore he couldn't have been ecstatic about the prospect of surrendering his privacy, even temporarily; yet for Nick's sake he was willing to put himself and his own interests on the line. Elyse wasn't so sure she was.

He studied her for several moments without saying a word. "And that's all that's bothering you?" The words could have cut glass.

In his most guarded moments Matt was all ice, yet never before could she recall him being quite so glacial, so contentious. Oh, she knew he could be prickly when questioned about a case he was working on or when asked about anything he was remotely averse to discussing—like his personal life or romantic involvements; yet never before had he been so cool toward her, so inscrutable. In the past, before Nick had died, she had always been *family* to him and

therefore been treated a little more sensitively than the av-
erage person he met on the street. Now his kid-gloves treatment of her had inexplicably vanished and his newfound
suspiciousness made her anxious. It reminded her of Nick.

She fidgeted nervously as he waited for her to reply. It
didn't help what she was about to say—that Matt had idolized Nick's surgical skill and medical genius. She knew his
whole family had seen Nick as a modern-day miracle
worker. She didn't want to be the one who told them that
it just wasn't so, that although Nick had been a gifted and
selfless doctor, he hadn't been a pathfinder of the caliber of
Pasteur or DeBakey. "Nick didn't perfect the artificial heart
valve or the swift new surgical techniques the hospital is
crediting him with," she admitted finally, hating to be the
one who broke the news. "He didn't do all of that work
alone." Although the way the family talked, you would've
thought Nick had done that and much, much more.

"He initiated those things," Matt argued, a perplexed,
disgruntled look on his face.

She grappled with the gentle, matter-of-fact speech she
had prepared in her head that evening. She'd known all
along she would eventually have to give it to Matt. And to
his parents. "True. But others carried on the work after his
death. It doesn't seem right to give one man full credit for
work he only started, work others finished. Nick wouldn't
have wanted the wing named after him, not for that reason.
Don't get me wrong. I have no quarrel with having Nick
honored," Elyse continued, wanting Matt to understand that
much. "I think he was a wonderful man, a wonderful surgeon."

"But you'd prefer the wing not be named after him."

"Honestly, yes, although judging from what I saw tonight
there's no way I can stop that from happening."

"And that's all it is?" His eyes measured hers.

The way he was watching her, she felt she was on trial.
That he was ready to hand out a life sentence. "Yes. What
else could it be?" she asked quietly, aware of a peculiar,

humiliating warmth spreading through her, flushing her neck, her face. He was making her feel guilty somehow, tainted, as if she had disappointed him and his family on every level. Why, how, she didn't know.

Furious he should be doing that to her when she'd done nothing to deserve it, she lifted her chin. Still he said nothing. Fury was thrumming through her. How could she not resent being treated so badly? He was subtle about it, true, but also a master at mentally degrading her. And all for no reason! "What are you getting at, Matt?" she asked in a clipped, harsh voice. "What are you trying to say? What do you want *me* to say?"

He laughed, and the sound was bitter in the silence of the room. "You're saying you have no idea?" He didn't believe that to be true.

"No."

Again he didn't believe her. His eyes narrowed contemplatively. "You're sure you don't want to get even with Nick?"

"Even with him—how?"

"By blocking the memorial. Making it impossible for it to happen."

"Why would I want to do that?" She had loved her husband!

Matt lifted his hands in an exaggerated display of innocence; his gaze never left her face. "I don't know. Maybe you should tell me."

There was nothing to tell! "I don't know what you're talking about," she repeated tiredly through clenched teeth.

"Don't you?"

"No." Her heart racing, she held her ground.

A disbelieving look on his face, he stalked closer and then simply waited, as if expecting, *wanting* some sort of ugly confrontation.

Suddenly she'd had enough. Before she could even realize what she was doing, she was advancing on him, too. "What is it with you, Matt?" she demanded coldly, despite the catch in her throat and the shaking of her limbs. She ignored the dark warning look on his face, a look that under other circumstances would have made her run. "What have I done to make you so angry? And don't give me any evasions! You've had it out for me for months!" Ever since Nick had died.

He didn't deny it, rather looked at her a long analyzing moment, then responded in a voice so thick with anger it made her shiver. "You want the truth? You'll get it. I know about your love affair with Lawrence Sears. Do you hear me, Elyse? *I know about your affair with Sears!*"

Chapter Three

"My what?" She stared at him in astonishment, his harsh words echoing in her ears.

"You heard me. I know about your affair with Lawrence Sears. I was here late one night before Nick died. I had planned to stop by, to talk to you; apparently I wasn't the only one with that idea." His voice lowered and he tightened his hands into fists at his sides, using every ounce of self-control he had as he continued in a low, tortured voice, "I saw you kissing him, taking him into this house. Damn it, Elyse, how could you sleep with another man in the same house you shared with your husband? Haven't you got any conscience at all?"

Her first instinct under his furious unfair attack was to tell him to get out. Her second, coming swiftly after the first, was to explain and clear her name. "I never had an affair with Sears," she stated through tightly gritted teeth. She was furious at having to defend herself yet determined to do so nonetheless.

He swore viciously, telling her very succinctly and crudely what he thought of her denial, then turned on his heel and stalked toward the doors.

She knew then that she had to make him listen to her. If she didn't, then anything she said later was likely to be discounted even more. She didn't want it ending this way. She didn't want him thinking the worst of her when none of it was true. She ran after him and, desperate to stop him, flung herself in front of him, barring the way to the door. When he tried to step past her, she moved with him.

"You're not leaving here, Matt, until you know the truth."

His steely-blue eyes glittered dangerously. "The truth or more lies? I'm not interested, Elyse."

She resisted the hands he put on her shoulders, and kept her weight wedged firmly against the door. "Well, whether you're interested or not, you're going to hear it! I never slept with Sears!"

Matt rested one hand on the wood above her head, his hand stretched out perpendicular to the flat surface of the door. She felt trapped. Her breath was coming quickly. She was all too aware of the heat of his body next to hers and the coiled tension in his tall, muscular frame. She knew her story sounded lame, yet there'd only been that one night, that one time.

He looked down at her coldly, his disgust at what she'd done shimmering in his eyes and the sardonic curl to his lips. "I suppose his coming over here while Nick was hospitalized was an accident."

"No. I invited him." There was a short silence. Elyse took a deep breath and sent Matt a beseeching gaze. "It's the truth, Matt. I was worried about Nick. Something had been bothering him, but he wouldn't talk to me about it or tell me what it was. I thought it might be related to work and that his partner, Dr. Sears, might have a clue about what that was."

"That might explain his presence here. It doesn't explain his kissing you. Or the fact that he was here at midnight. And you were in your robe."

Matt could still remember how pleasantly disheveled she had looked. No sooner had she opened the storm door to let Sears across the threshold than Sears had taken her into his arms. A light peck on the cheek Matt would've excused. But this was no casual hello kiss. Sears'd kissed her full on the mouth. And Elyse had made only a token effort to stop him. Seconds later, with a furtive look around, she had drawn him inside and shut the door. Matt had been able to see nothing more from where he'd been standing on the tree-lined street. In fury and frustration he'd gone back to his car and waited. It had been over an hour before Sears had slipped out of the house and gone back to his car as furtively as he had arrived.

And Nick…his poor brother Nick had been slated for surgery the next day. From that point forward Matt had never been able to look at Elyse without hating her. Part of him still did. Oh, he knew Nick could be a bastard at times and probably had been to Elyse. But he'd also loved her. And Nick had thought Elyse loved him. Which only went to prove what a talented actress she was, he thought, overcome by another wave of disgust.

Elyse surveyed him, reading the distrust on his face. She moved away and stood restlessly several feet away. "If you'll come in and sit down, I'll explain everything to you, Matt. Dammit, we owe each other this much." He said nothing, refusing to even look at her directly and she continued emotionally, "We can't leave it this way. We're *not* leaving it this way. You have to know what happened. I mean it, Matt. If you won't listen to me then I'll…I'll talk to your parents and then *they* can explain!"

"No," he cut her off sharply, whirling on her so suddenly that she gasped. "I don't want them involved in this!" The only reason he had kept quiet about what he knew so far was to protect them. They'd been through enough; he didn't think they could stand the disillusionment of knowing Elyse had taken another man into her bed the night before his brother died.

"Then you're going to have to listen to me," she repeated resolutely. Seeing he was still wary of her, she abruptly changed tacks, making her voice low and soothing, almost seductive in nature. "Matt, please. Just listen to what I have to say. Then if you still want to leave, I won't try to stop you.'' She ended on a note of sincerity.

He knew when to give up; if he didn't hear her out, she would go to his parents.

His jaw set angrily, Matt pivoted and stormed silently back into the living room. Rather than take a seat, he stood in front of the mantel. After a moment's awkwardness, Elyse sat down on the sofa. She leaned forward persuasively and began to talk in low, penitent tones, taking him back to the very beginning, as he'd half-suspected she would.

''Lawrence has always been a womanizer. I knew that. He'd chased me from time to time, but I'd always been very firm about telling him that we'd never…it was out of the question. I was insulted to even be thought of in that regard.''

Matt thought back; he'd never once known her to give out signals that she was ''available.'' As soon as he had the thought he suppressed it; why was he still defending her? ''Did you ever tell Nick he'd approached you?'' Matt asked roughly.

''No. I…'' She faltered, caught up in the pain of her memories. ''How could I tell him his partner made a pass at me? Made several? I knew what kind of stress Nick was under on a daily, weekly, hourly basis. He didn't need to handle that, too. I thought it was best for me to handle it alone, so I did.''

''It wouldn't appear you did a very good job of that,'' he cut in sarcastically.

She stood up, insulted. She put both hands on her hips. ''Do you want to hear this or not?''

Suddenly Matt did, if only to satisfy his own nagging curiosity. After a moment he nodded recalcitrantly.

She sat back down and exhaled wearily ''Back to that night.''

Grilling her in the same way he would a witness on the stand, Matt cut in bluntly, ''You're telling me there was only once?''

She gave him a withering glance. "Yes. Once. The night before Nick died."

Despite his intention not to listen to anything she had to say in her own defense, Matt began to relax. He'd never indicated on what day he'd witnessed the assignation, yet she knew. Maybe she was telling the truth after all or being at least partially honest.

Seeing the new attention he was giving her, she continued pragmatically, "I was concerned not only about the surgery but about Nick's state of mind. He was so depressed. I tried everything to get him to snap out of it."

"I never had any indication he was depressed," Matt interrupted.

"That's just it. No one did, not his parents or his friends. And he wouldn't talk about it, either."

"You had no idea what it was about?" Matt asked roughly.

"Just that it was work related. He felt very pressured." And she'd felt so terribly inadequate, such a failure because he wouldn't confide in her. "I tried to get him to talk to me of course. Or to talk to anyone. I didn't really care whether it was a colleague, his own physician, a friend. I just wanted him to talk to someone."

"And he wouldn't."

"No. And it was then that I—I suggested he see a psychiatrist."

"And?"

"He was livid. He refused."

Matt was staring at her silently, numb with shock. Elyse knew how Matt felt; he was wondering why Nick hadn't come to him.

"I can understand him concealing his depression from me," Matt said slowly at last, struggling to absorb everything Elyse was telling him. "After all, we hardly ever saw one another. But how is it possible he was able to keep this from my folks?"

They'd doted on Nick, his every mood or whim or wish....

Elyse continued in a voice that was low and roughened with fatigue, "Nick was always very 'up' when they were around. He didn't want them hurt. He didn't want anyone but me to know. You have to understand, Matt, this was very much an ego thing for him, a question of self-esteem. He was always a very firm believer in the mind over matter theory, a patient's ability to 'think' himself well—or ill. He was furious about being put in the hospital for stress-related colitis. As a physician he felt he should have had more control of the situation, of his own reactions to stress. He saw his illness as some sort of inner weakness, a failing on his part that went far deeper than just the physical. He blamed himself for the illness, for not being able to better handle stress, but at the same time he had no interest in trying to put an end to that stress or even discussing the reasons for it. With anyone. I was desperate to try and get him help. To prevent this sort of illness from happening again." Elyse became aware that her hands were trembling and slippery with sweat.

"I felt so helpless," she whispered in a choked voice, knowing her eyes were brimming with tears. "So after an awful lot of soul searching I finally called his partner. I asked him to stop over that evening after work. I couldn't say why on the phone...the hospital switchboard is pretty public and I couldn't take the chance that it would get back to Nick how worried I was because I knew it would upset him if he found out I had talked to anyone about him. So I was very firm with Lawrence about not saying anything to Nick or talking to anyone about it. He agreed. I didn't think anything about it at the time. Later Lawrence called to say he had to perform emergency surgery and that he couldn't come after all; I was very disappointed. I begged him to make it another time, as soon as possible. He agreed, after a pause, but didn't commit himself to any particular time. And again I didn't think anything about it."

She sighed and smoothed both hands through her hair. When she spoke again, it was in a weary voice laced with an undertone of bitter regret and resignation, "Nick didn't want me at the hospital that night, so I went home. I put the children to bed myself and went to bed early. When the doorbell rang, I got up and went to answer it. As soon as I opened the door, he…uh…grabbed me and kissed me. For a moment I was so shocked I admit I didn't do anything, but then I pushed him away." She shuddered, remembering. He could see the look of revulsion on her face.

Matt wanted to believe her, yet he knew all too well what had happened next. "And yet after that you still took him inside."

Her head lifted sharply and her voice filled with anger. "I was concerned about Nick. *He was very ill!* Ill enough to require surgery! I wanted to help him and I wasn't able to; I thought Lawrence might have the answers, so, yes, even after that, I led him in." She clenched her hands into fists at her sides and, with effort, lowered her voice. "I explained to him why I had called, I told him never to try to kiss me again." She gave Matt a level look, daring him to doubt her again. "And then we spent the rest of the time talking about Nick."

"You expect me to believe you didn't sleep with him at all that night?"

She stared at him haughtily, furious he should doubt her after all she'd confided. "Yes." She enunciated the single word so virulently he could almost believe it, and yet he knew Sears had been in her house for over an hour and that he'd left as furtively as he'd come.

There was a silence. She held her ground. After awhile he began to believe her, despite himself. The evidence was damning but it was also circumstantial. And much of her testimony had the ring of truth.

"All this time, you've thought I was unfaithful to Nick? Why didn't you confront me, Matt? Why didn't you just ask me what had happened, what was going on? I would have told you.''

He resented her shifting the blame for this mess onto him. He wasn't the one who'd had the bad judgment to invite Sears over for a tête-à-tête, if that was all that had happened. "What was I supposed to say?" He rhymed off a few possibilities that made her ears burn. "I was too angry then. And then the next day…there was no point during the surgery, with my parents there."

For long moments she was silent, remembering the day her husband had died. Sorrow softened her features.

Matt had his own pain to deal with, his own memories.

"You were so aloof," she whispered. She gave a short laugh; it had a slightly hysterical ring to it as she dwelled on the ironies of the past. "I thought it was worry and later, when we got the news Nick had died on the operating table, that it was grief making you so angry and unhappy. Anger at fate." There was a silence and then she looked up at him. "If only you'd come to me then, I would've explained—"

He'd wanted to, yet he'd also known his family had suffered enough. And with his mother near emotional collapse as it was…. "Nick was dead," he said in a clipped voice, restlessly pacing the length of the room. "I didn't see any point in it."

She got up to follow him. Her anger had faded. She was still confused yet determined to understand his point of view, to end the animosity between them. "And that's why you've stayed away? Why, except for the gifts you've sent the girls, you've never been in contact with me since?"

He faced the Elyse he remembered—compassionate, caring.

"I didn't want to start anything for my parents' sake," he admitted quietly, dealing with his own remorse and feeling vaguely ashamed. "I wasn't sure I could…control my emotions."

She stared at him steadily. The indignation that she'd been feeling earlier returned full blast. "How could you have thought that of me? Even for a second? Have I ever given you any indication I was promiscuous? Even once? Even a glimmer?''

He could understand her anger. If what she had told him was true—and he grudgingly admitted it appeared to be—then she was justified. "No, Elyse, you'd never seemed to be playing it fast and loose, but what I saw that night on the porch was pretty convincing."

Color flooded her cheeks but her jaw was set. "If you had come in that night, let me know you were there, it could've been a three-way conversation."

She let him know with a searing glance she could've used his help; he felt even more guilty. "How was I to know I would be welcome?" he shot back just as furiously.

"You could have asked, dammit!"

Silence fell between them. She put her head in her hands. When she looked up at him again, she seemed exhausted, emotionally drained. "Look, if there's nothing else—"

As it happened, Matt did have another question. "Did Sears know what was bothering Nick?" he asked curiously. He, too, had been worried about Nick. He, too, had intuited something was wrong.

Elyse shook her head. "No. Lawrence and I talked for over an hour that night—once I set him straight—but he had no more idea than I did as to what was bothering Nick. We did pinpoint the time the stress escalated to an untenable degree. It was three months before he came ill. Lawrence said he would look into it, try to get Nick to talk to him and, then, if he learned anything, get back to me."

"But he never did."

"No. After Nick died what was the point? There was so much confusion. Lawrence had to take care of his own patients as well as Nick's…as well as find a new partner for himself. It was a very tumultuous time."

"For us all," Matt said quietly.

"Then you believe me about what happened—or didn't?"

He looked at her. It was very important to her that he trust her. Suddenly Matt did. He knew his original estimation of her character was right. She had made a mistake, so had he. But she hadn't cheated on his brother, wasn't promiscuous now or then. "I'm sorry I didn't come to you sooner," he said after a moment, regretting the argument they'd just had but glad nonetheless they had cleared up the misunderstanding. "I thought that by keeping what I knew to myself I was doing us all a favor. I was trying not to make a bad situation worse."

"I understand. I still wish you had come to me, but—" she gestured obliquely, "Under the same circumstances I might have behaved the same. If I'd caught you with a woman, or—thought I had—I doubt I would have come forward to confront you."

Matt nodded, already feeling like they were getting back to more even ground. "Maybe if we'd seen each other more often to begin with," he theorized. "If I hadn't already been living in L.A. when you and Nick married—" If he hadn't been attracted to her himself, they would've been closer. He would have known for certain not to take what he saw at face value. As it had been, he'd been confused. Angry. Hurt. He'd wondered about his own ability to judge a person's character, to look past surface geniality and see the truth. He had never wanted to believe the worst about her, neither had he been able to ignore the evidence.

"It's all right," she said softly, wearily, her low tone colored with the depth of her discouragement. "I understand why you behaved as you did. I do." The elegant lines of her face were etched with pain.

He'd never felt like such a heel. Or that he'd been more wrong about a person. "Forgive me?" he asked after a pause.

Her gaze met his, held. "Of course." Silence fell between them. The awkwardness was still there but somehow it was less wounding. And he knew with a little effort it could be obliterated completely. "Maybe we just need to start over," he found himself saying before he could think. For his parents' sake, he knew he had to at least try to repair the damage he had done.

She watched him silently, testing him, trying to decide. "Maybe," she said softly, sighing. But at that moment she was too tired and emotionally drained to push it further.

"Uh, listen. About the memorial," he began reluctantly as she moved to show him out.

"I'm still not sure it's a good idea," she admitted slowly, walking him to the front door.

She had to admit that despite her lingering anger over his initial assumptions about her, it felt good knowing they'd cleared the air between them at last. And it helped her to know what she had done—or supposedly done—to alienate him in the past. Although she still had the feeling he was deliberately keeping himself at arm's length as he always had. Wanting him to understand her reasons for refusing to help, she chose her words honestly and elaborated further, "I think it might be very hard on the girls. So I might choose not to participate or to participate only minimally."

"Promise me you'll think about it before you decide," he urged persuasively. It would be several weeks before the hospital would be setting up a publicity and fund-raising schedule.

"I'll think about it," she promised quietly, "but I may not change my mind."

AS PROMISED, Elyse did give the memorial considerable thought over the next few days, and it was still on her mind when she went in to University Hospital for her interview with the director of nursing early Friday morning. Aware that the hospital was substantially understaffed, Elyse agreed to go back to work at the beginning of the following month. It was a little sooner than she had planned on; however, she felt sure she would be able to make adequate arrangements for the girls' care in that amount of time. Hence, her steps were lighthearted as she emerged from the personnel office and started down the hall. On her way out of the building, she saw many of her old colleagues. They all stopped to chat.

Not surprisingly Elyse also ran into Dr. Lawrence Sears. The fact that she had never liked him personally made it difficult for her to face him. She hadn't seen him since Nick's funeral; given a choice, she would never see him again.

"Hello, Elyse," he said breezily, pulling her into the staff lounge before she could do more than utter a token protest. "How are you?"

"Fine, thanks." She looked past him for signs of rescue; predictably there were none. Resigned to chatting with him momentarily, she surveyed him with a mixture of curiosity and dislike. In two years he had changed little. Not a particularly handsome man, he was nonetheless well-groomed and young-looking for a man in his early forties. His light blond hair showed no signs of thinning.

"I heard you were coming back to work!" Lawrence enthused, his dark brown eyes trained on her. "I think that's great, Elyse."

She smiled, pretending a cordiality she couldn't begin to feel. Lawrence was an indefatigable social climber with a reputation for doing almost anything to get ahead. She'd never liked him when Nick was alive; now she found his grating presence almost impossible to bear.

"I also heard about the memorial for Nick."

Elyse paused, focusing in on the jealousy she saw in his face and heard in his voice. "It's not definite yet," she said impassively, trying to edge past him.

He refused to let her leave gracefully. "Sure it is," Sears disagreed, his steely fingers biting into her arm. "They've even asked me to help—unofficially, of course." He forced another less sincere smile. "So what I'd like to know is how active a role are you planning to take in the memorial? I know they'd like you to do a lot."

He seemed to know she would shy away from any public

duties because of her dislike of being in the limelight. Sears
stepped closer, revulsion at his nearness flooded Elyse. She
wished she could extricate herself from his grasp without
turning their encounter into a wrestling match: knowing it
was impossible to elude him for long since he was bent on
saying what he wanted, she decided to brazen it out. She
acted as if being close to him didn't bother her in the least.
"Matt will be supervising most of it," she said firmly, ap-
pearing unshaken.

"From Los Angeles?" He frowned, as if worried about
them doing Nick's memorial justice, and his finger's un-
furled from her arm. "Elyse, they need someone closer.
Someone who'd know what Nick would've wanted," he
insisted. "I think *you* should take a more active part. If
you're worried about the complexity of the project, I'll help
you. Either at the hospital or at home, we can work something out. After all, I was Nick's partner," he insisted
smoothly.

And his betrayer....

Silence fell between them. Just being near him she could
feel her blood run cold. Suddenly she knew there was no
way she wanted him involved in Nick's memorial. Not at
all. And there was only one way for her to prevent that; she
had to take a more active role. "Thank you, Lawrence. Your
offer to help…well, I know Nick would've been very
pleased. And you're right, I do need to become more involved in this project." *If only to see Nick's interests really
were protected.*

"Then you'll allow me to help?"

I'll allow you nothing. Elyse smiled convincingly, knowing that the only way to get rid of Dr. Sears was to promise
him something, even if that promise eventually and deliberately amounted to zilch. With an ease fueled by past anger, she handed him a line of appeasement as easily as she
suspected he would hand one to her—or to anyone who got
in his way. Still smiling, she said, "I'll certainly pass the
offer along...."

"I'VE RECONSIDERED MY DECISION," Elyse announced to Nick's family several hours later. "I've decided to become very actively involved in Nick's memorial."

As expected, both Peter and Abigail were delighted. They praised Elyse extensively, promising to do everything they could to see that the work and responsibilities were shared as equally as possible. Matt was happy, too.

"What brought about the swift change of heart?" Matt asked casually, guiding her into the Donovan's kitchen for a cup of coffee. He knew only too well how only several days before, she'd been opposed to doing much of anything.

Briefly Elyse recounted her meeting with Sears. Matt's expression was grim by the time she'd finished.

"So you think he's going to try and have a hand in the way the memorial is run?" he asked, careful to keep his voice low enough so his parents wouldn't hear.

Elyse nodded. "Yes, I do."

Matt scowled. "Ten to one he's not doing this out of the kindness of his heart."

"I had that feeling, too."

"He's probably planning on grabbing some of the glory. Did he work on any of the experimental procedures with Nick?"

"No, he considered it a waste of time. He only wanted to operate." And, Elyse had to reluctantly admit to herself, in his defense, Sears was very good at what he did. Very devoted to his patients.

"Do you want me to ask him to bow out?" Matt inquired.

"No. After all, he was Nick's partner. He probably should be included on some level."

"But you don't want to work with him directly."

"How'd you guess?" She took a sip of her coffee. "Nor do I particularly want him talking to your parents a great deal. He can be fairly abrasive sometimes, especially when things aren't done exactly as he thinks they should be. You know surgeons, they're all perfectionists, all very demanding. Only in Sears's case, it's double the usual dose, which can often make him unbearable to be around.''

"Right. And I can certainly see where that'd be a problem.'' He exhaled slowly. "Well, if any problems should arise with him—and I hope they don't—I'll handle him,'' Matt promised.

"How, by phone?'' Elyse tried but couldn't quite keep the sudden note of discouragement from her voice. In the few days since they had cleared the air and called a truce, she and Matt had regained much of their former rapport. There were still awkward moments between them, to be sure, but on the whole they were friends again. In fact they were beginning to be closer than ever. Like everyone else in the family she didn't want him to leave again—it seemed his visit to Texas had been all too short—yet she also knew his vacation time was almost up and that Matt was set to return to California later that very weekend. He had responsibilities there including a job and a home. "Ma Bell's great, but I don't think anything you say long distance is going to have much effect on the unswerving Dr. Sears.'' The good doctor had a reputation for being very, very difficult; he was respected but not very well liked by most of the staff at University. No one in their right mind ever wanted to tangle with him because, win or lose, Dr. Sears invariably made things so nasty it just wasn't worth it the effort.

Suddenly seeming to have a great deal more than just what they were discussing on his mind, Matt grinned. He looked at her as if he had a big secret he was dying to announce. "I wasn't going to say anything just yet. I was going to wait and make a big announcement when you brought the kids over this weekend for dinner on Saturday night.'' He smiled happily as he looked over at her. "I've come to a decision the past couple of days. I've realized I can't run the memorial from Los Angeles, at least not the way I'd want it to be run. Hell, why beat around the bush? I miss Dallas, I miss my family. I think it's time I came back to Dallas, Elyse. For good.''

Chapter Four

"Mommy, I hurt my foot today." Caroline sat down in the middle of the kitchen floor and began peeling off her sock. She frowned worriedly, studying the injury. "The baby-sitter put a Band-Aid on it but it still doesn't feel good." She looked up at Elyse hopefully, the misery she'd felt earlier plainly evident on her face. "Maybe *you* should fix it," she suggested, her lower lip trembling slightly. "Maybe then it'll feel all better."

Elyse sighed, knowing just how her six-year-old felt—tired, disgruntled and lonely. Neither she nor her children were used to being separated all day. Although only a week had passed since she'd started back to work, she felt light-years older. "All right, sweetheart," she soothed softly, reaching over to give Caroline's shoulder a comforting pat. "I'll take a look at it just as soon as I get this spaghetti on to boil."

Returning to the stove, Elyse efficiently stirred precut spaghetti into the briskly boiling water on the back burner, then set the kitchen timer for ten minutes. Although she'd had the foresight to put the sauce in the slow-cooker before she left for work, she still had a salad to make, the pasta and hot bread to finish cooking. The table needed setting, the milk needed to be poured.... And all the girls looked like they needed a nonstop hugging and individual attention.

How had she ever assumed she could manage this? Elyse wondered.

"Mommy!" Four-year-old Betsy wailed from the portal, a stricken, panicky look on her face. "I can't find my blankie!" And she couldn't sleep without her blanket.

Elyse contemplated the whereabouts of the missing snuggly. "I think it's in the front hall, honey." She was pretty sure they'd remembered to bring that and everything else home from the sitter's house. "And if not there then try looking in the—"

"Mommy..." Nicole shuffled into the kitchen, then related in her most distressed tone, "I missed you today. I was lonely." Big tears rolled down Nicole's cheeks. Elyse knelt to give her youngest a hug. She knew how hard it was on all the girls to go to a sitter now, from nine to three every day. She also knew they'd eventually adjust, but right now she just wanted to make it easier on them. To somehow make the transition go a little easier. She wanted not to feel so guilty, so torn up about everything.

"Listen, girls." Elyse gathered them around her for a four-way hug. "I know this is an adjustment for you. It's hard on me, too. Change always is. But we've got to be patient. Try to help each other out as much as possible and give this time to work."

"What if it doesn't work?" Caroline asked, suddenly looking light-years older than her six years. "Will you quit then?"

Elyse sighed. She only wished she could but financially it was out of the question. Even if she sold her house.

Before she could formulate a reply, the door bell rang.

The huddle was instantly broken up as three girls chimed simultaneously, "I'll get it." They dashed off, a flurry of arms and legs.

Racing after her daughters, Elyse joined them in the entry hall and after running a hand through her hair, calmly opened the door. Her strained expression slowly faded as she stared up into Matt's face. If ever she'd needed to be rescued, it was now. And Matt was exactly what she needed…another pair of loving hands. Acutely conscious of her white uniform and shoes, she greeted him weakly. "Hi."

"Hi." He smiled back, looking a tad hesitant.

He looked handsome and self-assured in his dark business suit. He'd obviously just come from his law office, which was located in a downtown high-rise just off the Central Expressway.

Staring up at him, her stomach began to flutter and she was suddenly jumpy and on edge under the probing nature of his gaze. She was reminded again what a powerful man he was, how self-assured, and career-minded. While out on the West Coast, he'd had several very newsworthy cases. One had landed him briefly on the cable news service. She still remembered how he had looked talking to the press on behalf of his client, a very beautiful screen actress and former friend of Holly's. He'd been witty and protective, handling the reporter with tact and ease.

But unlike some men who did well only in the business world, Matt was a family person, too. When his parents had needed help straightening out their finances shortly after Peter had retired, it was Matt who came home for the weekend, put on a pot of coffee and sat with them at their kitchen table, his shirtsleeves rolled up, patiently explaining every detail until Peter and Abigail understood exactly where they stood. Elyse, who'd volunteered to do the cooking chores for her in-laws that weekend while Nick worked at the hospital, had tried to stay in the background as she moved from fridge to stove to dishwasher. She'd been impressed by Matt's patience, his ability to explain complicated tax shelters and retirement plans in easy-to-understand layperson's terms. Another time, several years before Nick had died, Matt had flown home just to help his parents relandscape their property. He and Elyse, in old sweatshirts and jeans, had done much of the physical labor. They'd worked for two whole days from early morning to dusk in the breezy, balmy spring air. They didn't finish until their cheeks were pink with sun, their muscles sore, their palms grimy and covered with blisters. Yet Matt, rather than mind or resent the demanding physical labor, had seemed to revel in the activity, as had Elyse. She'd admired that about him then, knowing he was willing to work with his hands as well as his mind.

Then he had been there primarily for his folks. For Nick, too. Now he was there for Elyse and her children. She liked knowing she could rely on him. She liked knowing he cared. And not just about his brother's children but about Elyse, too.

Oblivious to the ruminating nature of her thoughts, he quirked an eyebrow. "I hope you don't mind my dropping in—"

"Mind?" She leaned back against the portal and placed her hand just beneath her throat in a gesture of relief. "I'm delighted. Believe me, you couldn't be more welcome. Stay for supper?" she asked casually, trying not to notice how blue his eyes were, or how the elegant clothing emphasized his sculptured shoulders, trim waist and long, muscular legs. As he neared, she inhaled the tangy sandalwood and spice scent of his after-shave.

"You're sure?" Matt closed the door behind him and knelt down to give each niece an individual and heartfelt hug and kiss.

Elyse smiled, glad to see Matt's soothing masculine presence was already having a calming effect on the girls. She replied, "The spaghetti's almost ready and I could use some help setting the table."

"Done." Rising, he followed her brisk steps back into the kitchen, watched as she gave the boiling pasta another stir. As at home in her house as he was in his folks', he shrugged out of his jacket and loosened his tie.

"How's your new practice going?" Elyse asked, removing butter from the refrigerator. She sliced the French bread in half and buttered each side.

"Great. I'll start seeing clients full-time next week. I've already got appointments set up. I hired a secretary today."

Elyse checked the oven temperature and slid the bread into the oven. She wiped her hands on a towel and turned to Matt. "Any trouble leaving your old firm in L.A.?"

"No. I handed everything over to my associates when I was there last week. How's your job going?" Matt asked, settling the girls into individual chairs around the table.

"I've been very busy," Elyse admitted, giving the spaghetti another stir. She enjoyed getting back into nursing again, more than she had expected to. What she didn't like was the feeling of constantly being torn in half. Of wanting to be home with her girls full-time. Of thinking of them constantly, worrying, wondering....

"And their sitter?" Matt asked, coming to stand beside her and simultaneously lift glasses and plates out of the cupboard.

"She's also a registered nurse. I used to work with her at the hospital long before we both got married. She's doing a good job with the kids." Or as good a job as they would let her, Elyse thought. All three children still resented the idea of having to go to a sitter—period. And it showed. "I've been thinking about enrolling them in preschool for at least part of the day this fall, maybe this summer if I can find a place with an acceptable program."

"They might like that better," Matt theorized.

Elyse could only hope.

"I don't like Mommy's new job." Caroline spoke up.

"Neither do I," Betsy scowled.

Matt looked at the belligerent upturned faces, then turned to Elyse. His hips were wedged against the counter in an unconsciously masculine stance. He folded his arms across his chest and leaned his head towards hers. "Mutiny on the Bounty?" he murmured, his eyes lingering briefly on hers.

Elyse nodded, glad she had an ally there with her, someone who understood what she was going through. It meant a lot to her, having Matt back in her life.

Matt nodded thoughtfully, then moved forward to place the glasses and plates on the table. That task finished, he took a seat across from them and put his elbows on the table. He spoke to the girls like adults, "Pretty rough, huh, not having your mom here all the time?"

"Yeah!" This, in unison.

"I can imagine." He twisted his mouth into a fretful frown. "I'd probably miss her, too." He shrugged and sat back in his chair. "Course I bet some people at the hospital are mighty glad she's there. Don't you think? Doesn't she make you feel lots better when you're sick?"

"Yeah," Caroline nodded importantly. "She does. And she can make scrapes stop hurting. And she can take a Band-Aid off real quick so it won't sting."

Matt looked impressed. "Do you think the people at the hospital appreciate her, like having her around?"

"Well…yeah," Caroline admitted after a compassionately long pause.

"Probably," Betsy agreed.

Without skipping a beat, Matt launched his next question. "Do you think we should make her job harder or easier?" While waiting for their reply, he looked from one girl to the next.

Nicole took her fingers out of her mouth. "Easier!" Her older sisters, getting Matt's drift, mumbled the same.

"Well, I agree," Matt said quietly, linking fingers with all three girls. "And this is how we're going to start, by helping set the table and picking up our own toys and being brave about going to the sitter…if you want to go to preschool, that's okay, too. We'll talk about it."

Minutes later all was peaceful in the Donovan kitchen. Dinner passed in the same calm manner. Only after all the girls had been bathed and tucked into bed did Elyse and Matt have a chance to talk.

"Thanks for staying tonight," she said gratefully over a second cup of coffee. "I really needed the extra help tonight."

"My pleasure." His voice was suddenly gravelly and somehow very intimate. "Is it this rough for you every night?" He watched her intensely, waiting for her reply.

"I'm afraid so." Elyse sighed, running a hand through her hair. She exhaled lightly and tried to suppress a pensive frown. "Although it's only been a week."

"You look exhausted." He surveyed her from the top of her unswept hair to her white stocking-clad toe. She was still in her uniform of pleated trousers and a roomy white drop-shouldered top that buttoned up the front.

"Yes, well…"

He put his coffee cup aside. "You know I bought that big house—"

"Yes, your Mom told me about it and showed me pictures of the place." It was a twenty-acre ranch south of Dallas. A more beautiful house Elyse had never seen, although to this point she hadn't had the time to go out and peruse it personally. "You moved very fast," she admitted admiringly. Matt had found the house one day, gotten mortgage approval the next through a twenty-four-hour nationwide banking service and moved in several days later. Of course it helped that the ranch was furnished and he had little tying him permanently to L.A., save a small bachelor apartment he'd rented after his wife's death. And because of shrewd financial planning, he'd also had a lot of money in the bank.

"Like it?"

For some reason her answer seemed important to him. "Yes," she admitted frankly, "though what you're going to do in that big ranch house all alone—" His place was even bigger than hers, totaling six-thousand-plus square feet.

"Mom and Dad are moving in with me. They've agreed to help take care of the property—and to take care of me, Mom seems to think."

"Good for Abigail." Not that he couldn't take care of himself perfectly well; he could. But he deserved to have people who loved him in his life. He needed, maybe more than he knew, to be close to people again. He'd been away from them all too long.

"I think you could use some tender loving care, too. Why not move in with me, you and the girls?" Before she could speak, protest, he leaned forward persuasively and continued, "Mom and Dad would love it. I've got plenty of room. It'd make your house just that much easier to sell."

"Whoa, Matt." She put up a hand to stop his smoothly executed suggestion. She'd known he'd been mulling over something during the long evening. But she hadn't expected that. "Have you thought this through at all?" Her eyes widened in astonishment.

"No and yes. Meaning the idea just came to me a couple of days ago, but I like it. In fact the more I think about it the more convinced I am it could work. Think about it a minute. What could be better? If you moved in with me, you could go to work, know Mom and Dad were home looking after the kids—"

"Three children is a lot to take on full-time."

"We'd enroll them in preschool. They'd probably like that a lot better than going to a sitter anyway. And we'd hire help. A housekeeper/baby-sitter. Someone with experience. A grandmotherly-type person. As for the rest of the chores and upkeep, the four adults could split them. It'd be easier all the way around."

"What about the regular schools in your area? How are they?" Elyse couldn't move anywhere without considering that. "Caroline has already finished kindergarten. She's going to start first grade in the fall."

"There's a Montessori facility less than five miles from my place. They start with preschool, work up to junior high. I think it'd be perfect for all of the girls, but if you don't like that there're always the public schools in the area, which are excellent, too."

She smiled slowly. She knew Matt. He always did his research well, and once he made up his mind to do something, he generally accomplished the feat with Herculean speed. "You're determined to talk me into this, aren't you?" Oddly she was not too resistant to the idea, which was strange because she'd always been very independent. Maybe it was because she'd begun to realize she couldn't do it all alone anymore, especially now that she was working again. And her daughters needed a strong male role model in their lives. Someone who would guide and nurture them as Nick would've wanted.

"Yes." Matt grinned broadly. "I am. And when Mom and Dad find out they will be, too."

TWO WEEKS LATER Matt's wish had become a reality. Elyse knew she needed help, she knew she'd be a fool to reject the offer of a safe haven, at least until her house was sold. So she told Matt she would move in with him temporarily. Then if it worked out, well, they'd see. He had been elated, and his joy hadn't flagged even on moving day.

"Books, toys, bikes, clothes." Matt surveyed the back of the U-Haul truck he'd rented and turning to face her, concluded dryly, "The only thing we've forgotten is the kitchen sink."

Elyse grinned at his deadpan expression, then unable to resist teasing him, pursed her lips together in a contemplative moue. "Hmm. Well, now that you mention it, we could—I mean I've always *liked* that particular faucet."

He groaned and buried his head in his hands.

Her laughter spilled through the dark, crowded interior of the back of the truck. "You think I'm taking too much?"

He groaned even louder. "I think all women take too much."

She wasn't letting that remark go unchallenged. Hands on her hips, she lifted her chin remonstratively. "And you didn't bring a lot home from California. Books, fishing rods and reels, clothes, ski equipment...." She named a fraction of what Abigail and Peter had been sorting through while Matt had been at work.

A faint wash of color crept into his face. "On second

thought—'' he revised his first statement in an okay–I'm–crying–uncle tone ''—all men and women take too much.''

''We could have hired movers—''

''We're economizing, remember?''

Between his new house, the start-up costs for his new practice, her children's summer school fees and the part-time household help they'd employed, they were both spread thin financially. Neither was overly worried, however, because they both knew that would change when she sold her house and his practice got going. And in the meantime, with the family's three sources of regular monthly income pooled together, they would manage nicely at Matt's ranch, without dipping into Matt's savings or Elyse's remaining insurance money. In fact everyone would probably be better off.

Elyse needed reassurance. ''Are you sure you don't want me to call some college kids to help us move the boxes into the ranch house? I don't want you to hurt your back. And even with those mover's dollies, you've done a lot of lifting.'' Although, in Matt's defense, it was just boxes of belongings. She wasn't taking any furniture except the children's disassembled bunk beds. Consequently Matt had decided he could handle the moving chore himself. Certainly he looked in shape. He looked great! But they were both getting on in years…they weren't twenty-one anymore.

''Elyse, I lift weights and work out regularly. My back is fine.'' He cupped her elbows and guided her down the truck ramp. Seconds later the doors had been shut and locked. He turned to her, a grin on his face. ''It's your nose you should be worried about.''

''My nose!'' Her hand flew to her face. She felt her features flood with color. ''What—?''

He pulled a clean rumpled handkerchief from his back pocket. ''You've got dirt smeared across your face. Here and here…''

Soothingly, he rubbed at her cheek, the tip of her nose, a spot just left of her right eyebrow. There was nothing sexual in his ministrations. And yet without warning, she could feel her heart beating far faster than required. Her throat was unbearably dry. Her knees strangely rubbery and weak. She forced a smile and moved away from him. It had been a long time since any man had touched her so tenderly, that was all. A long time since she'd allowed herself to be taken care of in the least regard. If she was attracted to him...well, she wasn't. She couldn't be.

Matt, too, seemed lost in thought, though his gaze was directed back at her house. It was as if he were giving it a final inspection. "Ready to go?" he said finally.

Elyse nodded briskly.

"So, how's your job going?" Matt asked, once they'd both climbed up in the cab. He started the truck. The motor rumbled. The seat beneath them trembled with vibrations, disturbing the quiet of the spring afternoon. Because the truck was unairconditioned, they'd left the windows open. As the truck started to move, the breeze whirled Elyse's thick dark hair in wildly curling patterns around her face. She had to grab the strands of dark silk and hold them out of her eyes.

"You adjusting okay?"

It had been two weeks now and Elyse was loving every second of her time at the hospital. It was easier, too, for her to leave the girls, knowing they would soon be tended by family in her absence. Because they were moving in with Matt and his parents, they already felt more secure and, as such, were calmer, more cooperative. Indeed, Elyse's life was easier all around and it was all due to Matt. She knew he was doing it because she was family and because they were friends again. He cared about her and the girls and that was a comforting feeling. She liked knowing she could rely on him to help out.

"Work is fine," she assured him blithely.

"What about Sears?" Matt asked, downshifting with a screech. "Is he leaving you alone at work?"

A tingle of dismay slid across Elyse's shoulders. She

hated even having to think about Sears and what he'd tried to do to her. "Yeah, pretty much," she replied quietly.

Matt's mouth was set in a grim line. "Do you see him often?"

"Only...in the halls." So far, anyway, Elyse thought. That could change the first time she was assigned to care for one of his patients.

Matt continued, "Is it hard working in pediatric ICU?"

She nodded. "If a patient dies or doesn't recover fully it's very hard. But for every child that we lose, we seem to save five more, so it balances out, I guess."

"And you handle it."

"Yes," she said quietly, rubbing her temples. "I know I'm not God. I can't always control the outcome but I can contribute to a child's medical care to the best of my ability." She slanted him a compelling glance, wanting him to understand this much, "I like being needed. And no matter what happens I know the care I give a child makes a difference to the patients, to their families."

"I think it takes a lot of guts to do what you do," he said quietly.

She nodded, sobering. Sometimes it was very hard. And now that she was back at work, she needed family to come home to more than ever. She was glad she was going to be with Matt and his parents, glad the girls would have more ready access to their love, too.

Conversation slowed after that. Matt had all he could do handling the cumbersome truck, which refused to go faster than twenty-eight miles per hour no matter how much he stepped on the gas. Elyse was content to rest, look out the window and admire the countryside surrounding southern Dallas.

Matt's ranch was located south of the city, in a mostly rural area fifteen miles due south of Arlington. It was small compared to other ranches in the area, barely twenty acres in size. Thus far Matt hadn't had the time or inclination to purchase any horses or cattle, though he said he intended to do both within the year.

And it was beautiful, mesmerizingly so, in a uniquely "Texas" way. Dark brown split-rail fences surrounded the property. Trees were scarce, the land flat, the well-trimmed grass a yellow green in color. Elaborate landscaping—evergreen hedges, azalea bushes and patches of ivy—surrounded the sprawling two-story Georgian. The house was a soft rose brick, the wooden trim was painted a creamy off-white. The shutters were a contrasting glossy black. The wide front porch was supported by four massive white columns; it sported a huge outdoor chandelier midpoint, directly above the front door. At one end of the porch was a large chain-hung bench swing. A black wrought-iron patio table and chairs enhanced the other side. Decorative barrels of bright red geraniums framed either side of the leaded glass front door. The home, though imposingly large, already seemed welcoming, a safe port in a storm. It was private and serene and every bit worth the half-hour-plus commute into the city.

Inside, the downstairs was equally luxurious. The parquet floors were waxed to a shine, adorned with Persian rugs. The large kitchen at the rear of the house was done in cool beige tones with ceramic tiled counters and a matching Mexican tiled floor. Sunny windows overlooked the brick backyard barbecue pit, diamond-shaped swimming pool and private patio. Beyond that Matt had put in a swing set. The girls would love it here, as would Elyse.

"Regrets?" he caught her gaze as she began putting the kitchen utensils she'd brought with her into the pantry.

"No," Elyse turned to Matt with a smile. "No regrets." Strange as it was, she'd never felt more content, more secure. Was it just being with family? Or was it being with Matt?

MATT WAITED IN HIS NEW OFFICE two days later, anticipating the arrival of his first client of the day. The newly prepared file was in front of him as was a clean legal pad and pen, but Matt's thoughts were far from his next appointment. He was thinking about Elyse, what it had been like living with her in his house.

He hadn't expected her to be so cheerful all the time. Nor had he expected her to look so fresh and pretty, even after a hard day at the hospital. He hadn't known she would be so kind to him, so intuitive. She seemed to know when he hungered for conversation and when he wanted silence. She seemed able to adapt to his every mood, as well as those of Abigail and Peter. She was pleasant and easygoing, wonderful with her children, totally at ease. Which made his own discomfiture all the more ludicrous.

He should have been able to forget by now the brief moment near the back of the U-Haul when he'd gently touched her face, but he couldn't. The softness of her skin, the scent of her, the sweet evocativeness of her husky laughter, the way her eyes sparkled…it all haunted him. For weeks now he'd been unconsciously seeing her not just as a former sister-in-law but as a woman. He'd known that but thought—as he had in the past—that he could handle it, bury the desire he felt for her. It had taken the single gesture, the touch of his hand to her face, to bring it home to him that he could not. And by then it was too late; she was already moving in with him. He would be with her night and day. And there was no way in hell he could retract his invitation to live with him, not without explaining how he felt, how he'd always felt.

She was Nick's wife.

He wanted to be with Nick's wife. Not just in a physical way but in an emotional sense. He enjoyed talking with her, seeing her smile. He liked her interest in him. The gut-wrenching fact was that he was treacherously close to kissing her, man to woman. Even now he wanted her in his arms, her body beneath his, all soft and warm and giving. And it wasn't just the unconsciously sexy way she looked and moved. He wanted her as more than a friend or family member. He wanted her as the love interest in his life. It was crazy. Impossible. This attraction he felt couldn't go any further.

She was his brother's wife, or she had been. To be even thinking of claiming her as his own, to even try, seemed faintly incestuous, incredibly disloyal. Dammit, he owed Nick more than that. He would take care of Elyse, see that she was safe, see that her daughters were safe. He would be a friend to her but that was all.

"Matt, your client's here," his secretary buzzed him on the intercom, interrupting his thoughts.

Matt snapped to attention and prepared to begin work. "Send her in." As his client walked through the door, Matt greeted her cordially and offered her a chair. Intrigued that she had chosen him to represent her, he surveyed her casually as she sat down in front of him.

Melody Sears was a thin nervous woman with large gray eyes and strikingly blond hair. Matt estimated her to be in her mid-thirties, which meant she was about ten years younger than her husband, the illustrious Dr. Lawrence Sears. Her features, admittedly nondescript, were made up to the fullest advantage. She was well dressed and seemed to be simmering with repressed rage and determination. He'd been curious when she made an appointment to see him, but now he knew even before she spoke precisely what she was after.

"I want a divorce," Melody said, taking a cigarette and a lighter from her purse. "And I want you to handle it for me. But first—before you do or say anything to anyone about it—I want you to find out who Larry is seeing."

She's afraid, Matt thought, leaning back in his chair. That's why she wouldn't mention the word "divorce" on the phone, why she'd been purposefully vague to his secretary when making the appointment, citing it only as a personal matter to be discussed with Matt.

Had Sears physically intimidated her, he wondered? Was

she afraid for her health or her life? Or was it just money she was after? A hefty community property settlement?

Although Matt didn't relish divorce cases, especially messy high profile ones, he found himself wanting to take this particular case, wanting to nail Sears to the wall. But it had nothing to do with his client. His thirst for revenge was all tied up with Elyse and Nick and what Sears had done to them both. He knew that wasn't good. For a moment he thought of turning her down on personal grounds, then he decided he could handle it. After all he was a professional. And starting over again in a new city, he needed every client he could get.

"What makes you think your husband is seeing someone?" Matt asked.

Melody blew smoke rings up in the air. "Larry's a man of voracious appetites. He's seeing someone." Conviction radiated from her voice, eyes.

Matt began scratching notes on the legal pad in front of him. "Are you separated now?" His voice was clipped.

"Yes, informally. We have been for about three months."

Matt looked up calmly. "Does your husband know you want a divorce?"

She fidgeted with her lighter and evaded the question. "He knows I'm unhappy."

"But you haven't asked him specifically for a divorce."

Melody's jaw took on a stubborn tilt. "No. And I don't want him to know just yet. He's such an egotistical person, believe me, it'll never occur to him that I would even consider really ending the marriage unless I go to him and tell him. And even then, it probably won't make any sense to him since he won't understand why anyone would ever walk away from such a successful surgeon."

So, Matt thought, *Sears thinks this is just a whim on Melody's part, a whim to be indulged.* Poor sap, he hadn't the faintest idea what he was up against—not that a man like Sears didn't deserve to be raked over the coals. Judging from the way he'd treated Elyse and Nick, he deserved that and a lot more. Matt guessed shrewdly, "Timing is everything then?"

She forced a wry smile that was tinged with an underlying bitterness. "Something like that."

They talked some more. Matt learned Melody suspected Sears had been unfaithful to her off and on during their eight-year marriage, and that she probably would and could have handled that if it had been that alone. Unfortunately during the past two years he'd been also periodically abusing alcohol, belittling her in public. She'd hoped that walking out on him would shake him into an awareness of the way he was treating her. It hadn't.

Matt had one more question to ask her, one he asked all women in her situation. "Do you love him?"

Melody stubbed out her cigarette. She turned an unblinking gaze on Matt. "No," she said quietly. "I did once when I was very young and naive. Now the only thing I feel for him is contempt and pity. Larry needs love, but he'll never open himself up to either receive it or give it. And there's nothing I can do about that, not now, in any case."

Matt put down his pen. "I can hire a private investigator. It will be expensive."

Melody shrugged, put her cigarettes and lighter back in her purse. "A private investigator's fee will be no more expensive than my marriage has been to me. I want out, Mr. Donovan. And when I go I want to take everything I have coming to me. *Everything.*"

He studied her at length, seeing no compassion in her face, only vindictiveness and avarice. "We're talking a large settlement here?"

Melody nodded defiantly. "Every last dime I can get."

Chapter Five

"Hi. Is Matt home? I'm Bob Osborne. I used to work with him out in California at Smith and Lowe."

Elyse nodded vaguely at the man standing on the Donovan porch. Although she didn't remember Bob's name specifically, she did know Matt had worked with a lot of high-powered attorneys in the prestigious West Coast firm. Men like the silk-suited person in front of her. She looked past him, toward the dusty Mercedes with a California license in the drive.

"No, I'm sorry," she said in answer to Bob's question. "Matt's not home from work yet. Would you like to wait?" A burly six feet of solid muscle, Bob was in his late forties, with thinning grey hair. His features were rounded, pleasant. He had a guarded, almost self-protective expression as he entered the home.

"Yeah, thanks, if it's not too much trouble."

"Don't be silly. I'm sure Matt would want to see you." Bob nodded but made no comment.

"Did Matt know you were in town?" Elyse asked, fixing Bob a drink.

"I didn't call him. I thought I'd surprise him."

"Oh." Elyse didn't know what else to say. Suddenly it seemed as if there was a lot Bob wasn't telling her. Fortunately at that moment Matt walked in. When he saw Bob sitting in a living-room chair, his face drained of all color.

"What the hell are you doing here?" he demanded roughly.

"Matt." Elyse stared at him in surprise. She'd never known Matt to be that rude.

"Stay out of it, Elyse." Matt pushed past her and threw Bob a smouldering look. "I asked you a question, Osborne. What the hell are you doing here?"

Bob got slowly to his feet. "We need to talk."

Matt was unmoved by Bob's penitent tone. "I told you before you went to prison I wanted nothing more to do with you."

Bob didn't flinch. "That was three years ago," he said quietly, his expression hinting at the unspeakable experiences he'd been through. "Three years is a long time."

"Not long enough."

"I served my time, Matt."

Matt remained stone still. "Get the hell out of my house."

Bob tugged at his collar as if it were choking him. "Dammit, Matt, will you give me a chance? I need a job."

Matt's laughter was abrupt and unkind. He made no other response.

Moisture welled up in Bob's eyes, began spilling down his face. He begged Matt to have pity on him. "I've lost everything. My wife, my kids—the car and the clothes in the car are all I've got left."

"And I'm supposed to feel sorry for you, is that it?" Matt guessed after a sarcastically long pause.

"Matt—" Elyse tried to intervene again. Whatever had happened between the two of them had obviously been traumatic. But surely if Bob had been to prison he had paid for whatever he'd done. It wasn't like Matt to be so unforgiving, so rude and unmovable. She didn't want him doing or saying anything he would regret.

"Stay out of this, Elyse!" Matt snapped. Then to Bob, "Get the hell out of my house."

Bob swallowed hard, his Adam's apple moving up and

down as he recognized the depth of Matt's anger. "I'll be back," he promised softly but savagely. "This isn't the end of it, Matt. We were *friends*—"

"No," Matt said quietly, with an underlying vehemence that made Elyse shiver. His jaw was so rigid it could've been carved in stone. "A friend of mine wouldn't do what you did."

For that, Bob had no defense. He left the house without another word. Elyse sagged with relief as the door shut behind Bob. His car motor roared as he pulled away. She faced Matt. "You want to tell me what that was all about?"

Matt strode to the bar and poured himself a stiff shot of bourbon. He drank it straight up, grimacing as the liquor went down. "Bob and I go way back. We went to law school, trained at Smith and Lowe together."

"I don't remember you talking about him."

"That's because my interests were centered in family law. His were in the corporate division. About five years ago I caught him taking kickbacks from city officials. Our firm had been hired to handle the bidding for several major construction projects in L.A. Bob rigged the bidding process so selected firms would win; in exchange he got some hefty kickbacks under the table. I stumbled onto the scheme. He tried to buy me, too."

"So you turned him in?" Elyse surmised.

"Yeah, I did. He was indicted, sent to prison."

Matt sat down on the sofa. His knees were spread, his feet flat on the floor.

"What happened to Bob's family?"

Matt sat back in the sofa until his shoulders touched the cushions behind him. He looked glumly over at Elyse. "I don't know. His wife divorced him as soon as the scandal went public and took off for parts unknown." Matt apparently didn't blame her for leaving Bob, for wanting to protect herself and her children from the disgrace.

"Why did he do it?"

"Money. Why else?"

Elyse surveyed Matt silently for a minute. Contempt was etched in the lean, angular features of his face. "You really hate him for that, don't you?" she said quietly.

Matt's mouth tightened and he got up and restlessly paced the room. "I hate myself for not having realized what he was. For trusting him implicitly all those years." He shook his head in regret, as if unable to believe how naive he'd been then.

Elyse studied Matt further. "You think he lied all along then, that he cheated on more than just this one deal?"

"How the hell should I know?" Matt grumbled irritably. He spread his hands wide in a gesture of frustration. "That's what bothers me. I never had any inkling before that he was lying. Even now—you saw the performance he gave." His eyes narrowed. "I don't trust him," he said very low. "I don't want to be anywhere near him." He looked at her steadily and with a determination that was seared into his soul. "I won't be manipulated or misled again, Elyse. Not by Bob. Not by anyone."

SHORTLY AFTER DINNER with the family, Matt had gone outside for a swim. It was now ten-thirty and he was still sitting in the dark wrapped in a terry cloth robe. Elyse recognized by his remoteness that he was upset about Bob's unexpected reappearance into his life. She couldn't blame him. She was upset, too.

"Feeling better?" Elyse asked Matt.

"A little," Matt said curtly. An electric tense feeling touched her briefly. After a moment he said gruffly, reluctantly, "I'm sorry if I spoke harshly to you and my folks."

Elyse sat on the chaise next to him and switched on the patio light. "I understand you were upset," she said softly. Bob's betrayal had cut at Matt deeply. "And I'm sorry if I tried too hard to intervene, to play mediator."

Matt frowned, reflecting on his time with Bob. "You were right to chastise me," he said brusquely, shaking his head in silent condemnation over all that had gone on before, both that afternoon and five years previously, "although if I had it all to do over again I wouldn't change a thing, no matter what you said or did. However, having been brought up in a proper Southern home," he slanted her a slightly aggrieved look and finished in a deadpan tone, "I also know there's no excuse for rudeness. 'Whether you like someone or not,'" he continued with exaggerated cordiality, paraphrasing one of his mother's oft used sayings, "'you owe it to yourself to be polite.' Unfortunately I wasn't polite. You were upset. Bob didn't get half of what he deserved, the least of which is a boot clear out of Texas, but..." Matt shrugged and drew the towel tighter around his neck. He stared out at the lighted shimmering blue water before looking up at the black velvet of the night sky. "Anyway I was mostly angry at myself," he finished after a moment, once again giving voice to this thoughts.

Elyse understood that Matt prided himself on being cool and collected at all times; yet when Bob was there his voice had risen several times. "It still bothers you that you were gullible enough to befriend him, that you didn't see the flaw in his character sooner?"

"Yeah." Matt nodded. He ran a hand through his damp hair. "But that's not the worst of it. The worse of it is that on some level I still want to believe he had some excuse for what he did other than greed. But I know that's not true...so does everyone else who knew him." Matt sighed and swore, his frustration evident in the fiercely muttered words.

Impulsively Elyse reached over and touched his hand. She felt the tension running through him. "Don't be so hard on yourself, Matt. It's only human to want to forgive someone, to want to see only the good in them."

The distance between them was suddenly diminished. He turned toward her; momentarily they both ran out of words. He stared into the soft aquamarine eyes, scanning her face for a reassuringly long time, but whatever it was he needed from her, he didn't find. "Yeah, well you know what having a heart will get you," he said abruptly, extricating his hand. He stood and strode wordlessly toward the pool's edge. "Trouble every time."

That was an invitation for a question if Elyse had ever heard one. "What do you mean?" she asked quietly, striding over to stand next to him at the water's edge.

She wasn't in her swimsuit, rather shorts and a loose cotton top. Matt was shirtless, in a fashionably baggy knee-length surfer suit, the lone towel draped around his neck. She was acutely conscious of his near nakedness, the stirring of her senses. His well-muscled torso, arms and legs, were lightly covered with soft, downy black hair. His skin was tanned and damp, smelling of chlorine and after-shave. The hair on his head was damp and tousled, falling over his forehead in boyish disarray. She felt his misery as acutely as her own; she wanted to take him into her arms and simply hold him until this period of frustration passed.

He turned toward her suddenly. "You remember when Holly died?"

She nodded. "Of course." She and Nick had gone out to the funeral. There had been so many people around—family, friends, colleagues, not to mention the crush of ever intrusive paparazzi and reporters. She, Nick and Matt hadn't had more than a few minutes to talk. Nonetheless, Elyse could still recall all too well how torn up Matt had been. He'd looked grief-stricken, withdrawn. Now she saw that same look in his eyes, only this time she also saw regret and something else she couldn't quite identify.

"From the start I knew there was going to be trouble on that movie," Matt began. He paced restively back to a chaise and sat down. Elyse followed him, taking a seat opposite him.

"The director was an old friend of hers. He'd given Holly her first job. She felt indebted to him. I knew that. But I never thought..." His voice broke off and he was briefly unable to continue. "He'd had a string of losing pictures. He needed a hit. It was his first attempt at a comedy action film and he wanted to do a lot of close-ups on the stunts. Facial expressions, stuff like that. They tried it using doubles, but it wasn't as accurate as he wanted. So he talked Holly into doing a couple of her own pratfalls. The first ones were easy, falling over a sofa and a coffee table, and onto the floor. Jumping into a malfunctioning elevator that was already on its way down. She handled them extremely well—with even a bit more flair than the stuntwoman hired to do the film—and she began to feel more secure.'' Matt paused and his face paled.

"I don't understand."

Matt swallowed hard. "There was this car chase scene on a tricky freeway interchange. He wanted close-ups of her in the passenger side, during the pursuit and Holly wanted to do the stunt herself. So they rigged the car with a camera. It should've been all right. They had an experienced stuntperson driving. Holly was on the passenger side. But the stunt required her not to be wearing a seat belt. I didn't like that at all. Anytime you're in a car and especially at high speeds...."

"How did Holly feel about not wearing a seat belt?"

He shrugged. "She was a little bit nervous about that— the car was traveling pretty fast, twisting and turning, changing lanes within a hair's breadth of other cars, but in the end, as usual she was game."

"Did you object?" Elyse surveyed him carefully.

"No, I didn't. I didn't even know about it until later." *Until it was too late,* they were both thinking. His mouth compressed tightly. For a moment Elyse didn't think he was going to continue on, but finally he did, admitting candidly, "Generally speaking, of course, I didn't like the idea of her doing any stunts, but I also knew how much she felt she owed the director." Again he paused for an abnormally long time.

Elyse couldn't figure out what was bothering him. "Did you and Holly argue about her doing the scenes—any of them, the ones you knew about?"

"No, I just assumed, because she was the star, that she would be protected, that they would see to it that she wasn't put in any real or unnecessary danger. Maybe—maybe I didn't want to know. Sometimes I wish we *had* argued about it, talked more about what was going on then."

Elyse knew how he felt; hindsight was always better and so much clearer. But they couldn't live their lives in the past. Matt seemed to realize that, too.

"Of course I doubt that would've changed the outcome, even if I had argued with her," he said, shrugging.

"Knowing Holly, I'm sure it wouldn't have made a difference," Elyse said firmly. His wife had been very headstrong and goal-oriented when it came to her career. Much as she had loved Matt, Holly would not have let his reservations get in the way of her career.

Matt was silent another long moment. Finally he collected his thoughts and went on, "Anyway, I knew that the close-ups to be filmed or allegedly filmed during the car chase were crucial for the picture and that the more realistically they were filmed the more successful the film would be." His tone was pragmatic, accepting.

"Except it never got finished," Elyse remembered quietly, speaking before she could stop herself.

Matt's head lifted, his eyes meshed with hers and he nodded grimly. "Because halfway through the second take the car Holly was riding in crashed."

It had flipped over a guardrail into the air and then rolled some fifty feet down onto another freeway below. It had ended up wrapped around several concrete beams. Holly hadn't had a chance and neither had the stuntperson driving. Both had been killed on impact. Even worse, the movie company had film of the wreck, the horrible plunge to their death. And it had been played over and over on network news for days afterward. Even now Elyse could remember the horrifying scene with perfect clarity. She suspected it was even worse for Matt.

Matt stared out at the pool, continuing bleakly, "I've got

the same feeling now, Elyse, that same feeling Holly had then. Because Bob and I do go back, way back, on some level there's a very small, very trusting part of me that wants to help rehabilitate him, to give him a second chance if for no other reason than to validate my initial feelings of trust in him.''

''That's understandable.''

''Granted, he'll never practice law again. Not in California. Probably not anywhere in this country. But he could work as a law clerk or researcher—'' Matt's voice trailed off. He shook his head, discarding the idea as soon as it came up.

''But you won't help him,'' she guessed finally. The look on his face was regretful but determined.

''I can't,'' he said quietly. ''Sometimes, hard as it is, you just have to think coldly, react strictly by the book, forget about what you owe people or what they think you owe them and protect your own interests. And that's what I intend to do.''

Elyse understood. The truth was she wasn't sure about Bob either. He'd seemed nice enough on the surface. But so had Lawrence Sears when he and Nick had first been associated. Only later, as they'd gotten to know him better, had Sears' true personality emerged.

Again she had the urge to take Matt into her arms, to simply close the distance between them and hold him close but she sensed that if she did, he would think she was approaching him out of pity. And Matt wasn't the type of man to want pity from anyone. She got up and stretched. It was high time she went indoors. Past time. ''You're going to be all right?'' she asked quietly.

After a moment, Matt nodded. ''Yeah. I think I'll sit up a while longer, unwind.''

Elyse nodded, wishing there was more she could do for him. Some way she could help him feel better. ''Okay. I'm going to turn in. I've got a big day ahead of me at the hospital.'' And her girls would also be up bright and early.

Gratitude softened the lines of his face. His voice was soft and intimately low. "Thanks for talking with me to-night." His eyes continued to hold hers another moment.

She smiled, releasing the breath she'd been holding. "Anytime." It was the least she could do, considering all he'd done for her, helping her with her house, taking her in, helping to care for the girls. But it was more than simply obligation driving her to act as his sounding board and confidante. She wanted to know all about him, wanted to be there for him—maybe as more than a friend. The question was how did he feel about her? Was he seeing her as a sister-in-law or a friend? Both? Neither? Despite all the time they'd spent together, she hadn't a clue.

And even more disturbing was the sensation that Matt was still deliberately keeping a part of himself at a distance, that as candidly as he'd talked to her about Holly, Bob, himself, that there was still much he wasn't telling her, possibly wouldn't confide to anyone.

She wondered again about his marriage. He'd loved Holly very much. He was an intensely gallant, protective man. He'd said Holly hadn't told him beforehand that she was going to do the dangerous car stunt.

Was that because Holly had known instinctively that her husband would object and she hadn't wanted to argue about it with him? And if so, did Matt feel betrayed by that? He hadn't indicated so, at least not in so many words, and yet surely he must've been hurt. That was an important life-and-death decision on Holly's part. Surely Matt would've wanted to be told that she was going to do it, if not consulted beforehand. As her husband, didn't he have a right to know? Elyse wasn't sure. She did know Matt must feel that Holly had betrayed him somehow, whether deliberately or not was anyone's guess. She wondered what that meant about the state of his marriage in general and if there had been other secrets between Matt and his wife. Had he really been as happy with Holly as Elyse—and everyone else— had once thought? Or had there been trouble in his paradise, too? Elyse wondered if Matt would ever feel close enough to her to confide in her. She wanted to be with someone who wouldn't be afraid to tell her anything ever, who would always tell her what was on his mind, even if it hurt. Because she knew that without that kind of emotional intimacy there could be no real love, no real closeness.

When she'd first known Matt, she'd judged him to be the strong but emotionally inaccessible type. Since he'd returned to Texas and she'd moved in with him and his family, she'd reversed her opinion on that. She'd seen his defenses come tumbling down one after another. She'd seen how giving and loving and understanding he could be. Indeed that very evening he'd told her more about his wife's death and his friend Bob than she would've expected him to.

And yet that nagging feeling came at her, signalling that Matt was once again withholding every bit as much as he was telling. He was censoring his words and feelings every bit as much as Nick had at the end. Matt was suppressing his pain, his hurt, bottling everything up inside, trying to keep anyone—everyone—from knowing how he really felt. So far Matt seemed to be handling everything. True, he was moody again—for the first time in weeks—but anyone in his position, having had such an ugly confrontation with Bob, would have been upset. What did any of this mean? Was Matt keeping secrets from her—or if not secrets, at least his feelings? Could it possibly be that Matt was more like his older brother than Elyse had ever guessed?

Chapter Six

"Can you believe it?" Elyse rejoiced, dancing spiritedly round Matt's office with the signed sale papers clutched to her chest. "We not only sold the house in less than two months but we also got every penny we asked for it, too!"

Matt grinned and leaned back in his swivel chair, propping his feet on his desk. He, too, was filled with a sense of accomplishment and euphoria, and not all of it was due to the financial unburdening of his former sister-in-law.

In the five weeks they had lived together as family, he and Elyse had become increasingly comfortable with one another. She obviously felt there wasn't any subject she couldn't talk to him about. She knew she could go to him and he would be there for her. And he knew the reverse was true for him. It was a comfort to him, having her in his life. His handling of the legal aspects of the sale of her house was only one more favor in a seemingly limitless exchange of mutual kindnesses between them.

"I'm glad it's over, too," Matt confided honestly as Elyse sat back into a chair on the other side of his desk. Peter and Abigail had taken the girls to a movie and dinner out; neither Matt nor Elyse was in any real hurry to get home.

He surveyed her carefully. "You know, I wasn't quite sure what your mood would be today," he began casually. He'd been afraid it would be tears. Instead she was joyously happy. In fact in all the time he'd been back in Texas, including the four weeks he'd had her living under his roof, he'd never seen her looking so beautiful. He'd done a double take when she'd arrived at his office that afternoon for the closing, and it had been all he could do to keep his eyes off of her. He'd managed to keep his demeanor businesslike as they went through the official sale process with the buyers and the two real estate agents. Now, however, he and Elyse were alone again. He could relax and look at her—this once anyway—until he'd had his fill.

She was wearing a simple wedgewood-blue silk dress, a white silk blazer and wedgewood-blue heels. The understated and expensive clothes made the most of her slim figure, the slim skirt drawing attention to her beautiful legs. She wore a simple strand of pearls around her neck. Her dark hair was loose and free, in a coiffed cloud around her heart-shaped face. Her aquamarine eyes were sparkling joyously; color flooded her pronounced cheeks.

"What do you mean you weren't sure of what my mood would be like?" she queried.

He shrugged. "Most people get incredibly sentimental about leaving their homes, even when they want to move." And Nick had intimated privately to Matt on more than one occasion that it was Elyse who had coveted the prestigious home in a fashionable city neighborhood. Elyse had fallen in love with the home and insisted they buy it. And Nick had consequently wanted her to have whatever she desired, even if it meant terrifically high mortgage payments.

"And instead I'm acting like an enormous weight has been lifted from my shoulders," she responded drily, studying the confusion on his face.

Matt grinned and pointed out in a teasing tone, "You were the one dancing around my office, waving sale papers as soon as everyone else left."

"True." She grinned back. "I take it you expected tears?"

"I had my hankie all ready." He pulled a folded white

square of cloth from his inner suit pocket, and waved it in front of her like a sign of surrender.

She laughed and rolled her eyes. "Sorry to have disappointed you."

Had she disappointed him? Matt was surprised to discover that perhaps she had. Maybe he'd wanted the excuse—any excuse—to hold her in his arms and comfort her. He pushed the unbidden thought away. Forcing himself to continue the conversation, he asked a little gruffly, "The house was a burden to you, then, even before Nick died?"

"From the very beginning," Elyse affirmed, meeting his gaze honestly.

"I don't understand." Matt stared at her incredulously; he remembered how much the place had meant to his brother. And supposedly to Elyse. Had Nick really known so very little about his wife? Matt wondered. Had they all?

Some of her happiness faded. He saw a glimmer of the anxiety that had been in her face when he'd first returned to Dallas. He cursed himself for having put even the slightest hint of unhappiness in her eyes.

Quietly she explained, "I never wanted anything that elaborate. I would've been happier living a lot more simply. But Nick felt that because of his position in the community we should live in Highland Park. No matter we could barely afford it...never mind all the repairs we'd need to make to insure it was livable." She shrugged and her voice trailed off. "I don't know. Maybe he didn't understand what renovating and refurbishing a house from the inside out entailed, or how much it cost."

Matt stared at her in astonishment. "I thought he had a sizable income." Nick had said as much to Matt, never naming an amount, of course, but telling him what he charged for various surgeries....

"He certainly could have had if he'd operated only on wealthy or well-insured patients. The truth of the matter is he did a lot more charity work than anyone knew. And he was sensitive about others knowing about his generosity toward his patients. He didn't want to be thought of as a pushover by some of his more financially shrewd and ambitious colleagues. Or worse, he didn't want to portray himself as a 'self-crowned martyr'—I think that's how he put it. He always said charity didn't count unless one could donate anonymously—without public acclaim.''

"He got that from my mother."

"I thought so. I seemed to remember Abigail and Peter saying it more than once."

"They were always involved in public service projects," Matt related. "They always gave to UNICEF and the American Cancer Society—at least as much as they were able to afford."

"Well, you can see where he got his need to be a hero," she said softly, pride radiating in her voice.

When Matt thought of the financial shape in which Nick had left his widow and three children, irritation stiffened his spine. It was all well and good for Nick to have taken on the role of Good Samaritan, but surely he'd had an obligation to his own family first, an obligation he'd neglected shamefully from the looks of it. "You didn't mind?" he asked.

Elyse shook her head, confirming his suspicions about her generosity of heart. "No, of course not. I wanted him to help those less fortunate."

Matt nodded understandingly. His brother had possessed a chivalrous streak and obviously that appealed to Elyse. It was unfortunate, however, that Nick hadn't been as circumspect with his own family. However, Matt would take care of that now.

"About you looking for another house," Matt began carefully. Elyse had stipulated from the first that her living with him would only be a temporary arrangement.

"I know I should get on it."

"That wasn't what I was going to say. The truth is I'd like you to stay on and think about investing the profits from the sale of the house for the girls' education.'' The idea appealed to her, he could see it in her eyes.

"I'd like that, but as for you continuing to put us up when you've already done so much...." Appreciation could be heard in her voice. "I don't know, Matt. What if you remarry?"

As far as Matt could tell, there wasn't a chance in hell of him remarrying. Nor did he even want to think about it. To soothe Elyse, however, he said, "Then we'll cross that bridge when we come to it. Find you a house then."

She bit into her lower lip and continued to survey him. "Living with three little children can get very overwhelming," she warned.

"So I've seen," he said sincerely, holding her gaze. "It hasn't bothered me yet."

"If it did—"

"I'd tell you. Come on, Elyse. We can work this out. We already have."

"I know that. I'm just not sure. Matt, I don't want to impose. I don't want to be a burden to you. And I'm afraid if we did stay on that eventually you'd come to resent me, and the lack of privacy."

"Elyse, if I thought for one moment that would happen, do you really think I'd be extending this invitation now?"

"No—"

"Well, then?"

He waited. He could see her resolve faltering as before. He waited, sure he was doing the right thing. "All right," she said finally. "I—we'll stay. But only as long as we're not in the way."

"You won't be."

She smiled hesitantly, extending her hand in a gesture of gratitude and friendship. He clasped her hand warmly, knowing all the while that gratitude wasn't what he wanted from her. Nor did he want her to feel obligated to remain with Nick's family simply because together they could provide better care for Nick's children. He wanted her to remain at his house because it was where she wanted to be. Because she was enjoying living in the same house with him, as much as he was enjoying having her around. His life had been lonely as hell before she moved in with him. If she were to go, he'd miss her and the girls terribly.

"Well, it seems my affairs are settled more quickly than I'd anticipated," Elyse smiled. "Now it's my turn to do a favor for you."

"Oh, yeah? Like what?" Matt asked, trying not to notice how the soft material of her dress seemed to gently and seductively outline her slim form. He grabbed his jacket and slipped it on.

"Let me take you out to dinner." Elyse brushed her hair into place with her hands. She straightened the lapels of her white silk blazer and centered the belt on her dress. "Your choice of restaurant. Only I'm warning you now—" her enticing smile widened "—it has to be fancy."

Her cheerfulness was contagious. "No chili burgers, hm?"

Elyse groaned and laughed. "Please! I'll take something elegant and quiet—"

"Adults only—"

"No mustard on my chair—"

"No clattering forks or spilled milk."

"Just a few quiet hours alone. In a place with background music—"

"And a wine list—"

"And a menu *I* can read."

Which ruled out French and Italian…not to mention that German place. "No snails?"

Her eyes danced. "Not even a hint of escargot!"

THEY ENDED UP at Kirby's Charcoal Steaks, the oldest steak house in Dallas. The fare was basic but substantial, both had charbroiled steaks, baked potatoes and crisp green salads. After the lengthy real estate transactions, they were ravenously hungry and consumed every last morsel.

More than the hushed atmosphere, however, Matt enjoyed the company of the woman he was with. She was pleasant and charming, a good listener, interested in his every thought no matter how off-the-wall or mundane. She also seemed to have a sixth sense about his moods and seemed to realize that, more than ever, they needed simply to relax, to shut out the world and concentrate only on themselves for the evening. She also reminded him with her bright gaze that they had much yet to learn about one another as individuals. He found he was getting impatient. Living with her, he had time with her, but the vast majority of that time was spent with her children and his parents. That left them precious little time to simply talk to one another alone. In fact since that night at the pool when he'd told her *some* of what he knew about the circumstances surrounding Holly's death, they hadn't had any real private time alone. It was a shame, and then again, maybe it was for the best. Because like it or not, he was beginning to be very attracted to his former sister-in-law.

"Why did you choose to be a lawyer?" she asked when they'd finished their dinner and the talk had, as always, turned to their careers. "Surely there were other things you could have done, too. Weren't you especially good in math?" Her eyes widened curiously as she waited for his reply.

He grinned, knowing she'd been listening to his mother, whose capacity to brag about his past and present accomplishments never ceased to amaze Matt. "Yes, I was, but I was never really interested in becoming an actuary or a math professor. On the other hand I liked knowing there were rules to guide us. An organized, systematic way of doing things, assuring equality for all of us. I don't know. Maybe it came from being a younger brother, watching Nick's childhood travails and escapades, but from the very first I could see what happened to a person when he followed the rules and what happened when he didn't."

"Chaos versus peaceful coexistence."

"You got it."

She leaned back to allow the waiter to serve her coffee. When he'd gone, she stirred in a generous amount of cream. "Do you get frustrated when you lose a case?" She lifted the cup to her lips.

"Lose!" He puffed out his chest pompously and pretended indignation. "What a question! Woman, you offend me mortally!"

She laughed softly and put the cup back down on its saucer. The sound of her voice was low and enticing.

"I'm serious."

And beautiful. And kind. And sexy as hell even in the most demure yet sophisticated clothes. "Sure, I get frustrated," Matt admitted, leaning back in his chair. "Who doesn't? Aren't you sad when a patient doesn't heal as rapidly or as well as you'd like?"

"Yes."

"But you continue to work as a nurse because you love it."

"Yes."

"And I love the law." Matt's voice turned unconsciously caressing as he spoke about the work he loved. He was unsure whether it was his imagination or not, but as they talked, Elyse's eyes seemed to grow luminous. She was as aware as he of the intimacy settling around them. Remembering they had to go home to the same house, he tried valiantly to fight the feeling descending upon them. He roughened his voice and finished practically, "I admit I like the law best in its pure form, in the perfect administration of it, but I also like it when it's screwed up."

She laughed. "Because there's always an appeal."

"Right." They both laughed and Matt couldn't resist teasing her a little; she looked so serious as she questioned him. "Are you sure you're not interested in the law, as a career, I mean? Just now when you were talking about an appeal you seemed to have a dazzling legal mind—"

"No, Matt," she refused dryly. "I'm not going to law

school. You'll have to find someone else to recruit as a
protégé. Maybe one of my daughters?''

"Maybe."

They lingered a while longer over coffee and dessert,
talking about nothing and everything. Eventually they realized the time, knew they both had to leave because they
had to go to work the next morning. Reluctant to let their
time together end, Elyse paid the check as promised and
allowed Matt to escort her to his car.

They drove south of the city in silence. Elyse was quiet
beside him, listening to the Phil Collins tape he'd put in the
tape deck.

Matt, too, became caught up in the ballads.

Returning home, Matt parked the car in the garage. Together, he and Elyse walked the moonlit path to the front
door. Abigail had left the porch light glowing in welcome;
the porch was bathed in soft yellow light. Beyond the house
was dark and silent. Again Matt felt depressed, deprived
somehow. He wanted more of her time, more than she had
given him thus far, and by the same token he knew he had
no right to ask it of her. Or did he? It wasn't as if she were
still married to Nick. But how would she feel, knowing that
Matt's feelings toward her were beginning to be anything
but familial? Would it frighten her? Dismay her? If only he
had a clue, if only she weren't always so cautious around
him....

Elyse was nearly to the door when she turned toward him,
"Thanks for going with me tonight, Matt. I haven't had
such a good time in, well...I can't remember when."

This even feels like a date. He reached up to tuck a wisp
of hair behind her ear. He knew he had to do or say something to break the unabashedly amorous mood that was descending upon him. Swallowing hard, he concentrated on
keeping it light. Then, unable to resist teasing her one more
time, he reminded her softly, in his best bad boy fashion,
"Hey. You picked up the tab—"

She smiled, looking up at him, taking in his rumpled hair, the dark suit.

"So I did," she admitted softly. She turned slowly toward the front door, as if knowing it was time for them both to go in, yet not wanting to. She looked suddenly as if she, too, wanted to linger in the darkness, to treat this as a romantic opportunity....

And he knew then that the battle he'd been fighting for years was over. No longer could he deny his feelings for Elyse as a woman.

Maybe he should feel guilty.

But he didn't.

Nick was gone.

Elyse was here. He was here. And he cared for her more deeply than he had imagined possible.

"Elyse—" he whispered softly, urgently, knowing the time to further their relationship had come. He had never wanted a woman in his life with the same urgency he wanted her.

At the sound of his voice, her breath caught in her throat. She turned toward him, then was motionless, looking up at him, as if she were powerless to move away. As powerless as he felt.

He couldn't fight the attraction he was feeling toward her. He didn't want to. His hands were coming up to grip her shoulders, guide her nearer. He was aware of the feminine softness of her body beneath his hands, the slight sway and give of her knees, the way she seemed to melt into and against him as he drew her ever nearer, until they were touching from waist to knee. One hand cupping her shoulder, his other slid midpoint to her spine. Bringing her closer still, he rested his cheek against hers. He inhaled the sweet scent of her hair, the flowery scent of her skin. She was gasping in reaction and murmuring his name. And then he was doing what he'd wanted to all night. His mouth was lowering to hers. Her eyes were closing. Their lips were touching, gently at first, and then with growing intensity.

She tasted sweet, so sweet, and her lips were so giving, slanting perfectly against his, returning the pressure, opening to allow his tongue entry into her mouth.

It had been so long since he'd held a woman he cared about, a woman he could love…might love….

Shock waves rolled in, claiming his attention. What was he doing?

As involuntarily as he'd embraced her, he released her.

Stunned by the suddenness of his withdrawal from the embrace, she swayed slightly on her feet, then took a halting single step back and away from him. Within seconds the look in her eyes went from a soft kind of dreaminess to an expression that mirrored the confusion, the inner pause he felt. *Was this what they both wanted?* He knew they were both asking, wondering the same. And he knew also that for the moment they had no answers. They would both need time. And solitude.

In the meantime, if he'd hurt her….

It appeared he had, at least on some level, by first kissing her, then releasing her as he had. Oh God, he thought, that he didn't want. Not when she'd already been through so much, when she'd begun to mean so much to him. "Elyse—" he said hoarsely.

"Don't, Matt." She put a hand up against his chest and turned her head away, then pivoted even further so he couldn't possibly see her face. Both her voice and breath were ragged. "I shouldn't have let that happen. But I did and I'm sorry—"

"Elyse—" He wanted to apologize, she wouldn't let him.

"I let this feel like a date. I shouldn't have. I—I shouldn't have. I'm sorry."

When she turned back to him she was in control again and as untouchable as a woman could be. He was silent. He wanted to touch her, to bring her close and simply hold her again. Had they not been residing under the same roof, had her daughters and his parents not been involved, he might've done just that. As it was, he knew he had to consider other people's feelings—especially Elyse's. And distance from him, time apart, was what she most seemed to want. If the guilt for her was more than she could handle...

"Look, let's just forget it, okay?" Elyse turned toward him, a raw note of desperation in her voice. "I—please?"

She seemed to want to go back to where they'd been before that evening. Friends only. Good friends now, to be sure, but that was all. That wasn't what he wanted at all; he knew he had to give her time.

"All right," he said quietly. "If it's what you want, for now, I'll forget it." Or he would try. From the way he had kissed her, the way she had responded, he doubted either of them would have very much success at all.

FOR THE NEXT SEVERAL DAYS, Elyse and Matt managed to avoid each other as much as possible, deliberately allowing themselves no time or opportunity to so much as be in the same room alone with one another for more than two or three seconds at a time. This all came to a halt when they found themselves face to face at the breakfast table on Saturday morning. Abigail had made her famous waffles and was serving them piping hot with fresh strawberries and confectioner's sugar. There was no way Elyse could avoid eating with the family, nor would she ever risk hurting Abigail's feelings by not partaking in the lovingly prepared feast.

Looking at Matt, however, was another story; had she been able to, Elyse would've avoided that completely. For all she could think about whenever she was near him was his kiss, how she'd responded, how tender his embrace, how right his arms felt around her. Never once during her marriage had she ever harbored a desirous thought toward him, and yet now she wished they were closer still. The truth was she'd wanted the kiss when they'd returned from the outing that had felt like a date. Even worse, she wanted him to kiss her again.

She knew she was behaving like a foolish kid. So was

he. To bring that fact home all she had to do was remember the look on his face when he had released her. When he'd realized what he was doing, and with whom. He'd already once thought of her as promiscuous. Did he think the same now, because of the way she had kissed him, because of the way she had allowed him to kiss her?

That fear alone had made her quell the emotions she'd shown him, to deny they'd existed.

The heart of the matter was she'd come to rely on his friendship. She couldn't lose that and, on many levels, didn't want to risk it. Yet something was happening between them. She knew it, Matt knew it. Sometimes she thought even his parents had noticed it. With the exception of the past tumultuous seventy-two hours, Matt was letting his guard down with her, allowing her into his life. And she was doing the same with him. Was it because they were compatriots, approximately the same age? Because they'd both been lonely and widowed and had much in common? Or was it beginning to be more than even that? And if it was, could she adjust to the idea of having Matt as her beau, her lover? Could he? Could Abigail and Peter?

"...so what do you think, Elyse?"

With a start, Elyse realized they'd been making plans for the evening's fund-raiser, the first on Nick's behalf. And caught up in her problem-ridden reverie she'd heard less than two words of it!

"I've already got a sitter," Abigail continued expansively as the three girls finished their meal and ran back to watch the rest of their favorite Saturday morning cartoon, "but Peter and I don't want to stay the whole time."

"But we think someone from the family should be there from beginning to end," Peter added. "So, Matt, if you and Elyse wouldn't mind going together, your mother and I can take our own car," Peter finished.

"That way we can duck out early." Abigail smiled. "Whenever we're tired."

"Sure," Matt said, after only a very slight pause. He

turned to her questioningly, "Elyse? That all right with you?"

Elyse took a deep breath and looked at Matt. There was nothing in his gaze to indicate he even vaguely recalled the other night. The fact that her pulse was racing…she was being silly. It was just a kiss after all. They were both experienced adults. She'd asked him to forget it; he had.

So why then did she suddenly feel so bereft? As if she were a teen without even the prospect of an interesting date? "Sure," she smiled, with an insincere tone of tranquility. "That'll be fine with me." Now, if only she could get over that kiss….

"READY?" Matt asked some eight hours later.

"As I'll ever be," Elyse volleyed back lightly, picking up her wrap. Because she was so nervous, she found herself making jokes to lighten the tension between them. "Why is it I feel like I'm going into the lion's den?" she queried, ignoring the light but possessive grasp Matt had on her elbow as he escorted her to the door. Was it the fund-raiser, or the prospect of spending time alone in a car with Matt? Time when they were both dressed up. Time when she felt and knew it looked as if they were on a date. Another unofficial one…. *He's taking me only because his parents asked him.*

"Is it that bad for you, the prospect of making it through tonight, mingling with all the guests—and, we hope, contributors?" Matt asked, once they were en route to the gala.

The truth? Elyse thought for a moment. Yes, it was that bad. But not wanting to sound ungrateful for all the hospital was trying to do for Nick, Elyse said only, "Maybe it's silly but I get very nervous when I'm in the public eye." And the director had already indicated several newspaper reporters as well as a few people from the television news crew would be there very early in the evening. It was more than that, though. She was afraid someone would ask her too many questions. Like details of Nick's illness. What stresses were upon him at the time of his death. How would it look for Elyse, his wife, to admit that she had had no earthly idea, that whenever Nick had been under stress of any kind that he'd pushed her away, put her almost totally out of his life? Remembering hurt her still. She didn't want any reporter latching onto her pain and insecurity, or digging deeper, or eventually revealing things to the general public that would hurt not only Elyse but Nick's daughters as well. For how could her daughters respect a mother who had failed their dying father so miserably? Why should they have to live with the guilt and the resulting questions that belonged only to Elyse? Wasn't it enough that her daughters had lost their father at such an early age?

"Tonight's mostly mingling with people who have money to burn," Matt said casually, merging onto the freeway.

In black tie and white shirt, he looked very handsome. At ease. Personable. Everything she wasn't at that moment.

She grinned, trying for a more easygoing manner as she responded to his observation. "Well, I guess I can handle that." For Nick's sake. She fingered the catch on her evening bag. She caught him looking at her again and felt compelled to add softly and honestly, "The fact of the matter is that I'm no saleswoman. I hate pressuring people—however subtly and elegantly—to make a donation." It just wasn't right, putting people on the spot, expecting them to dig out their wallet. It felt almost like extortion in a social setting.

Matt shrugged, both hands circling the wheel. "I would think as a doctor's wife that you'd be used to it." He slanted her another compelling glance. "Don't the medical auxiliaries do this sort of thing all the time?"

"Yes, they do." She winced, remembering without warning how she had disappointed Nick in that regard. "I never became overly active in charity work."

"Meaning what, that you did enough to get by or—?"

She grimaced, admitting, "Next to none." Now these

were the kinds of questions a reporter would ask. Questions that would automatically and perhaps fairly put her in a bad light because in the past she hadn't been a great philanthropist. No, it had been Nick who volunteered all the work in their family. Elyse had concentrated on raising the kids, keeping the home fires burning. Before that she'd worked as a nurse. There hadn't been any time in her life for altruistic ventures.

His eyebrows raised and lowered in silent contemplation of her regret-filled statement. "How did Nick feel about that?" he asked compassionately.

Again Elyse fingered the clasp on her handbag. "He wished I had done more, I think."

"You didn't talk about it?"

Why was he suddenly so interested in her marriage? she wondered. And why did she want him to think the best of her, while simultaneously letting him know there had been problems in her marriage—numerous problems. They were problems that to this day she wasn't sure she could ever have fixed, at least not in any lasting way. "We argued several times," Elyse answered finally, not sure at that point where her loyalties were. "He wanted me to do more—again mainly it was a 'position in the community' thing. But I didn't have the time, and finally he realized that and let it drop." She paused, looking out at the skyscrapers on her right. "I probably could have done more, though."

"I doubt it, not with the girls so young." Matt came to her defense with surprising quickness as he handled the considerable freeway traffic with ease. He gave her another brief glance that communicated understanding. "I think you're being too hard on yourself. I'm sure, even if Nick was disappointed in you for not being more public-spirited, that he understood how busy you were with the children, how committed you were to them."

She supposed so. Maybe it wasn't that bothering her so much as the idea of meeting up with Dr. Sears. For she knew he would be there and would be difficult, pushy, perhaps even angry that Elyse had made no further moves to include Sears in Nick's memorial despite his demand that she do so. And although Elyse knew she could and would handle Sears, she wasn't looking forward to it.

"I guess I do owe Nick this one last project," she said quietly, mentally bracing herself for the night ahead.

Matt smiled at her newly conciliatory tone, keeping his eyes on the road. He left the freeway and the car's speed slowed accordingly. "Does that mean you'll give it your all tonight?"

She could see how much it meant to Matt that she do this for his brother, that they all participate on Nick's behalf. "I'll try." And she would.

They lapsed into silence.

"Anything else on your mind?" Matt asked as they neared the University Park mansion where the fund-raiser was to be held.

How was he able to sense her moods so accurately, Elyse wondered, to know when even the tiniest thing was bothering her? Even Nick had never been able to do that, not in almost ten years of being together.

"It just feels strange to me, doing this on Nick's behalf now," she said slowly, trying to put her feelings into words. "I almost feel like I'm playing a role. Like I've got to prepare myself in a theatrical sense. I've gotten out of the habit of thinking of myself as Nick's wife. In my own mind these days, I'm just me now, a single woman alone with three kids to raise. Now suddenly I'm back to being part of a half." A half that no longer existed.

"And you want to go forward?" His brows rose questioningly but he was careful to keep his expression unreadable.

Elyse shrugged, suddenly getting very emotional. "You're a widower," she said softly, the words spilling out of her before she could think. "Don't you simply want to go forward? Don't you want to forget the past and just make a new life for yourself, a life without all that grief and pain?

How would you feel to be emotionally linked with Holly again after all this time?"

"Especially when I've finally gotten my life in order."

Matt pulled up in front of the mansion. Cars were already lining both sides of the street. He cruised forward, looking for a parking place, then braked at a stop sign. "Look, I'm sorry. I hadn't realized when I got you into this memorial how upsetting this was likely to be for you."

Nor had Elyse known. Not until tonight. Not until she'd gotten dressed and put on her social mask as "Nick's wife."

"I'll handle it," she reassured him.

He watched her carefully, his eyes darkening perceptibly, then nodding, drove on to find a parking place.

Elyse's thoughts once again turned to Nick. She wasn't ungrateful or even forgetful of the good times she and Nick had shared. She just wasn't anxious to make a saint or a martyr out of him, either. She wanted to remember him as he was—good, kind, decent and very human. Very real. She wanted to stop dwelling on the way she had failed him at the end, through all periods of stress. She wanted to prevent others from delving into the same.

Maybe she just needed to act more assertively, help others remember Nick the way she wanted her daughters to remember him.

Matt parked the car, then turned to face her. He studied her preoccupied expression, then cautioned gently, "If you need me—"

She smiled, humor her saving grace. "I'll just whistle," she teased, paraphrasing a line from an old movie they'd both recently watched on television along with the rest of the Donovan family. "I do know how to whistle...."

Now. If only it were that simple.

Chapter Seven

The grandfather clock chimed midnight just as Peter and Abigail threaded their way through the throngs of elegantly dressed people to where Matt was standing next to the buffet. He'd been engaged in conversation with a neurologist at University; noticing his parents wanted to talk to him, he excused himself and made his way past several groups of men and women. "Hi, what's up?"

"We wanted to tell you we're ready to leave," Peter said.

Matt noticed his mother and father were both looking weary. Happy, but weary. He, too, was glad the memorial was off to such a good start. Donations, large and small, were already pouring in, now that the word was out.

"Say goodnight to Elyse for us, will you?" Abigail asked, patting Matt's arm affectionately. "I'd do it myself but it would probably take me half an hour to find her in this crowd."

Matt knew what she meant. There were over five hundred guests milling about the sprawling mansion. People spilled through the many downstairs rooms, outdoors into the formal gardens and beyond over moonlit lawns. In a corner of the patio a country and western band played the latest hits, as well as countless old standards. About twenty couples were two-stepping to the music while others crowded long food-laden tables. "I'll do that, Mom."

Once his parents had left, he set out in search of Elyse.

He hadn't seen her for at least an hour, he realized at once. In fact they'd been split up almost as soon as they arrived. Now he found himself wondering if she was all right.

She was. At least in a manner of speaking, Matt noted, when he found her at last. She was among the guests dancing on the patio. He didn't know the older gentleman she was with. Because she looked perfectly content, he stood back awhile just watching her, intending to go and claim her for a dance when the song ended.

Meanwhile he surveyed her from afar. She was beautiful tonight, there was no doubt of it. Her rich brown hair was worn loose and free; the silky strands tumbled around her slender shoulders, curled softly against the slender arch of her neck. She was wearing a cranberry evening dress made out of a glittery material. The dress was boat-necked and body hugging in front; the floor-length skirt flared out in a hundred tiny accordion pleats from her waist. The back view was something else again; it dipped in a vee nearly to her waist, making her look both sophisticated and sensual, twice the woman she'd ever been with Nick.

He'd never been more acutely conscious of the fact that she was single or that he wanted her—as his own. Sometime in the past few days he'd gotten past feeling disloyal toward Nick. After all, Nick was dead. It wasn't as if Matt had ever entertained designs on Elyse when they were married; he'd never really even looked at her then. But now he looked at her often. And as much as he looked, he couldn't seem to get his fill.

The dance ended. Matt slowly pushed away from the wall and started forward. Before he could claim Elyse, Lawrence Sears had come up behind Elyse and taken her into his arms. Elyse looked both startled and dismayed; nonetheless she recovered quickly. Matt's first impulse was to stride forward and break it up immediately. His second was to hang back, to watch. If Sears was hassling Elyse, it'd be easy enough to spot it and then give Sears the warning of his life.

There was no evidence this was the case, however. In

fact, to all the world, they both looked like the best of friends, old friends, Matt noted, his brow furrowing in consternation. What the hell was going on between them? he wondered. Was Elyse still involved with the man on some level? He'd thought she hated Sears, yet there was no evidence of that emotion now on her face. Or was she just a better actress than he had ever guessed? She *had* promised to go all out to raise funds tonight, Matt remembered with chagrin.

With the music playing softly in the background, Elyse followed Lawrence's lead. Sears talked continuously but Matt couldn't make out anything he was saying. While Sears spoke, Elyse's head was turned slightly to the side. When she looked up at Sears again, her gaze was very intent but otherwise emotionless. Matt shifted to better see Elyse's face. She was talking to Sears now, her voice soft and low. She appeared animated; it seemed whatever she was saying to him was very urgent, very necessary and persuasive....

Sears reacted to whatever she was saying with a crocodile smile. He said something back. Elyse blinked, froze, then resumed dancing. Sears talked some more and then his hand, which had been resting lightly on her waist, moved up ever so slightly. His palm grazed Elyse's bare skin. She moved away from his palm instinctively; the movement sent her closer into her partner's embrace. Sears trailed his fingers lower across her skin to the bottom of the vee. There was no mistaking his intentions or the fact Elyse had done absolutely nothing to stop the man, rather was staring at him, her face revealing a look of dread or, conversely, of mute acceptance. Again Sears slid caressing fingertips up her spine. And still Elyse remained in his arms, listening to him talk, looking as if she could not care less that the man was touching her, blatantly coming on to her in a dance area full of people. Matt's jaw clenched and a red mist clouded his eyes. Before he could think, he was moving toward her, tapping Sears on the shoulder and rudely cutting in. "You promised me a dance, Elyse."

Startled, Elyse looked up into Matt's face, easily reading the angst along with the blame and anger in his expression. How could she have let Sears even slightly close to her again, Matt wondered furiously, especially considering all that had happened between them in the past? Why hadn't she entertained the good sense not to dance with him at all? Especially on this night when Nick's memory was being honored?

"I guess I did promise you a dance, Matt." Elyse's artificially bright smile faltered.

Sears looked from Elyse to Matt, then said, "Well, don't let me interrupt. Elyse, we'll talk later," he finished firmly, his low tone rife with a message only Elyse could decipher.

At the unspoken intimacy flowing between Elyse and Sears, Matt's jaw clenched. Sears slipped away, not waiting for Elyse to reply.

"What was that all about?" Matt asked tersely. He knew he sounded jealous; he couldn't help it. He was holding her too tightly, possessively. He didn't care. No way was she sidling out of this one until she'd told the truth.

"I—" Elyse bit her lip. "It was nothing."

She didn't even try to meet his gaze; another pronouncement of her guilt. "Nothing," he repeated sarcastically between clenched teeth. "Like hell it was nothing. Don't lie to me, Elyse—"

At the plainly accusing timbre of his voice, her face changed. Using her hands as leverage, she pushed herself as far away from his chest as she was able. Not about to let her go, he kept his hold on her and continued dancing, giving her no choice but to match his deceptively fluid motions. She stumbled once, twice, her thighs bumping his. Still, he held on, holding her upright, holding her close. Closer than she wanted to be held.

The hands against his chest trembled. "What exactly are you accusing me of, Matt?" She looked unsettled but her voice was haughty, and there was an icy smile on her lips. Lips that could—and apparently had—driven men wild.

Matt pushed the ugly thought away. She wasn't promiscuous. Just because once before circumstances had led him to see...because someone else had...it was over, it was in the past.

Eyes narrowing, he picked up the threads of their whispered conversation. "I want to know what's going on with you and Sears. Why you were dancing with him, why he had his hand here—" Matt placed his palm flat on her skin; defiantly touching, caressing the soft smooth skin of her back. Elyse gasped softly as if he had branded her. She tried without much success to pull oxygen into her lungs. Her eyes took on a panicky, hunted look.

Matt had seen that look before on countless others in court. Men on the witness stand. Caught cheating, they lied about even the most flagrant infidelities, then floundered even more when presented with explicit proof. Matt often wondered why, even after they'd been caught, they continued to lie. Why didn't they just admit to the truth, take their lumps and be done with the whole ugly mess? He guessed it was because they were afraid. Like Elyse was afraid now.

More convinced than ever of her guilt—if she wasn't guilty why would she have continued to look so frightened and uneasy—Matt continued gruffly, "I want to know why Sears wants to talk to you later." *And you'd better have a good explanation....*

She swallowed hard. For a long tense moment they stared at one another. "Back off, Matt." She looked past him and smiled at the other couples surrounding them on the dance floor.

"No way, Elyse."

The dance ended. He wasn't about to release her. Realizing that, she stepped on his foot, driving the heel of her shoe into his instep. Matt let go involuntarily. His lips compressed as he bit down on a string of curse words.

Her composure intact, Elyse stepped back out of reach and smiled up at him prettily. Her aquamarine eyes flashed warningly, signaling him she'd had enough. "I don't have

to listen to this and I'm not going to. When you calm
down—if you calm down—let me know. We'll talk then.''
Oblivious of the others who were staring, she stalked away
from him, her high heels clattering on the stone patio.

Matt let her get as far as the open French doors before
he caught up with her. His arm closing around her elbow
in an unshakable grip, he guided her back into the house.

"Let go of me.'' She pushed the words through tightly
gritted teeth and a frigid smile.

"No." They walked past the buffet, his steely grasp giving her no choice but to move along at the swift but easy
pace he had decided upon.

"Dammit, Matt—'' she hissed between clenched teeth.

He turned to face her and stopped so abruptly she collided
against his chest. "You want a scene?'' he asked simply,
meaning it. "You want everyone to hear what I have to
say?'' Her face whitened and with satisfaction he continued,
very low, "Perhaps I should call Lawrence Sears over here,
too. We could *all* talk about what's going on, rehash old
times and we'll start with—''

"No!" Her denial was sharp, almost pleading in intensity.
The rest of the color drained from her face. She looked
shaken, upset.

He looked down at her, hating the guilt he saw in her
expression, the fear. The way even now she was struggling
to breathe, to maintain her composure. He didn't want to be
placated. He wanted her to level with him, tell him the truth.

"Fine,'' he said curtly. The resistance sapped from her
and Matt continued his quest for a moment alone with her.
They spun through the kitchen, past a sea of gaping caterers,
out through the servants' entrance and into the darkness of
the night. His steps never faltered nor did hers; he felt a
certain grim satisfaction in forcing her to keep pace with
him by just lightly touching on her elbow.

As they walked, muted sounds of the party filtered
through the windows, reminding them of the gathering inside. To the side, couples clustered on the lawn. He headed

in the opposite direction. Too far, and they'd end up with the valets near the cars. Midpoint…midpoint he might just find a spot for them alone.

Under the cover of darkness, Elyse started to struggle against his grip. Ignoring her attempts to pry his hand from her arm, he pulled her through a couple of photinia bushes, past a towering live oak with innumerable branches and around the corner of the house. Finally finding a deserted spot in the corner next to the chimney, he backed her up against the brick. "Now we're alone," he said on a grim note of satisfaction.

Relieved because they at last had no audience, she muttered an insulting description of him. With effort she regained her former composure, then in a droll tone that was in direct contrast to her racing pulse, asked, "Had enough drama for one evening, Matt?"

"Not on your life," he echoed back smoothly.

There was a brief silence in which neither moved, they barely breathed. She recovered first. "Well, I have had enough!" she hissed softly and started to step past him.

He didn't make a physical move to stop her, not then. Yet there must have been something on his face to imply what he intended to do, for just as swiftly as she'd broken free, she paused, changed her mind and moved back again. Her back against the wall, her whole body trembling, she simply waited, her breath catching in her throat.

He should have been pleased to finally have her where he wanted her; he wasn't. He felt only remorse that they should be having this conversation at all, that Sears had come on to her again and she had allowed it. Dammit, what was wrong with her anyway? Did she enjoy leading men on, making them suffer?

He exhaled slowly, struggling to find the last shreds of his patience. "I repeat. What's between you and Sears, Elyse? Is he harassing you? Making a play for you? And if that's the case, why didn't you tell me? Or do something to stop him yourself?'' After all, she'd done a fine job of stomping on Matt's instep!

She bit her lip, sidestepping his questions entirely. "He hasn't bothered me at work."

She was lying by evasion. Matt's frown deepened.

Hastily she raised both hands in surrender and added, "I'll admit being around him does make me uncomfortable—"

"Then why were you dancing with him?" His eyes never left her face.

She squirmed uncomfortably and avoided his eyes. "Because I couldn't get out of it without making a scene."

Maybe, Matt thought, maybe not. "Couldn't, or didn't, want to?" Matt asked with an outward calmness he couldn't begin to feel. He had no idea *why* he was so angry. He just knew the sight of her, in another man's arms...a man who had once desired her...kissed her...the remembered images set off an explosion of rage inside him. A rage that now had nothing to do with Nick, but was restricted to Matt alone. It was Matt who felt betrayed. Led on somehow, cuckolded...

Elyse stared at him as if seeing a stranger. "What's wrong with you?" she whispered, stepping forward. "Why are you behaving this way?" She took a deep, placating breath. "It's not like you to be so jealous and suspicious, so overly protective!"

Matt knew. "You should be thankful I'm here—" he said roughly.

Her chin tilted up stubbornly. "Well, I'm not. Dammit, Matt, I've given you no reason to mistrust me!"

He gave a brief, cold laugh. "Haven't you?"

She exhaled dramatically. Her lower lip trembled. "I explained about that one time—"

"With Sears coincidentally," he interrupted.

"Matt—" The word was strangled; suddenly she was close to tears. Stung by his tone, she stared up at him. Her eyes grew huge and dark and desperate.

He, too, was close to the edge. Perilously close. He laughed bitterly, all the emotions he'd suppressed coming to the fore. "You know, I almost bought your innocent act. I might still buy it now if I hadn't known—" He caught himself just in time. He had promised Nick Elyse was never to know about that.

"What?" she demanded.

Suddenly, promise or no promise, he knew he had to tell her. "That Nick mistrusted you, too," he said quietly.

The color left her face. She didn't question the validity of his statement, merely asked in a harsh whisper, "How do you know that?"

With satisfaction, Matt noted she wasn't denying it. "Because he came to me several months after Betsy was born." Matt's words were clipped. "He said he thought you were having an affair."

She reeled backward in shock and confusion, her skin draining of all color. "I never—"

"Oh, I know you were innocent then," Matt interjected tersely, remembering what hell he'd been through while sweating out the results along with his older brother. Fortunately for Nick, long weeks of surveillance had given *him* the peace of mind he needed. "The private investigator's reports confirmed it." Nick and Matt had both been able to forget until the night Matt saw her with Lawrence Sears. Even then he hadn't wanted to believe she was capable of infidelity. He still didn't want to believe it. But neither could he deny that she was covering up something about her current relationship with Sears. Her mute acceptance of the man's caresses on the bare skin of her back said as much because under normal circumstances, Elyse was not promiscuous. So, something had to be going on. But what? Blackmail? Was she trying to sleep her way into a better nursing position? What?

She stared at him in stunned silence. "You had me followed?"

He nodded and she swore furiously, beginning a recital

designed to infuriate him, "You self-righteous, interfering, presumptuous—"

Matt hadn't wanted to arrange it, but Nick had been his brother and when he'd come forward, asked, Matt hadn't been able to refuse him. Not when he'd realized how tormented Nick had been. How obsessed. "I didn't want to do it," he admitted calmly. "I had to." Nick had protected him for many years. Matt had owed him. It had been that simple.

She shook her head, suddenly as unforgiving as he was. "No, you didn't," she said quietly. Her cool, hard stare told him exactly how betrayed she felt.

He returned the look. "For what it's worth, I tried to dissuade him." Then, he'd thought she was innocent, too. He would have sworn to it. But that was before Holly's accident. Before he'd seen Elyse in Sears' arms. He swallowed hard, recounting harshly, "I thought Nick was a fool for even suspecting you of fooling around. But now I can't help but wonder if where there's smoke there's fire." He moved closer, backing her up against the wall, trapping her there with the length of his body. His hands gripped her shoulders, first caressing her, then holding her still. His voice dropped to a supposing whisper. "Why did Sears come on to you that night, Elyse?" His breath whispered across her brow. He could feel her heart beating against his chest, hear her quickened breaths. She was hiding something from him, he could feel it, see it, and the idea she might be deceiving him, too....

"Were you really all that blameless?" He lowered his voice, handling her as he might handle a hostile witness on the stand. He knew on one level that his tactics were unfair. But he also knew that if he were ever to have any peace of mind he had to get to the truth. "Or were you as enticing to him then as you are to me now? Was it some sort of ego trip for you, Elyse? A way of confirming your appeal as a woman? Or does it go deeper yet?"

She stood stone-still. "Stop it, Matt. Just stop it." She spoke without looking at him.

He knew it then, they were getting near the truth. He was all the more determined to uncover what she was withholding. A hand beneath her chin, he tilted her face up to his. Slowly he shook his head letting her know that he wouldn't stop. "Not until you tell me what I want to know."

Tears glimmered in her eyes. "I won't—"

His jaw set just as stubbornly, he interjected coldly, "Then we'll stay here all night."

"The party—" Her protest was a strangled moan of desperation. She moved against him defiantly and shoved at his chest. "We can't just walk out on it." She twisted against him, her thighs brushing the rock solidness of his, once, twice. Seeing it was useless, she leaned back against the wall, apparently making the most of the bare half inch space between their adjacent bodies. Unbidden, he felt the beginnings of desire, pushed it aside and continued to refuse to let her go.

"I don't give a damn about the party," he said grimly, losing patience with himself as well as her. "I want to know about you and Sears!"

"I've told you everything there is to say," she repeated tiredly.

He was unconvinced. "Like hell you have."

"Matt, please, someone might see us here."

It was a lame excuse, one neither of them really believed, given all the care he had chosen in selecting the spot for their tête-à-tête. "Funny time to start wondering about talk, don't you think?" Sarcasm dripped from his voice, and he finished in a lazy insinuating tone, "Especially after the way you just let Sears—"

"Shut up! Just shut up!" Her hands came up to flatten against his chest, to wedge distance between them. "I can't stand being accused of something when I've done nothing to deserve it, and for you to even suggest—! Damn you, damn you to hell, Matt Donovan!" She shoved with all her might then and still cursing him, she brought up a hand to slap his face. Stunned by the vehemence of her reaction, he

initially did nothing to fight her off. The fast rising hand
propelled him into action. With no time to spare, he blocked
the intended blow, pushed her hands aside, the struggle
bringing them closer together. Furious at being subdued so
easily, she twisted and turned, her legs chafing against his,
her breasts brushing the hard surface of his chest.

Suddenly it was too much. Too much sensation. Not
enough contact. Where his hands cupped her wrists, her skin
was hot, her pulse racing. Her thighs were tensed, her knees
slightly apart beneath the long, flowing skirt. He wedged a
knee between the two of hers, for better control of her. Unbidden, he felt his desire spreading in a low, fierce ache. He
turned his head slightly in an effort to catch his breath and
instead inhaled the light, sensuous aroma of her perfume.

All conscious thought fled. He was only aware of the
small helpless sound she made in the back of her throat.
Turning back to her, he saw her lower lip tremble. He saw
her eyes grow wide and luminous. He felt her fear—and her
passion. No longer able to deny the emotional impact she
was having on him, or the fact she'd recently become far
too important to him, he caught her up short in his arms and
stared down at her wordlessly, wanting everything and
wanting nothing. Only that they be together, this once, that
he have her lips and feel how soft and giving she could be.

Looking up into his face, she saw his intent, gasped softly
and murmured his name. And then he was doing what he'd
wanted to all evening; he was taking her upturned mouth
and kissing her as if his life depended upon it. She resisted
at first, struggling to keep some part of herself separate and
free, but it was useless and after another few seconds she
gave in to the desire plaguing them both. Her mouth opened
beneath his and her whole body softened. Without being
aware of what he did, he lightened his grip to a caress. Her
hands came up to first touch his shoulders, then circle his
neck. His lips gentled on hers, tasting and savoring, drawing
deeply from her mouth. She murmured a soft sigh, an en-
treaty, and leaned back against the wall, as if her legs would

no longer support her. Feeling as if he were drowning in her softness, the solace her lips offered, he moved with her, molding the length of his body to hers. And still he kissed her with the slow, hot whisper of experience, his tongue touching hers, seeking, reassuring, searching. She was real. She cared…about him…and he cared about her.

When at last the kiss came to an end, he drew back breathlessly, giving her yet another searching glance. He hadn't received any answers to his questions. Yet he had all the information he wanted. It had been there in her kiss, in the way she'd surrendered to him. It was there in her face as she looked up at him.

"ARE YOU GOING TO CONTINUE the silent treatment all night?" Matt asked Elyse several hours later, guiding his car into the garage.

For a moment Elyse didn't answer his question. She didn't have the strength. He had taken all she had to give and more in that one haunting kiss. No matter what happened between them from this point forward, she knew she'd never forget the way he'd looked at her then, with his face gilded by moonlight; the shadowed, mesmerizing eyes, the intent line of his mouth, the slight flare of his nostrils, the sharpness of his features. Although she'd fought it— both physically and mentally—it hadn't taken more than a few seconds for all will, all sense to seep out of her. She'd wanted only his kiss, the liquifying pleasure only he could give. She'd wanted the sense of belonging he seemed to offer her, the intimacy that mingled with his strength, his instinctive need to dominate, to control—not just her but life, fate. Even now, just thinking about the hot, slow caress sent turbulent waves of raw feeling through her. She'd wanted that…she still wanted him.

But he didn't trust her.

And that, she couldn't live with.

"I don't want to fight with you, Matt." She wearily lifted herself from the car.

"I don't want to fight with you, either." He fell into step beside her as they left the garage.

He touched her elbow, guided her around to face him.

"Look, about me having you followed. I'm sorry but I had no choice."

She saw his regret, knew it was genuine. "I don't blame you for doing what Nick asked. If it hadn't been you overseeing the investigation for Nick, it might've been someone else." She was very sure of that. Funny how, prior to tonight, she'd almost forgotten the jealousy she'd lived with, the fights. How could she have put Nick's possessiveness out of her mind? she wondered. Because coupled with his customary neglect of her, it had often almost been enough to destroy their marriage, at least to make her think of divorce. But that hadn't come about, and with Nick's death she had tried to put those jealous episodes behind her.

They continued walking toward the porch. "Do you want to talk about it?" Matt asked before they went into the darkened house.

No, the truth was she didn't. But if she didn't talk about it, there would always be questions on his part. She'd see them every time she looked at Matt's face. And she couldn't bear that. She dropped her house key back into her purse and moved over to sit on the chain-hung swing on the porch.

"Why did Nick suspect you of being unfaithful?" he asked quietly, sinking down beside her on the swing.

"I don't know why he was so suspicious. I never gave him any reason to think that I would so much as look at another man. But it was a problem almost from the day we were married." If Matt knew enough to have her followed for Nick, he probably knew this, too. "On the one hand, I knew his jealousy was just a symptom of stress, a way for him to vent the emotion he couldn't allow himself in his work," she said, her voice laced with weary resignation. "I knew what a high-pressure job he was in, how much it took from him physically and emotionally and mentally. I knew he felt guilty about the long hours he spent away from me and the children.'' And the fact was they'd made love very infrequently because he was so tired, so drained when he did come home. She shrugged off the unhappy memories, the remembered feelings of loneliness, adding, ''That's why, even now, I can't stand to be accused. Why I overreacted tonight when you made those insinuating remarks about Sears.'' Her hands curled into fists in her lap. ''I hate feeling guilty and condemned when I've done nothing to deserve it.'' She stared out at the serene darkness of the Texas night sky.

''Why did you stay married to him?''

''Because when I married, I married for life. Because I loved him. I wanted it to work. We had three children we both loved....'' Her voice trailed off.

''Then it was a good marriage?''

Elyse was silent. Slowly she put her thoughts into words, ''At the time I thought it was. Now, looking back, I'm not so sure. I think we could have had a much stronger partnership if he hadn't let stress drive us apart.'' She shivered though the night air was still warm and balmy. Matt pulled her closer, into the curve of his arm, and she continued emotionally, confessing, ''I never want to go through that again, feeling so alone.'' Remembered pressures tightened her nerves. Solemnly she related, ''Adversity should make a couple closer; I know it can, I've seen it happen that way dozens of times in the course of my work at the hospital. A couple becomes much stronger, more united because they're fighting their battles together.''

''And you and Nick never had that,'' Matt ascertained softly.

''No, never. And that's what I want. If I ever get married again, I want to know in advance I can always count on my spouse to share not only the good times but the bad times with me. I want to weather the storms of life together.'' Without thinking about it, she rested her head against Matt's shoulder.

''Sounds reasonable to me.''

"Well…maybe." It hadn't been to Nick. He'd always taken on everything alone. And because of that, he had died alone, denying Elyse and everyone else the chance to know what was really on his mind. However, there was no way she could change that now, she realized. All she could do was think about the future and try not to make the same mistakes again.

"About Sears tonight—"

Elyse straightened, knowing he'd had every right to be angry, jealous. Because like it or not, she and Matt were getting involved…and Sears, the sleaze, had slid his hand up her spine. She'd wanted to belt him but she hadn't because what he had been saying to her at the time, in that cool well-modulated tone, had held her immobile.

She noticed Matt was still looking at her, waiting for an explanation from her. Something, anything to explain what had gone on, what he'd seen. If only she could tell him everything…but she couldn't. She hadn't even had a chance to really absorb Sears's filthy lies or to check up on the proof he claimed existed. And until she did…no, she wouldn't, couldn't involve Matt yet.

What an irony that was, she thought. All she'd ever wanted was a man she could confide in. And here she was, keeping secrets about Nick.

But she couldn't tell Matt what she'd heard. "It was nothing. He was just putting in his two cents about the memorial." Still censoring madly, she injected boredom into her tone. "As usual he'd like to do everything his way, have a lot of input. I tried to politely tell him the family was handling it and what we didn't decide, the hospital would."

Matt's features relaxed at her plausible—abridged—version of what had occurred. "Did he buy it?"

With effort Elyse met Matt's steady look. "Probably not. But at least he knows now he'll get nowhere with me." She wouldn't be blackmailed. Everything Sears had said was a lie, and soon as she had proof of that, she would tell Matt, involve his whole family.…

Matt frowned. "I don't want him hassling you—"

Neither did Elyse, but she wouldn't get anyone else involved in Sears's treachery unless she couldn't avoid it. "I told him to go to the hospital board with his suggestions for the memorial."

"Do you think he will?"

She shrugged uncaringly. "Probably." And knowing most of the members of the board, who saw Sears as a money-grubbing social climber, they would probably ignore him. It was too bad medical talent didn't automatically erase character flaws, she thought. Unfortunately doctors were people, too, and very human. Sears was among the most flawed.

Matt hesitated. "His promise to talk to you again—"

"Lawrence said he'd get back to me after he speaks to the board," she admitted quietly. "I'd rather not be apprised, but…he'll do what he wants anyway."

"If I can help—" Matt stood and helped her up from the swing.

"I think in this case the less we do the better, but if he does bother me, Matt, I'll let you know."

"Promise?"

"I promise."

His protectiveness surrounded her like a warm cloak. Without warning she knew she needed Matt more than she'd ever needed anyone. He seemed to be feeling the same. He reached for her wordlessly, folded her close. His lips touched hers tenderly, infusing her with warmth, bonding them together in an intimacy that was deeper and more compelling than any she had ever known. She knew he was telling her he was sorry, that he cared. She knew she cared about him, too. She might even be falling in love….

Looking up into his eyes, she knew finally that everything was going to be all right. It had to be….

ELYSE RETIRED TO HER ROOM, with every intention of falling into a deep soundless sleep. But as she had half feared it would be, rest was impossible for the duration of the night. All she could think about was Lawrence Sears, the time she'd spent with him on the dance floor. She hadn't believed a word he had said. Which was another reason why she wouldn't repeat his filthy lies. Not to Matt or to anyone else. She shuddered, recounting the scene....

He'd started out chiding her for avoiding him at the hospital, which was true; she'd done so with a vengeance. Any time she saw him coming, she went the other way. Then he'd moved on to the subject of Nick, the memorial. Although his voice had been cultured and politely soft, his jealousy had been apparent from the start. "Nick didn't do all this work alone, Elyse. He had help from me as well."

Maybe in their practice. "You didn't help with the research," she pointed out tranquilly.

"But I covered for him in other ways."

"Of course you did." Elyse had smiled just as politely, though her nerves were already stretched to the limit. "The two of you were partners!"

Lawrence's eyes took on a diabolical gleam. "What I did for Nick went well beyond being partners. It bordered on the illegal. God knows it was unethical, too, morally reprehensible...enough to put Nick in the hospital, anyway."

Her mouth dry, Elyse had nearly stopped dancing at that point. She'd never known what had caused Nick's stress-related illness. Nor had Lawrence—then. But he had promised to find out, then when Nick had died, he had never gotten back to her with any facts or theories. Was it possible Lawrence was telling the truth now, that he alone had discovered whatever it was that had sent Nick into a deep depression? Her throat dry, she protested, "I don't know what you're—"

"Then let me tell you. Nick had good reason to be ill, Elyse, because he was solely responsible for the death of a ten-year-old boy. One of his prized patients."

At that her spine had stiffened. Noticing people were

watching them, she'd forced a smile. "I don't believe you—" Sears was exaggerating.

"I've got medical proof." Sears had spun her around the dance floor, gripping her tighter, his hand snaking up her bare back, his voice a whispery menace in her ear as he uttered his final threat. "And unless you want that knowledge made public, you'll help me out, Elyse. You'll see that the new wing is named not just after Nick but after me as well. The Sears-Donovan wing. It has a nice ring to it, doesn't it?"

Elyse had stared at Lawrence in shock, and it was then that Matt had strode forward to cut in. His fury, his jealousy had diverted her, as had his kisses and her unexpectedly passionate reaction to them. Now...now Elyse knew she had just been avoiding the real issue. Nick's alleged guilt. She didn't believe it, not for an instant.

But unless she could prove Lawrence wrong, what would happen next? She'd wanted to tell Matt what had happened. She'd thought about it as he escorted her irately from the dance area and through the host's house over to a quiet spot where they could talk alone. That was why she hadn't really resisted his high-handed treatment of her, even though at the time Matt had clearly been too jealous and upset to deal with rationally. Because she had wanted to tell him first what Sears had said.

Then she remembered Bob Osborne, Matt's unforgiving nature, his ironclad sense of right and wrong. And a tiny knot of fear had begun to form inside her. Something had been bothering Nick greatly before his death. If Sears was right, or even partially right, and Nick had been negligent in even the slightest regard, what then? If she told Matt would he insist they go to the proper legal and medical authorities immediately and let them handle it? Would he turn in his brother as surely and swiftly as he had turned in his ex-friend and colleague? And if he did do that, what would happen? Would Nick's name be tarnished permanently, whether he was guilty or not? She knew how the

press could be; they crucified a person first and printed re-
tractions later—somewhere in a tiny column on the back
pages because scandal sold news, innocence was a yawner.

With the plans for the memorial winding up, Nick—and
the question of his fitness as a surgeon—would be big news.

Lawrence Sears's allegations would be front page news,
a major scandal, no matter how the investigation eventually
turned out. A traumatic event like that would hurt the entire
Donovan family. Elyse couldn't allow that. Nor did she
want Matt being put in the difficult, heart-wrenching position of having to turn in his own brother for medical malpractice. He had been devastated enough by the Bob Osborne episode. Even now, just thinking about it hurt him
terribly. To have to face even the *prospect* of defaming his
own brother, too. She didn't know if Matt would be able to
handle it. Or, even if he could handle it, if Peter and Abigail
would be able to forgive Matt for having even the slightest
hand in such a painful process. She remembered how upset
and how hurt they had been when she had balked at becoming involved in the memorial. If either she or Matt were to
do this…no, she doubted they would be able to handle it.

She also had her daughters to think of; for their sakes,
she wanted Nick's reputation kept intact. And it was also
important that his memorial continue. Were even the hint
of scandal to come out, the memorial would probably come
to a crashing halt. Nick's parents would never forgive her
if that happened. And she and her daughters couldn't manage without the Donovans' support, their love and devotion
and continuing kindness.

That meant there was only one other solution. She would
have to embark on her own investigation. And only when
it was concluded, when she knew the answers and she had
positive proof of Nick's innocence, would she be able to
decide what to do. Only then would she be able to go to
Matt and tell him what she knew. Only then would they be
able to figure out a way to get Lawrence Sears out of their
lives, once and for all.

Until then, like it or not, her knowledge, her secret fears, would simply have to remain an undisclosed barrier between them. It was either that or risk hurting all the people she loved. And that she categorically refused to do.

Chapter Eight

Elyse sat in the car outside the post office, the file on Ronny Dilmore in front of her. Less than a week had passed since Lawrence Sears had told her Nick had been responsible for a child's death, and in that time she felt her whole world had been turned upside down.

It hadn't been hard to discover which child Sears had meant. Nick hadn't lost many patients; of the three he had lost in the months before his death, only one had been ten years old. She'd gotten his folder from Nick's file cabinets, which were now stored in the attic in Matt's home. Reading through the file, she'd discovered nothing at all to indicate negligence on Nick's part. There had, however, been a one-year gap in the child's medical history, when he was four to five. She had sent for the appropriate records air express, using Nick's old stationery and his "new" post office box number. The doctor in Arizona had complied readily.

The heretofore missing files easily explained why Ronny had died during surgery: undetected internal bleeding in the abdominal area. He'd had a previously treated and medicinally cured stress ulcer when he was five. His parents, the veterans of many moves and countless doctors, had forgotten to list this illness on the presurgery forms, so technically Nick couldn't be held accountable. They had, however, listed the doctor in Arizona. It had been up to Nick to send for the records and see that he had them before he ever operated, just to be sure. He hadn't received the records, maybe hadn't even sent for them. He also hadn't noticed the omission. That was his fault. And when he'd realized this, he'd probably felt very responsible, perhaps even negligent in Ronny's death. For had Nick known about Ronny's previously cured ulcer prior to surgery, Nick would've been on the alert for any signs of unexpected complications, including abdominal bleeding during the open-heart surgery. He hadn't been prepared, and as a result, Ronny had died.

Obviously somewhere along the line, Nick had discovered this sobering fact, too. Maybe in a postdeath talk with the child's bereaved parents or in a subsequent investigation into the records. But one thing was for sure, it hadn't come out in the hospital's routine investigation of Ronny's death. For whatever reason, Nick had covered up his carelessness at the mortality conference with the hospital's medical review board. Whether it was out of panic, fear or guilt really didn't matter. What did matter was that as of the moment, only two people, Elyse and Lawrence Sears, knew of the irregularity.

Which left her wide-open to blackmail. Sears undoubtedly knew how much a revelation like this would hurt Nick's parents. It would destroy the fund-raising operation, cast a shadow on all the research Nick had done, all the good he had done. It would destroy his memory, and Nick's memory was all her daughters had left of their father.

Although she wanted to tell Matt, Elyse felt she couldn't. He would probably insist they make the scandal public. Find out if anything criminal had been done. Find out if there was a case against Nick for medical malpractice.

And for what? Both Nick and his patient were now dead. Nothing could be gained by dragging both their names, their families through the mud. The best thing to do, Elyse decided pragmatically, was to forget.

If only Sears would let her do just that! But he wouldn't. Not unless she were able to make it a joint memorial.

Which brought her to her next problem. Matt would never

agree to sharing Nick's memorial with Lawrence Sears, even if she could get Peter and Abigail to approve of the idea and move forward. She would have to go to the hospital committee in private then, suggest the hospital wing become a joint memorial called the Sears-Donovan wing. Only that way would they ever be safe, could she ever forget. Only that way would Sears leave her alone.

Fortunately for Elyse, Sears was temporarily pacified when she carried through her decision and told him about her private talk with the director the next day. He wasn't happy about the fact that they would have to wait six to eight more weeks minimum before the officials reached a decision, as several of the high-ranking hospital officials were now on extended vacations out of the country. Knowing she was free from any more pressure or blackmail for a while at least, she went home that evening more relaxed than she had been all week. Unfortunately not all was well at home.

Matt was downstairs on the hall phone when she walked in the door. Betsy was curled up on the sofa, her cheeks flushed. Caroline and Nicole were playing very quietly in the dining room. "What's up?" Elyse asked, putting her car keys and purse aside.

Matt put down the phone. "Betsy's sick. I've called her pediatrician. She'll see us at her office in fifteen minutes." He frowned impatiently, then asked in a quiet aside only the two of them could hear, "Where've you been anyway? I've been trying to get you since three o'clock. The hospital said you'd left the office early."

She had left work, but needing to tell Lawrence Sears what she had done on his behalf, she'd met him briefly in the park adjacent to the hospital. From there, though, she had come straight home.

Elyse hated lying to Matt, but in this instance she had no choice. It was for his own good. "I had some errands to do." Elyse walked over to touch Betsy's forehead. There was no doubt about it, the child had a fever. All business in her concern for her child, she asked, "Have you taken her temperature?"

Matt nodded, trying not to show his worry. "One hundred and three."

Abigail came into the hall. "Oh, Elyse, thank goodness you're home. You're going to the doctor with Matt?"

Elyse met Matt's eyes and nodded. Though she could take Betsy alone, now that she was home, she preferred Matt go with them. "Yes."

"Well, don't worry about anything here. I'll feed the girls." Abigail walked over to Betsy and kissed her forehead gently, promising, "And I'll have something for you when you come home. Whatever you want."

Betsy smiled wanly in response. She sat up groggily, pushing a fringe of sweat-dampened curls from her forehead. "Thanks, Grandma."

Dr. Marilyn Howard met them in the waiting room. Everyone else had already gone home for the day. It didn't take long for her to examine Betsy. By the time the exam was finished, Betsy was dressed and playing with the wooden train set up in the waiting room. "It looks like strep throat again," she informed Elyse, consulting the chart. "You realize this is her fourth episode in six months?"

Elyse nodded slowly, dreading what she sensed was coming next.

"Those tonsils are going to have to come out, Elyse. I know you don't want to do it and I wouldn't suggest it if I thought it weren't absolutely necessary, but in this case, to prevent reinfection—"

Elyse knew that if they put off surgery Betsy would continue to suffer as she had the past six months. "When?" she asked succinctly.

"Just as soon as I can arrange it. I'll let you know. In the meantime, you might want to prepare her. Or would you prefer I do it?"

Elyse smiled, concealing her inner conflict. Since Nick's death during surgery, she'd felt an irrational terror of any operating room procedure. And to have her four-year-old child go through it…this was going to be rough, pretending she wasn't at all worried. "Maybe it would be better if you did." Marilyn was young, kind and very good with young children. And more importantly she was calm about the procedure.

"Okay."

Betsy was brought in. Using a model of the throat, Marilyn explained what would be done. She finished it with a pep talk concerning University hospital. "And of course you'll be able to have all the ice cream you can eat.…"

Betsy perked up at that. "Any flavor I want?" she croaked hoarsely, brightening for a moment.

Marilyn smiled and promised, "Any flavor—if I have to tote it in myself."

"All right!"

"She took the news well, didn't she?" Matt remarked several hours later, when Betsy had been given her first dose of antibiotics and acetaminophen and put in bed for the night.

Elyse looked up from the needlepoint she was trying to concentrate on. So far she'd put in fifty wrong stitches, torn out half of them and put in thirty more that were equally as bad. "Yes, she did."

"You don't look as confident," Matt remarked quietly.

Elyse took a deep breath. Leave it to him to zero in on her weakness immediately. She glanced up at him. "Is it that obvious?" she asked quietly. Suddenly her heart was pounding for no reason, her hands were clammy with perspiration. She felt weak all over, faintly nauseated.

Matt continued to watch her carefully. Wordlessly he moved to sit next to her on the sofa, removed the half-finished pillowcase from her hands and put it gently aside. "I don't think Betsy knows you're worried. My parents—maybe. It is going to be all right, Elyse." He stressed every word. "Betsy will come through this operation with flying colors."

"I know." Tears welled up in her eyes; she blinked furiously to keep them from falling. Several escaped anyway and rolled down her cheeks. She swallowed hard. "I just can't seem to stop shaking. Every time I think about it—" her voice broke. She couldn't finish.

Matt understood all too well. As a result of what had happened to his brother, he had his own fears to deal with. He put his arm around her shoulders. His touch felt strong and comforting. "Would you like me to come to the hospital with you?"

Embarrassed by her weakness—surely as a registered nurse she should be able to handle this—Elyse wiped at the moisture on her cheeks with the back of her hand. "Would you mind?" She needed him there with her.

Matt shook his head slowly, his nurturing gaze never leaving her face. "I'd be glad to be there with you."

A WEEK LATER, both were waiting in a reception area in the pediatric wing. It was seven in the morning; Elyse and Matt had already been at the hospital for three hours. Although Elyse had brought her needlepoint and several new magazines with her, she couldn't concentrate on anything but what was going on in the surgery rooms beyond. Intellectually, of course, she knew she had nothing to worry about. Betsy's pediatrician was in the operating room with the surgeon—the best throat man in Dallas. Betsy's presurgery work-ups had been fine. Her medical history was complete and, except for the recent rash of strep throats, free of any indication that complications would ensue. Nonetheless, Elyse couldn't calm down, couldn't seem to fight the panic that filled her throat and weakened all her limbs.

"You're thinking about Nick's surgery, aren't you?" Matt crossed the distance between them, his low courteous voice breaking into her anxious thoughts.

"How can I help it?" Elyse said quietly, getting up to pace the waiting room with long restless strides. It was agony for her, knowing her child was in there, being operated on that very minute. She wanted to be with her; she couldn't. "I don't want Betsy to go through this. I wish she didn't have to." Tears welled up in her eyes. "I don't want her to be scared. And Matt—when she wakes in the recovery room—that first moment when she's all alone and disoriented from the anesthetic, maybe even crying, I—"

"The nurses will be there to comfort her."

"It's not the same." Elyse wanted to be there. Had she been more together emotionally, because she was a nurse, she might—*might*—have been able to wangle permission to sneak in to see Betsy. But she wasn't composed. So there was no question of her breaking the rules to accommodate herself. It would be better, in this instance, to follow the rules strictly. Elyse knew that. She even accepted that, as a cool professional. As a mother, however, it was killing her to be so far away from her daughter. Especially after the way Nick had died. In this same hospital. During another essentially "routine" procedure.

Oblivious to anyone who might see them together, Matt crossed the distance between them and from behind her, put his arms around her tightly, holding her close. Elyse's arms were crossed tightly at her waist. His arms were over hers. She leaned back against the warm welcome curve of his body. She was aware she was shivering uncontrollably now—out of pent-up emotional reaction and anxiety—and that his arms felt strong and right.

Since the night of the first fund-raiser, he hadn't kissed her again. But he'd been thinking of it often, always. She saw it every time she looked in his eyes. She knew they needed more time together to sort things out before deepening their relationship, and she wanted that, but since the night he'd kissed her there had been little opportunity for them to share more than token moments alone. Far too many other things had gotten in the way of their being together— Sears, Betsy's illness, the surgery. Yet, maybe that was for the best, she rationalized quietly, considering the enormity of the secret she was keeping from him now.

Hysterical laughter welled up in her throat and she had to work to suppress it. It was funny, ironic really, that the qualities she had wanted most in a relationship—total honesty, emotional intimacy, sharing even in times of stress— were now completely out of her reach because she was protecting the man she cared about. Because she was protecting Matt from finding out the disillusioning truth about his brother, from having to act on it and then live with the consequences. What she was doing for Matt was right, she had no doubt of it; but her actions were also keeping them apart.

And would continue to do so, at least to some degree, until the matter was resolved once and for all. When the board acted in Sears's favor, Elyse would be able to put Sears's blackmail behind her.

Matt, knowing nothing of what else was worrying her, turned her slowly to face him. His arms lightly circling her back, he said quietly, "I know you're scared. I am, too. We'd be crazy if we weren't frightened by surgery because even in the most ordinary of circumstances, things can go wrong. But nothing is going to happen to Betsy. *You have to believe that.*" He did. His faith was so strong it was tangible.

"I want to—but I'm so scared," she whispered emotionally, holding him tight. She kept reviewing every detail of the day Nick had gone into surgery, the day he'd died in the O.R. Matt had been at the hospital that day, too. Only that day he hadn't held her, hadn't offered any comfort but had stayed off by himself, talking only to his parents every now and then. When the news came of Nick's death, they had all cried. But the grief had been a solitary emotion for Matt, and for Elyse, nothing like the shared anxiety they had now.

It was easier, Elyse realized, going through a traumatic event with a man you cared about at your side. And she did care about Matt, very much.

"Betsy's going to be all right," Matt said firmly, holding her even closer.

Elyse looked up at him through a film of tears, not seeing the man who stood just outside the portal—Lawrence Sears. "She has to be, Matt. She just has to be."

"STRAWBERRY?" MATT GUESSED, his eyes focused on the picture Betsy was drawing on the pad in front of her. She shook her head no, then clutched at her throat before resuming her communicative artwork.

"No, uh…hm." Matt twisted his mouth into a perplexed frown and squinted his eyes to better survey his niece's artwork. "Orange? Peach! That's it! Peach! You want peach ice cream!" Matt deducted triumphantly, remembering finally that it was her all-time favorite.

Betsy, still unable to talk, nodded vigorously.

Smiling, Elyse looked at the familial scene. As Matt had predicted, Betsy had come through the surgery with flying colors. She would be going home in the morning. But for now, she was recuperating, enjoying the attention she was getting from her mother and Uncle Matt. Elyse, too, felt much much better now that the operation was behind them, though she'd broken down and sobbed uncontrollably when Marilyn Howard had come out with the surgeon to tell Elyse Betsy was doing great, beginning to wake and asking for her Mommy and her Uncle Matt.

"Peach it is then," Elyse smiled, bending to give her daughter a quick kiss on the top of her head. She went out to the nurses' station. Prior to the surgery, she'd stocked the ward's freezer with a pint of every flavor she'd ever known Betsy to eat. What was left over would be doled out to the other children on the ward.

When she came back, dish in hand, Matt was sitting next to Betsy on the bed, his arm around her. Betsy was cuddled in the curve of his arm, looking more content, Elyse thought, than she had since before Nick had died. Matt was reading softly to her from a book about the Berenstain Bears and too much television. So engrossed in the story were they, they didn't hear her come in. Elyse stood against the wall, watching, content to let them finish, not wanting to interrupt.

Betsy pointed to a picture of the papa bear with his children. "They have a mommy and a daddy," she said, hoarsely, forgetting for a moment in her excitement over the story that she wasn't supposed to talk. She looked over at Matt. "Could you be my daddy?"

Elyse swallowed hard.

For a split second Matt looked both surprised and touched, but the suspicious moistness in his eyes disappeared almost as quickly as it appeared. "Well, no one will ever take the place of your daddy," Matt said. "He'll always have a special place in your heart. But I can do things with you. Love you. We can go places together and give each other presents at Christmas, and when you get old enough to have homework, I can help you with that—"

Betsy's brow furrowed. "What's homework?" she whispered hoarsely.

Matt laughed and explained. Moments later they were reading the story again.

"What were you thinking?" Matt asked, hours later as Elyse walked him toward the elevators at the other end of the pediatric wing. He was going home. Elyse was staying the night at the hospital with Betsy.

"I was thinking how much the girls have come to love you in the past few months."

"That was something, wasn't it," he murmured emotionally, "Betsy asking me to be her daddy?"

Betsy's request had brought on an emotional reaction in them both. "Yes, it was." Elyse swallowed around the lump in her throat. "Did you mind?"

"No." Matt smiled affectionately, looking down at her. Nothing could've made him happier.

They paused by the elevator, waiting for the doors to open.

"The truth is, Matt, I don't know how I would've gotten along without you the past few months. You've helped me so much." Oh, she knew she would have managed. Somehow, she always did. But he'd brought joy back into her life, peace. Even some much needed challenge now and then. And she wanted to be with him now more than ever. But still there loomed the specter of Sears between them, the devastating knowledge about Nick only she and Lawrence were privy to. How could she begin a relationship with Matt knowing she would have to continue to lie to him for several more months, maybe longer, in order to protect Matt and Nick both? In order to protect the whole Donovan family, herself included? Oh, she knew in her heart Matt would understand why she chose that particular route. But intellectually—that was another matter entirely. Intellectually, he was a lawyer. He believed in justice, the system. He believed in public truths, no matter how much they hurt the individual.

"Is that all it is between us—?" he asked softly, focusing in on her preoccupied look. The elevator doors opened. He ignored them. Touching her shoulder lightly, he guided her back into a corner so they might talk privately, and unobserved for a moment. "—gratitude?"

Elyse looked up into his face; she knew she was beginning to feel much more than gratitude or friendship. She was beginning to rely on him for a multitude of things. She was beginning to love him, not just as a friend or a brother-in-law but in a very permanent way. In a marital sense. Yet how could she tell him that now? Knowing of the lies she still had to tell him, for his own sake, as well as hers. Maybe it would be better to wait for just a little while until this blew over, or until Sears was out of the way. When Sears was no longer a threat to her happiness and to Matt's, she could be honest with him, completely honest.

"No," she murmured, aware of her own awkward breathing, "it isn't just gratitude."

If she were sensible she wouldn't say anything more—

anything that would put him off or make him feel uncomfortable around her. She didn't want to risk the friendship they'd built day by day, minute by minute. She remembered all too well his elusiveness, his coolness in the past. She didn't think she could go back to that...to having Matt withdraw emotionally every time she got anywhere near him.

And if she were to admit how she felt...if he didn't feel the same as she thought he was beginning to...oh God, what then?

Dammit, she'd been sensible for weeks now and where had it gotten her? Face it, she had to take a risk and it might as well be now. "It isn't just gratitude," Elyse repeated in a stronger voice, before she could lose her nerve. Her mouth dry, she searched for words that would adequately express her feelings. "I like knowing you're there for me, to talk to or be with. I like being with you." She liked living with him and seeing him morning and evening.

"And I care about you," he interjected quietly, his eyes never leaving her face. His eyes darkened to a silvery blue and he seemed to be steeling himself against the possibility of hurt, too. Of rejection.

"But you're not just a former sister-in-law or member of the family to me," he finished in a low, provocative voice.

Her heart was pounding against her ribs. She could see a pulse working overtime in his neck and felt a warm flush stealing up into her cheeks, coupled with a happiness that had been a long time coming, a very long time coming. In fact, even now, she could hardly believe...

He exhaled slowly and continued watching her, silent and subdued. "But then you knew that, didn't you?" he whispered, moving closer still. "You knew I'd stopped seeing you as Nick's wife weeks ago. That I've been thinking of you—seeing you—as a woman." A woman he desired.

"Yes," she whispered fervently, wanting to but unable to lower her gaze from his. She knew it. And she was afraid of it. Afraid he would find out what she was withholding from him if she let him get too close. Afraid they'd rush

into love, only to lose everything because of a very necessary deception on her part. How frustrating, to finally have
everything she wanted and yet be kept from obtaining it
because of Nick's past....

"Tell me what you're thinking, what you're feeling," he
whispered, running his hands gently up and down her arms.

And suddenly she couldn't evade anymore, not about this,
no matter how frightened she was. "Oh, Matt, everything
is so damn complicated," And she wanted everything to be
easy. And free. And open. She wanted to be free to love
him, to have no past. Only a future...

"I know."

"It'd be easier if we weren't living together."

"I know that, too," he said, his arms tightening around
her. But he didn't want her to leave his house any more
than she wanted to pack up and leave with her children.

He was still watching her, waiting. Elyse swallowed hard.
"It's not just Betsy who wants you more a part of our life.
I care about you, too," she whispered back, saying the
words and knowing they were true. "I care about you very
much."

His hands were gentle on her, pushing the thick hair from
her face. Unmindful of the possible intrusion of others, he
eased her against him, his arms warm and strong around her
shoulders. They needed this time out together and they were
taking it. It was that simple.

His grip on her tightened possessively. She could feel his
heart beating double time in his chest. Holding her gently
in his arms, skimming his jaw on the softness of her hair,
he said only, "When Betsy's well again, when everything's
back to normal, I think we should take some time just for
ourselves, on a regular basis." His voice was husky yet
underscored with fierce determination. He held her slightly
away from him so he could look at her. His eyes were full
of wonder and delight, as if he couldn't get used to the idea
that he could have allowed himself the luxury of touching

her. Of holding her in his arms. She knew how he felt. She didn't want to let him go, either, didn't ever want to move. "Yes," she whispered, giving in all too willingly to his request. "I want that, too." She wanted to explore all the possibilities of a relationship with Matt. She wanted to know him in every way possible and vice versa. It wouldn't be easy, but somehow, some way, they would find the time, the way to be together. At least for a while, without interference. From anyone. Releasing a pent-up breath, she softened her body against his. She had needed this all day, needed to feel him next to her, needed to physically soak up some of his strength. And it wasn't just the stress of Betsy's surgery bringing them together. What they were feeling for one another had been building very slowly for a long time. The day's events might possibly have hastened the inevitable just a bit, but it would have happened no matter what.

She looked up at him, her eyes blazing a path between them. Studying him, she was filled with a tenderness that was almost overwhelming. There was no doubt about it; it had been an incredibly draining day for both of them. His hair was rumpled from running his hands through it. His eyes were alert, but there were shadows beneath them alluding to the fact that he'd been missing as much sleep as she recently. His jaw, though clean shaven at four a.m. that morning, was now stubbled with the faint shadow of a beard. His open sport shirt and pressed trousers were also a little worse for wear—the latter stained with a little of Betsy's coveted peach ice cream. And yet to Elyse he had never looked more heart-stoppingly sexy.

He lifted a hand to gently stroke her hair. Her pulse leaped, flooding her with warmth. "It would be sort of an informal courtship," he delineated gently, looking very much as if he wanted to kiss her then and there. His voice dropped another husky notch as he raised a hand to her cheek and gently traced a line along the pale golden curve, "To let us know if what we're feeling now is real. Lasting."

It is, she thought joyously, *in my heart I already know it is.* Matt was everything she had ever wanted in a man and more. She'd never expected to find happiness like that again. Now that she had, the feelings were almost overwhelming. She felt twice blessed, as if suddenly the world were full of possibilities for her and for him. She felt like she could begin to dream again....

She could smell the lingering traces of his after-shave, mingling with the bolder masculine fragrance of his skin. Everything about him, she thought, was so appealing. And yet there were plenty of roadblocks in their path. Tension stiffened her spine. "What about your parents?" What would Abigail and Peter think? Would they approve and if they didn't, what then? It may have been foolhardy, but she didn't want anything interfering in her relationship with Matt. She wanted time alone with him, time to savor and explore the newness and fragility of what they were feeling.

"If you don't want to tell them yet, we don't have to," Matt promised quietly, understanding her reservations about going public before they knew better where their relationship was heading.

"I'd rather not," she decided pensively after a moment, her mind whirling with images of the past and fears of the future. If this thing with Lawrence Sears did blow up...no, better to keep it as simple as possible. For now.

He studied the mixed feelings he saw reflected in her face. She felt the tension inside his body, saw the confusion in his eyes. She wanted to comfort him but she didn't know how.

"I don't mean to push you. I'm sorry if it seems to you if I have. But I wanted to be honest with you. I don't like being forced to keep my feelings for you under wraps— even for propriety's sake." His voice dropped another mesmerizing notch as his gaze roved lovingly over her face. He seemed to be committing everything about her to memory. "Especially when they feel so right."

At his confession, Elyse didn't know whether to laugh or

cry. God, her life was a mess. And all because of Sears and Nick. She'd wanted an honest, open relationship. Matt was offering her that; ironically now it was she, not the man in her life, who was having to put up roadblocks to that kind of perfect intimacy and sharing.

He studied her silently. "What is it? What else is bothering you about this?"

"I—" she floundered, not knowing what to say that would sound plausible but still protect her secret.

Misreading the reason behind her anxiety, he finally asked quietly, "Do you want to go out with someone else? Is that it?" For him that wasn't a joyous prospect.

Nor was it a pleasing thought for Elyse. "No, I—no." There was Matt and only Matt. Of that, she was very certain. The other men she had dated since Nick's death were nothing to her. She looked down at her hands. "It's just because of our past relationship...this is going to be very tricky. We're going to have to handle it carefully."

"I agree." An announcement that visiting hours were over sounded over the loudspeaker. He paused reluctantly, knowing he had to leave. "I better be going before they kick me out of here. I'll see you in the morning?"

Elyse nodded. "Betsy and I will be waiting. And Matt, thanks for everything. You really helped me today." She didn't know how she would have gotten through it without him.

His eyes darkened; his voice took on a emotional huskiness. "I wouldn't have wanted to be anywhere else."

Nor would she have wanted him to be, Elyse thought, turning slowly and heading back up to pediatrics. Maybe this would work out after all. All she needed was a little more time, until the memorial was behind them and that chapter of her life with Nick was closed forever. Once that happened, she and Matt would be able to make their feelings known to others—provided everything worked out as she hoped and thought it would. Maybe then Elyse would be able to stop looking back and only look forward. To love, marriage. Matt had made her realize that she wanted to be married again, she wanted to share her life with a man. The truth was she wanted Matt and the love and caring and gentle protectiveness only he could give.

Betsy was sitting up in bed watching television when Elyse returned to the room. "Did Uncle Matt go home?" she whispered hoarsely.

Elyse straightened Betsy's covers and tucked them in around her. "Yes, he did."

"Will he come back tomorrow?" Betsy asked.

"Yes, he's going to come to the hospital to help take you home," Elyse smiled, sitting down next to her daughter and taking her hand in hers.

"I'm glad," Betsy said. "I like him a lot. I miss him when he's not here."

Elyse smiled and nodded. "Me, too."

OVER THE COURSE OF THE NEXT WEEK, Matt and Elyse spent as much time together as possible. One night they made popcorn together and along with the children watched a Walt Disney movie on cable. Several nights they had a late swim alone. On Wednesday they were able to sit out front on the porch swing and talk long after the others were in bed. They shared trivial and important things, looking forward to the future when they would have more time alone.

Saturday evening found them in the shopping mall, planning a surprise anniversary party for his parents to be held at the end of July. Together they selected a gift for them— a beautiful silver serving tray and tea service. Finished with their errands but not anxious to go home yet, they wandered through the mall. Matt wasn't touching her, wasn't even holding her hand, yet Elyse had never felt closer to another man in her life. She liked the fact that he was taking it nice and slow and yet she was impatient, too. She wished their lives were less complicated, less entwined in a familial way. She wanted to be able to see him and be seen with him freely. Yet she knew for many reasons that just wasn't possible yet. Foremost was the gossip such an action would cause and the probable detrimental effect on Nick's memorial. Neither Matt nor she would jeopardize that now. Their own wishes would have to be put on hold just a little while longer. They would have to be patient, careful, accept what little time they could manage to set aside for themselves.

Oblivious to her thoughts, Matt was watching intently as a mother and daughter quibbled over a wedding gown in a nearby bridal shop. His next question revealed his interest.

"Do you ever miss being married?" He turned to Elyse expectantly.

She did now. Before Matt had come back in her life, though, it had been a different story. "This may sound strange, but I kind of enjoyed my freedom for a while. Now though, yes, I'd like to be married again." *But only to you,* she thought.

Matt looked back at the mother, watching as they disappeared into the dressing room. "I miss being married, too," he said quietly. "I didn't at first, though. Right after Holly died, I didn't want anyone else close to me, intruding on my space. On the heels of that came an indiscriminate dating stage—I went out simply so I wouldn't have to be alone."

"I know what that's like," Elyse said softly.

"But that wore thin after a while." He turned and headed for a nearby ice cream stand.

"For me, too,"

He bought them both a cone. They found a quiet bench and sat down, their packages on either side of them. Matt continued, "Lately I find I miss being intimate with a woman. Not just physically intimate, although that's a part of any good relationship, but emotionally intimate. I miss the late night talks. The private times. I miss having someone to talk to, day or night, waking up and finding the woman I love in my arms."

The yearning in his voice brought home her own feelings. "I miss all that, too," she said quietly, although she felt her time with Nick perhaps hadn't been quite as ideal as Matt's marriage to Holly seemed to have been.

"Was your marriage a happy one?" she asked quietly, as they finished their cones and started strolling again. He had changed after Holly's death. At first she had chalked it up to a simple postloss depression. Now she wasn't so sure that was all it was. He rarely talked about Holly. In some ways, it was as if he half pretended she never had existed. He talked about Nick a lot though, to his parents, to her, to her children. So why did he avoid talking about his first wife? Was she making too much of this? Maybe it just hurt, remembering. She could understand that.

Matt looked straight ahead. He answered carefully, "Yes and no. I was a lot younger then. Holly and I were both pretty self-centered, career-oriented. I don't think she would've ever wanted to have children. I think I would have missed that."

Knowing how much he loved her children, Elyse agreed. "Then you do want children of your own?" Elyse ascertained. He would be a wonderful father.

He nodded. "What about you? Is three it for you or could you see yourself having more children—if you married again?"

Her answer was important to him. "I could see myself having one more child," she said softly. "Maybe two. Whatever I did, I'd want to make sure I had time enough for all of the children, though."

He nodded approvingly and his hand lightly touched the middle of her back as he guided her, single-file, through a throng of laughing teenagers. "What about working?" he asked when they were alone again and had stopped to admire a display or richly crafted leather accessories. "Is that important to you, too?"

She took a deep breath. That was a harder question. Since she'd gone back to work, she'd had both high and low days. "I think, given a choice, I'd stay home until my children were a little older and then just work part-time. Enough to get out of the house and into the world and keep my skills up, not enough to exhaust me.''

"That sounds practical.''

To their left, a store owner pulled closed his gate and locked his front door. Other shop owners followed suit. Elyse was stunned to realize the mall was closing for the night. Matt looked at his watch. "Guess it's time to head home.''

"I guess so,'' Elyse said reluctantly. They'd been at the mall for three hours. It seemed more like thirty minutes, and selfish as it may have been, she didn't want their time together to end. "It didn't seem like we were here that long,'' she commented as she and Matt headed for the mall's exit.

"To me, either.'' He grinned and juggling his packages to one hand, held the door open for her. "As a first 'time out,' I'd say it was pretty successful, wouldn't you?''

Elyse nodded. "Very successful.'' It was getting so she couldn't imagine her life without Matt.

Chapter Nine

"I need your help, Elyse," Bob Osborne began late the following afternoon in the hospital cafeteria. He'd come to the hospital earlier, then waited around her until she had a break. Elyse hadn't really wanted to talk to him; it felt disloyal somehow, to Matt, for her even to be there with Bob when she knew how Matt felt about the man. But at the same time he'd looked so lost, so pathetic. And Elyse had never been able to resist rooting for the underdog. So she'd given him fifteen minutes of her time.

"I've decided to write a book."

Elyse stirred sugar into her iced tea. "Good for you." She wanted to see him on his feet again, if for no other reason than to ease Matt's guilty feelings about ending the man's legal career. And she couldn't help but note dispassionately that Bob did look better than he had the last time she'd seen him. Now he was more in command. The wan look around his eyes was gone, but perhaps that was due to his recently acquired tan.

"I've even got a publisher lined up, but here's the hitch. They insist on a balanced view of the entire situation. They want to interview some of the other principal people involved, and since Matt is the one who turned me in—"

"They want him to talk about it, too," Elyse guessed.

"Right. Only I can't even get him on the phone."

Elyse knew; Bob had called the house a few times, only

to be turned away there, too. "I don't know what I can do, Bob. Matt is still upset about your being here in Texas. I think he wants to forget the whole thing."

He gave her a minute or two's grace. "I can't forget the whole thing." His misery reminded her of how his life had been ruined. Without the book contract what chance would he have to rebuild it?

"No, I guess not." She sighed.

"You think I'm being unreasonable, asking for Matt's help?"

Elyse picked at her salad. "Unrealistic may be more like it. I just…Matt isn't a very forgiving sort of person. He sees things in very black and white terms. He believes in the system."

He grimaced unhappily, stared past her at a spot on the floor. "The whole time I was in prison he never wrote or called or came to see me once. He deserted my family. We were friends, Elyse."

Bob was behaving as if the hurt were one-sided; it wasn't. "Maybe that's what makes your betrayal so hard for him to bear. It probably would've been a whole lot easier on him if you hadn't been friends, if he hadn't taken the whole thing so personally."

Bob sat back and spread his hands wide in a gesture of supplication. "It's not as if I tried to frame him for what I did."

"No, but your actions did reflect badly on the whole firm. They hurt the reputations of all the lawyers at Smith and Lowe."

Bob was silent, reflecting. His jaw jutted out resentfully. "You'd never know it to see the firm now. They're as busy as ever." While he was out of a job.

Elyse was curious. "Why did you do it, Bob?" To hear Matt talk when he had first known Bob, the man had been a saint.

Bob shrugged. "Money. We never had enough of it. I wanted to give my family everything."

She could understand that. "And did you?"

"For a while."

"What happened to make you…well, get into trouble?"

"That's the funny part. It was an accident."

She looked at him blankly. "I don't understand."

Bob leaned back in his chair and began to talk in weary tones. "It was shortly after I started at Smith and Lowe. I went to this car place. I was in the market for a Mercedes. I wanted to buy my wife a new set of wheels for her birthday, something really special to make up for all the years of sacrifice when she'd put me through law school. Anyway, they were all out of my range. I couldn't even lease one for her. Then out of the blue this guy comes to me. He owns the car dealership, has heard I work at Smith and Lowe. He wants me to be his lawyer. If I agree he says he'll give me a special deal on the car, kind of a professional courtesy. All right, I knew it wasn't exactly…legitimate, but I figured what the hell? Then a couple months later, along comes another guy. A builder who'd gotten into some trouble for not complying exactly with the local building codes. If I'd get him out of trouble, he'd help me get a really nice place, at cost. Well, one thing led to another. Before I knew it, I had deals going all over the place."

"And the kind of life you'd always wanted."

Bob nodded, looking miserable. "Then when the last deal came along, I—I didn't want to get involved. I knew it was risky, but the people involved knew a lot about me. They said if I didn't help out they'd see that my family paid."

"You were involved with the mob?" She sat up incredulously.

He shook his head. "Nothing that organized, but they were a very powerful group."

Elyse knew what it felt like to get caught up inextricably in an unsavory situation. "So you went along."

Bob nodded. "And got caught." His mouth compressed unhappily.

"Why didn't you turn yourself in? Matt said if you had he would have helped you."

He shrugged. "It was too late. I knew if I did I'd lose everything I'd worked for, get disbarred. I was just trying to hold on to what I had." Perspiration broke out on his forehead, dotted his upper lip. "I begged Matt not to turn me in, begged him." His voice turned cold as he remembered. He got a handkerchief out of his pocket and mopped at the moisture on his face. "Anyway, that's why I'm writing the book. Part of it is to make money. I do need to support myself. But the other half, the more pressing half, is so I can tell others what it's like, how easy it is to get in over your head, to do something a little bit shady, and then something else, and then something else, until finally there's no going back. If I could just save one man from losing all I did, it would be worth it. So please, Elyse. Talk to Matt. Try to get him to at least see me?"

"I saw Bob Osborne today," Elyse began, later the same evening. The kids were in bed. Abigail and Peter were watching a television miniseries about China. She was sitting on the porch swing. Matt had come out to join her.

Matt stiffened. The swing momentarily stopped. "And?" His tone was anything but cordial.

"He's writing a book."

Matt swore profusely beneath his breath. Knowing he didn't want to hear of it, Elyse nonetheless plodded on, recounting to him everything Bob had said.

Matt remained unmoved. "I don't want anything to do with him." He pushed away from her and stalked to the far end of the porch.

"He says he's sorry—"

Matt whirled to face her. "Like hell he is! And even if he were—the man betrayed me, Elyse. Do you understand that? He betrayed me. I can't trust him. I can't even look him in the face."

She was silent. She knew how hurt Matt was. She had

sympathy for that. But she also knew the rage he felt toward Bob was eating him alive inside. "You can't go on like this, avoiding him," she pointed out calmly.

"Why not? I've done it for three years. The man is a master at playing people, Elyse. Don't you think I know that? Hell, I was one of his prime patsies! If I hadn't caught him red-handed, he'd probably still be playing me for a fool." He swore again, this time more loudly. A muscle worked convulsively in his cheek.

She got up and moved to stand by him. "Whether you help him with the book or not is for you to decide, but life is too short to carry grudges." Especially when the feelings Matt harbored were so destructive and stressful. "I think maybe you should see him again, try one more time to make peace between the two of you."

"I can't forgive him, Elyse," Matt repeated roughly between clenched teeth.

Nor would he forgive her for withholding the information about Nick. Information that was just as treacherous. A chill went through Elyse at the thought. He won't find out about Nick, she thought. I have nothing to fear.

And yet…another part of her was not so certain she was safe from discovery. She took a deep breath and tried one last time to reason with Matt, to help him become a more tolerant, forgiving person—if only for his own well-being. "Bob paid the price for what he did. He went to jail, he served his sentence. If society has forgiven him, why can't you?"

Matt was silent, looking at her.

"You'll never be free, Matt, until you do."

ELYSE'S WORDS STAYED WITH MATT all the following day and the next. Several times he reached for the phone, only to put the receiver back. He wanted to please Elyse, to believe he'd been wrong about Bob, but he just couldn't. In his gut he knew the man was the worst kind of traitor, a master at manipulating others. Matt had no intention of letting Bob hurt him or anyone else in his family again. If it meant carrying that grudge permanently, so be it.

In the meantime he had a private investigator's report to peruse, Matt thought decisively, opening an envelope that had just been delivered to his office by a cross-town courier. Melody Sears would be there in half an hour. And when she arrived, she'd want a full report.

The first week of surveillance was as Matt expected. Sears had been in surgery or at the hospital ninety percent of the time. The rest he'd apparently been home alone, sleeping. Ditto the second week, except for the night he'd attended the fund-raiser in Nick's honor.

The third week...

Matt stopped, blinked, sure he wasn't focusing right.

The third week he'd been seen twice in the company of Elyse Donovan. Matt shuffled through the rest of the papers. The first time they'd met at a little bar several blocks from the hospital. The second time was in a park just outside the hospital.

He opened a second manilla envelope. Inside were several glossy photos of Elyse in the park, sunglasses on, arms folded at her waist, talking to Sears. Another of Elyse sitting in a booth, her jaw taut and angry. She looked tense, hassled.

Matt went back and checked the details on the meetings. Both incidents had been brief—not lasting longer than ten minutes. There'd been nothing to indicate the two were having an affair, the investigator said—but the exchanges had been of an intimate, hushed nature. Mrs. Donovan did not look like she was having a good time or enjoying Dr. Sears's company. Beyond that, there was nothing out of the ordinary to report.

Matt flashed back to Melody Sears, the first day in his office, "Larry's having an affair, I know it. He's always been a man of voracious appetites...."

And then again, another scene. Sears dancing with Elyse, his hand inching up from her waist to the bare silky skin of

her back. Elyse's seeming acceptance of the man's touch.
The guilty, hassled look on her face afterward, when Matt
had confronted her about Sears's actions. Her initial refusal
to tell him anything about what had gone on between the
two of them. Her almost too pragmatic explanation later.

Had Elyse been telling him the truth? Matt wondered.

Or was she betraying him, too? Was Matt wrong to believe in Elyse, as wrong as he'd been when he'd once believed in Bob Osborne?

His secretary notified him his client had arrived. "Mrs.
Sears is here to see you."

Matt responded promptly. "Send her in."

"So, did you get the goods on Larry?" Melody asked,
sauntering into the office. She draped her handbag over one
chair, and as she sat down in the other wing chair in front
of his desk began inching off her gloves.

"He's not seeing anyone on the side right now." Matt's
reply was automatic; he felt guilty as hell. He had never lied
to a client before or even deliberately held anything back,
yet he felt his first responsibility in this instance was to
Elyse.

"You're sure?" Melody took out her cigarettes, her ex-
pertly made-up eyes concentrating on Matt's face.

"Positive," Matt said. Sears hadn't seen anyone except
Elyse. And he was certain she had an explanation for that.
At least she'd better....

Melody's mouth twisted into a pout. "You must've hired
a lousy P.I.—" She blew smoke circles up in the air.

With effort, Matt kept his voice flat. "I hired the best
group in Dallas. The fact is your husband is keeping a com-
mendably low profile these days. Maybe because he antic-
ipates a divorce?" Now, if that were true, Matt thought, it
could explain a lot.

"Maybe." Melody frowned again. "Money means a lot
to him. More than I ever did." She pounded her left fist on
the arm of her chair. "Damn, if only they still gave ali-
mony—"

Matt was tempted to laugh at her mercenary approach; maybe Melody and Lawrence were a perfect match, more so than they knew. "You're entitled to half your community property—"

Melody scowled and put out her cigarette in the ashtray on the corner of Matt's desk. "*What* community property? Aside from the house, the cars, Larry spends everything he brings in. Bad investments, ridiculously expensive vacations—you name it, he's done it."

So what does that have to do with Elyse? Matt wondered. Why is Sears seeing her outside the hospital? Why had Elyse allowed it? And why hadn't she mentioned it to him?

Those were answers he would have to get later. "Do you want me to keep trying?" Matt let Melody know how much it was costing, day by day, to keep constant tabs on her husband.

She frowned. "No. If he's not playing around now... damn. After all this time of reeling in everything in sight, he lives like a monk."

Except for Elyse.

Matt pushed aside the ugly thought. "About the divorce—"

Melody began putting on her gloves. "Don't do anything for the moment. I need time to think."

Matt studied her closely. "You're reconsidering?"

Melody shrugged insouciantly. "I'm not going to live on poverty row. If it means staying with him..." She gestured as if she couldn't care less what happened, either way. "Well, we'll just have to see...."

FOR MATT, the rest of the day passed in a confused haze. For one thing his conscience was bothering him. He hated lies. He felt ambivalent about handing a story to Melody Sears, and yet under the circumstances what else could he have done? Beyond that, all he could think of was Elyse. He got out the pictures of her and Sears several times. He studied them relentlessly. But no answers came to him. For those, he knew he would have to talk to her—alone, with no children present, no interruptions of any kind.

Matt's chance came later that same evening. By ten o'clock his parents had retired for the evening. Elyse was in the downstairs utility room, folding clothes.

"Here, let me help you with that," he remarked casually, taking a basket of towels. He tried to subdue the frustration and fury he felt inside him. If he wanted answers from her, he had to stay cool.

"Thanks," she smiled, tossing him a few towels. "I can use a spare hand." Her eyes were bright and lively as she inquired, "Get your work done? I noticed you were poring over papers in the library tonight."

She was so damn innocent. He could almost believe…but he'd seen the pictures, dammit!

"I was writing a few thank-you notes on behalf of the family," he informed her implacably. The list of contributors was growing by leaps and bounds. Personal letters were also coming in. Though the memorial hadn't been officially announced to the public, dozens of people were aware of it. Many were writing to let the family know how Nick had positively affected their lives. Matt found it comforting to read the letters, to know that even though Nick had died at a very young age, he still had been able to help so many people.

Elyse looked guilty for a moment. "You should have told me. I would have been glad to help."

He knew, but he'd needed to be alone to sort out the questions he had. "Is there much talk at the hospital about the memorial?" he asked casually.

Elyse paused reflectively. She was barefoot, wearing a loose cotton jersey top and matching slacks. She looked rumpled and desirable in an at-home-casual sort of way. "No, not really. I mean everyone's hoping the money will get raised, of course, and almost everyone has made some small contribution, but other than that…."

"What about Sears?" Matt asked casually, picking up

another towel. "Is he bothering you at all? Did he go forward to the hospital board with his suggestion that he take a very active role in the memorial?"

Elyse paused briefly, then resumed folding towels with brisk, economical gestures. "Yes, he did. They turned him down."

Matt jammed his hands in the pockets of his jeans. His frown became more pronounced. "Bet he wasn't happy about that."

Her eyes were large and unhappy. "No, I guess he wasn't." Elyse turned toward the dryer. With unusual concentration, she removed the last of the clean clothes, then began transferring a wet load from the washer into the drum.

Matt noticed she wasn't meeting his gaze. Another clue that something was wrong. He lowered his voice to a gentle, coaxing pitch, then asked, "Has Sears been harassing you about it—again, trying to get you involved?" And if so, why wouldn't she tell him? Unless she were afraid of another jealous scene, like the one they'd had at the fundraiser. Suddenly he couldn't blame her for not coming forward, not after the asinine way he'd behaved the other night, dragging her off into a side yard like some sort of caveman.

Elyse's breath escaped in a wavering sigh. She turned toward Matt and met his probing look. Something gentled in him. As always he wanted to protect her.

"Yes," she said finally, sighing deeply. "He has been bothering me a little." Relief swept through Matt that at last Elyse was levelling with him, telling him what he needed—wanted—to know.

Seeing he wanted her to be more specific, she swallowed hard and said carefully, "He's approached me several times about going forward to the board on his behalf. He thinks they'd be inclined to listen to the family."

"He's bothering you at work, then?" Matt asked.

She shook her head, then looked at him directly. "No. He—both times we've discussed it outside the hospital."

Matt noticed she didn't say where.

Elyse, reading his dismay despite his attempts to suppress the nature of his thoughts, said quietly, "Once in the park, once at a bar near the hospital. Both meetings only lasted a couple of minutes. There was nothing to them, really."

"But you went—" Matt couldn't help it. He began to get angry again and as a result his tone was grim and accusing.

Her mouth curled in exasperation. "It was either that or get into it at the hospital. Frankly I'd rather not see him at all, but I know how he is. If I didn't do as he asked, then he'd just bring his requests home, to the family. And I'd rather not have your parents involved in this at all."

Matt believed that. He, too, sheltered his parents whenever possible. "You could have sent Sears to me," he said gruffly. Her decision to handle the man's harassment alone left him feeling hurt and angry. The pale, miserable look on her face only added to his discontent.

"I tried." Something inside her raged like a tug of war. "He said the two of you had never really hit it off. If I wouldn't deal with him, he preferred to deal with your parents. Naturally I decided to act on behalf of the family."

"By refusing him."

She stiffened at the annoyed note in his voice, then made a seesawing motion with her hand, correcting with weary coldness, "Putting him off. I didn't say no exactly, just that I'd...try and figure out something when it came to the dedication ceremony." Unexpectedly her voice became tentative, pleading. "He was Nick's partner, after all—"

To have her defending Sears after what the louse had done to her and to Nick was more than Matt could take. He closed the distance between them sharply, loomed over her. She backed up against the washer, her hands out on either side of her, gripping the machine for balance. Her face whitened yet another shade. She looked frightened and upset.

Matt felt equally defensive as he corrected, "He stabbed Nick in the back." Had she forgotten Sears had tried to cuckold Nick on the night before his death?

But to her, for whatever reason, Lawrence's passes at her

no longer mattered. She let out a frustrated breath. "You and I know that. People at the hospital and your parents don't. Lawrence thinks it will look odd if he isn't involved. That people will talk, wonder why he wasn't invited." She paused and wet her lips. "Frankly, Matt, I think he has a point." Her hands gripped the cold enamel more tightly.

Matt bent closer, unsure of whether he wanted to kiss her or shake her. He just knew he'd never been more angry in his life, not even when Holly had... "I don't want him involved in Nick's memorial."

She seemed not as convinced it could be avoided. Finally she said softly, honestly, "The truth? I don't either."

Matt believed her. He still had the odd sensation she wasn't telling him everything. Though what else she could be hiding, he didn't know. She saw his questions; she gave him no clue as to what she was thinking. Matt sighed. He hadn't known he could be hurt like that, and her seeing Sears at all hurt him. "If he comes to you again—" he began wearily.

Her chin lifted defiantly. "I'm hoping he won't."

"But if he does," Matt interjected firmly, placing both of his palms flat against the washer on either side of her. "I want to know about it—then, that moment." He was standing so close to her he could feel her body heat.

Elyse hesitated, the pulse throbbing frantically at the base of her throat. "I don't want to cross him, Matt."

She really was afraid. Why? And why wouldn't she tell him everything? Why did he have to keep dragging details out of her bit by bit? "You don't want to cross me, either," he said silkily, before he could think.

She reacted as if she'd been slapped. Her body took on a deathly stillness. Bright new color flooded her face. Her jaw clenched. Her head lifted. "Is that a threat?" She seemed almost daring him to say that it had been.

He knew it had sounded that way. Suddenly Matt was ashamed of himself, of his jealousy. He had to stop being so protective of her, so possessive. She'd given him no real reason to mistrust her. True, she hadn't come to him with everything, but as of yet he had no right to expect her to do so. It wasn't as if they were committed to one another, not yet, anyway. So they'd had one date—in the loosest sense of the word. He hadn't even kissed her that night, deciding instead to continue to take it slow. He had to believe in her, trust her; if a lasting love did develop between them, he knew she would come to him then. But only if he showed her beforehand that he could handle anything she had to say. He couldn't risk flying off the handle with jealous speculations the way Nick had. Because if he did back her into a corner that way, make her feel guilty and condemned for no reason, he'd lose her for sure. And Matt didn't think he could stand that.

"Matt, I can handle him." Elyse came forward. She rested both her hands on his forearms. Matt felt his anger flee. "You're sure—" He wanted her in his life.

She nodded emphatically. "I just need you to trust me, to believe I can handle this—not just for me but for the whole family."

She seemed so capable then, so in control. Although it went against everything he stood for—he'd always wanted to protect the woman he cared about—he knew he had to give her the freedom to make her own decisions, use her own judgment. Because only if they met as equals would they ever be able to build a relationship worth cherishing. "All right," he nodded reluctantly, "I'll do it, for you."

Chapter Ten

"Whose idea was it to dress the children up as flowers and tree trunks anyway?" Matt grumbled, bending over the sewing machine.

"I don't know. The teacher's, I guess." Elyse glanced over her shoulder, pleased with Matt's skill. She'd just shown him how to use the sewing machine several hours earlier. Predictably it hadn't taken him long to get the hang of it.

"It figures," Matt laughed and shook his head over the silliness of the costumes they were creating.

Elyse smiled. "Welcome to the wonderful world of preschool, *n'est-ce pas*?" She was ironing the costumes as Matt finished sewing the last of the seams. Never the most patient person when it came to domestic work, he was operating the sewing-machine pedal at high speed. Fortunately he seemed to have good control of the material he was passing beneath the flashing silver needle. "How are your seams coming over there?" she asked. Until that evening he'd never been near a sewing machine in his life. And he probably still wouldn't have been had Abigail and Peter not been away on their long-yearned-for Bahamas cruise. Generally all sewing in the Donovan household fell to either Abigail or Elyse.

"Well…" Matt peered down at his handiwork. "They're all right, I guess." He paused and peered a little closer. His lower lip twisted into a reflective frown. "It's a little crooked in places, maybe an eighth of an inch past the five-eight markings. Want me to rip it out and do it over?"

"Heaven's no! If we do, we'll be here all night! Besides I don't think it has to be that perfect. After all the kids are going to be up on stage—"

Matt grinned. "Singing their little hearts out."

"Who's going to notice if the bark is straight or not?"

"Not me, that's for sure." He flashed a dazzling paternal smile. "I'm going to be so busy videotaping their first school play—"

"You're serious."

"I want Mom and Dad to be able to see it when they get back from their cruise. I know the girls will want to see it afterward. And I also figure we'll want to run it several times."

Elyse smiled. She'd enrolled the three girls in the summer session of the Montessori school at the beginning of June. So far, three weeks into the program, they were enjoying it tremendously. She credited their enthusiasm to the loving dedication of the teaching staff and the small child to teacher ratio. "You know, this is the first school program they'll all be in together." Caroline and Betsy had been in previous programs at their former church-run nursery school in their old neighborhood.

They went back to their respective tasks. "Have you had to do this often?" Matt asked. Clearly costume making was the part of parenting he least liked.

"Just for Halloween. These are my first school costumes."

Matt sighed, taking the last garment from beneath the needle and clipping the threads. "And I thought being a lawyer was hard work."

"Not cut out for seamstressing, hmm?" Elyse teased as he walked over to hand her the garment.

He pressed the fabric into her hand, momentarily resting

his palm against hers. "Not cut out for anything involving great manual dexterity."

"I thought you did fine." She held the garment up and, with the exception of a few slightly crooked seams, found no other discernible flaws.

"Yeah, well, thanks. You should see me put together a model. As a kid—" he spread his hands wide "—my models were incredible disasters! Most of the time you couldn't even tell if it was supposed to be an airplane or a ship, and that was before it was painted. When it was painted, it was even worse—never failed to look like anything but a giant multicolored psychedelic blob."

"Fortunately you don't need that kind of dexterity to be a lawyer." Elyse turned off the iron and put the last flower costume on a hanger. "For that, you only need brain power and a propensity for logic and that—" She winced, feeling the unexpected cramp in her neck. Her hand covered the sore muscle as her breath hissed in.

Matt was at her side instantly. "What is it?"

"It's nothing." Elyse frowned, massaging the place where the muscle was knotted. "My neck and shoulders always get stiff and sore when I'm sewing. Tension, I guess."

"Here, let me see if I can work it out." Before she could protest, his hands were on her shoulders. Moving slowly at first, his hands pressed down on the tense muscles. Increasing the pressure slightly, he rubbed and stroked. It was the most mesmerizing, relaxing sensation she'd experienced, and Elyse felt her tension dissolving.

She sighed, leaning back into his chest. "Oh that feels good."

Her eyes shut as the rhythmic kneading motions of his hands brought on a delicious lassitude. Her breath slowing even more, she relaxed against him.

The next thing she knew the massaging motion had stopped and she was being turned around. Her eyes fluttered open in surprise. She had a brief second to see the intent look on his face, and then his hands were on her shoulders, sliding down her back, guiding her closer still, until they were touching everywhere. He stared down at her for a long quiet moment. She knew he was going to kiss her, knew it and wanted it with every fiber of her being.

His mouth pressed against hers in absolute command and it was a command she responded to completely. She had always yearned to be needed like this, desired; his kiss left her no doubt she was the only thing that mattered to him. Surrendering just that swiftly, she lost herself in the sinewy cradle of his arms, the give of his mouth. He was everything she'd ever wanted, more giving than she could have imagined.

The trembling began in her knees, whispered through her thighs to settle deep inside her. He felt her response and encouraged it. His hands moved over her body, gently at first, molding her against him with a conviction not to be denied. His fingertips grazed her breast, the heat of his touch descending easily through layers of fabric. Her mouth clung to his, needing, wanting more of the magic only he could give until they were thinking, reacting, touching as one. After seconds he lifted his head and stared down into her face, not speaking, simply gauging her reaction, accepting the fact that she knew what she was doing and wanted more, wanted him completely, body and soul.

She knew then that she loved him and had for some time. She couldn't tell him when her feelings for him had changed, only that they had. "Matt—"

"I love you," he said quietly, beating her to the punch.

For a moment she basked in the sound of his words and the tenderness in his gaze. And then she was speaking, too, telling him what was in her heart, what had been for a very long time. "And I love you," she said softly. "I love you."

"YOU LOOK HAPPY," Matt said two weeks later, sitting down next to Elyse on the sofa. The house was quiet save for the muted sounds of the television program Elyse had been watching.

Elyse switched off the remote control television and cuddled next to Matt. His arm was draped across her shoulders, her cheek against his chest. He'd just had a shower and she could smell the soap and talcum powder on his skin. "I am happy," she confessed. Since Abigail and Peter had been away, her relationship with Matt had blossomed into something very special.

"It's been nice, having the house all to ourselves in the evening after the children are in bed," Matt mused. He closed his eyes and drew her nearer; she was aware of the strength of his arms, the pressure of his body next to hers, the desire curling deep inside of her.

"Having late dinners on the patio," she reminisced.

"Talking until three a.m.—"

Elyse smiled, remembering that they had indeed stayed up that late one Saturday night. And what a romantic yet peaceful night it had been. But then Matt made everything seem romantic—even the most mundane household chore—because they did it together. They'd become a team in so many ways; she liked having him as a partner. She liked that they were free to talk and laugh, to just be together every night.

"I liked dancing in the dark."

Matt grinned provocatively and tilted his head down until his lips just brushed hers, back and forth, back and forth. "And necking—"

Elyse tried but couldn't suppress a small shiver of pleasure as she gently returned the light, fleeting kiss. "That, too." At her confession, he growled his delight and guided her more fully into his arms. He held her against him tightly and they kissed more passionately until her whole body was alive with golden currents of sensation and frissons of fire. When he finally let her go, she moaned, soft and low in her throat. She felt shaken, vulnerable—and very much loved. "I don't want this to end," Elyse whispered, clinging to

him, her mind whirling with images of she and Matt together, of feelings of love and warmth.

"I don't either," Matt dropped a tiny kiss on the sleek
crown of her head and held her tighter still, as if he never
wanted to let her go.

Seconds ticked past. Matt made no effort to kiss her
again, to further the intimacy. Although it was something
they'd never spoken about directly during the past few days,
the constraints of their current relationship were still a concern to both of them. They sighed in unison, knowing there
was just one thing keeping them apart now. But it was a
stumbling block that had to be removed before they took
their relationship any further. "We have to tell your parents," Elyse said quietly, her lips pressed against the throbbing pulse in his neck.

"I know." Matt's arms tightened around her possessively. "And we'll do it as soon as they get home."

"And have had a chance to recover from the traveling,"
Elyse stipulated firmly, thinking, *please, let them understand*. Yes, she had been married to Nick once and she had
loved him. But her marriage to Nick was over. Now she
wanted to go on. She wanted and needed their approval.
Matt felt the same way.

But, as it happened, it wasn't necessary for Elyse and or
Matt to try and orchestrate just the right time to talk to her
in-laws. Abigail came to her. "Something on your mind,
Elyse?" Abigail asked the morning after they had returned
from their cruise. "You've been unusually quiet since we
returned."

Matt had gone to the office early to complete work on an
upcoming court case. Peter was off at the hardware store,
picking up some new washers for the upstairs faucets.

Elyse looked up at her mother-in-law, feeling her inner
trepidation knot her stomach. Okay, this was going to be
hard. But Abigail had already given her the opening she
needed to begin the discussion. Perhaps she already knew,

in her heart of hearts. "It's about Matt," Elyse said finally, swallowing hard. "And me."

Abigail nodded sagely, her level gaze silently reassuring Elyse. "The two of you have become very close while we were away."

So, they weren't totally unaware of what was happening under their roof, Elyse thought with a sigh of relief. She saw nothing but calm curiosity on Abigail's face. "Yes," she admitted quietly, "we did."

Abigail groped for a chair—her only sign of nervousness—and sat down. "How close, exactly? Are the two of you...are you dating or—?" she asked calmly, struggling to understand.

"I think I love him," Elyse said, wanting to be honest, yet wanting to be gentle. And suddenly, she knew she couldn't be both. She would just have to be frank...and let the chips fall where they may after that. "No, scratch that," she amended firmly, gulping again. Her eyes filled with unshed tears. Her voice shook with suppressed emotion. "I do love him. I just...I don't know how to say it. I don't want to hurt you and Peter. And with me in the same house—"

Abigail's expression softened compassionately as she urged her daughter-in-law to continue. "I understand, dear. And as for Matt and you...well, let's just say Peter and I have both had our suspicions for some time now. We only wondered when and if... Oh, dear, this is awkward, isn't it?"

Elyse felt herself flush. "Very."

"How does Matt feel?"

Elyse swallowed. She didn't know how Matt would feel about her speaking for him. But she might as well just blurt it all out now that they were on the subject. And besides, Abigail didn't look all that upset. In fact, upon closer inspection, she didn't look upset at all. "He loves me, too." Her words were halting, but heartfelt.

Abigail smiled slowly. She held her coffee cup between her hands. "I thought so. I thought so. That's one of the reasons Peter and I finally decided to go away. We thought maybe the two of you would enjoy some time alone. Time to figure out what's really going on.''

Gladness filled Elyse's heart Abigail was taking this so well. ''Then you don't mind? You don't object?''

''Elyse, had this happened two years ago, yes, I would have been upset. But Nick is gone. You have to continue with your life. If you don't mind my saying so, you couldn't find a better man than Matt, or vice versa.''

''Peter—''

''Is even quicker to accept these developments than I am. So you can relax.''

Elyse sighed her relief and sat back in her chair. ''You don't know how much better this makes me feel.''

''YOU TOLD MY MOTHER we cared about one another?'' Matt asked, several hours later. En route to the hospital, Elyse had stopped at his office, to tell him what she'd done.

''Yes.'' She nodded firmly, reading the mingled surprise and anxiety on his face.

''How'd she take it?'' Matt got up from behind his desk and crossed the room to her side. His arms automatically went around her waist.

''She wasn't even surprised.''

Matt leaned forward, until his lips lightly touched her hair. ''Figures,'' he murmured dryly, inhaling her scent. His arms tightened around Elyse. She'd never felt so protected or cherished.

''Mom always has been able to read me like a book.''

Elyse leaned her face against his shirtfront. ''So you say,'' she teased. ''To hear her talk, you're the original mystery man.''

Matt grinned. Several heartbeats passed before he angled his head back and looked down at her. His fingertips lightly stroked her face. ''I think this calls for a little celebration.''

''What?'' Her question was a breathless caress.

His eyes darkened and took on a romantic gleam. "Dancing and dinner?" he asked softly.

She couldn't think of anything she'd rather do. "You're on."

Because Matt had a court case that would run late, they agreed to meet at his office. When Elyse arrived, he was still shaving in the small private bathroom adjoining his private office. At seven-thirty everyone else was gone for the day. Elyse found the silence comforting. She tossed down her handbag and keys and sauntered over to join him. She leaned in the open portal, feeling very content just being near him once again.

"Hectic day?" Matt said, easing the razor across his well-lathered jawline.

She watched with fascination as stripe after stripe of smooth tanned skin was revealed. "Very. Three new admissions while I was on duty."

"Everything okay at home?"

She nodded. "I spent some time with the girls before I left. They said to tell you hello."

Matt walked out of the bathroom. He was shirtless, a towel slung around his neck. The smell of his after-shave hung in the air. He went to the small coat closet, pulled out a clean pressed shirt that had come straight from the cleaners. He unbuttoned it briskly, then started to put it on without realizing he'd neglected to unfasten the second to last button. Seeing immediately what the problem was, Elyse moved forward impulsively. "Here, let me help." Both hands reaching around his waist, she found the fastened button, released it. The ends of his shirt fell forward. Matt didn't step away.

Looking up at him, her breath caught in her throat. "It's only been a couple of hours," he murmured, drawing her close. His eyes filled with a fragile, indecipherable emotion. "I feel like it's been three years."

She released the breath she'd held captive for too long. Her voice was underscored with ragged emotion, suppressed longing. She could have sworn he understood her better than she understood herself. "I missed you, too." More than he could ever know.

His hands slid up her back, past her shoulders to tenderly encircle either side of her neck. His thumbs beneath her chin, he tilted her head back. She knew what was coming and she wanted it with all her heart and soul. And yet...

The kiss was searching at first, a gentle hello. "Matt," she murmured, her hands against his chest. Everything was moving a little too fast. She wanted time. And she wanted to be able to be completely honest....

Then she realized that it hadn't been just the Donovans that had been keeping her from being with Matt, it had been Nick and Nick's secret....

At that thought she took a breath, her heart beating frantically, a vulnerable little shiver chasing up her spine. Panic rose in her throat. She wanted to flee, to evade, to put it off just a little longer....

But Matt's great supply of patience seemed to have ebbed. He was a man with needs, with desires....

Knowing she was nervous, misunderstanding the reason why, Matt bent and gently kissed her collarbone, her throat, the silky hollow just beneath her ear, the fragile lines of her neck. "You don't have to be frightened," he murmured soothingly. His hands slid up to knead the aching swells of her breasts, every touch, every caress a tender urging to become a part of his sweet hunger. It was so tempting to just give in to that demand, Elyse thought. Already her breasts were aching for the touch of his mouth, her lower half flaming and tightening. "I won't take this any further than you want me to take it."

Her breasts rising and falling rapidly with each intake of breath, Elyse said hoarsely, not meeting his eyes, "I know that." And she knew she loved Matt, too. Knew it and wished more than anything there was nothing destructive between them. No lies. No evasions. No half-truths or secrets...

"And?" His hands were suddenly lazy, waiting. They shifted down to her waist and lower still to her hips.

She saw him watching her intently. "What is it?" he asked, softly, compassionately. And then, his face hardening, he queried bluntly and unhappily, "Is it Nick?"

"No, I—no." Her denial was quick and heartfelt.

His eyes narrowed consideringly. He saw the conviction behind her words but relaxed only slightly. And suddenly she knew he needed to know it was him she wanted. Not anyone else. Not his brother. She couldn't bear for him to be hurt that way, for him to think...

Standing on tiptoe, she wreathed her arms about his neck. She kissed his mouth and his cheek and his neck, and then his mouth again. "It isn't Nick," she whispered emotionally, tasting the salt on his skin. Nick had been a distant memory for a very long time. "It's just that I'm nervous...." *And that I want you so badly I ache.*

That, he could understand. And did.

His hands closed around her waist. He guided her closer, his mouth covering hers. He kissed her long and hard and deep. He was relentless in his pursuit of her; she welcomed the newfound abandon. This, this was what she wanted, only feeling...passion...sensation and more sensation. The sense that he cared about her, cared tremendously, the sense that she was his and that he was never ever letting her go. She kissed him back, putting everything she felt for him in that single caress.

Matt's laughter was warm against her ear, husky and very male and enticing. "I said I'd stop but...I'm no saint, Elyse. We're never going to get out of here if we keep this up." It was a last warning. She had perhaps sixty seconds to call time. She let the sixty seconds come and go.

"I know," she said softly, "I know." She was feeling reckless and abandoned...and very much a woman. And all because of Matt.

She relaxed against him as his lips made a lazy trail down the slope of her neck and back again to the sensitive spot just below her ear. His touch was electric. She cuddled against him, cuddled and trembled, this time from sheer desire. Needing desperately to get closer to him, she parted the edges of his unbuttoned shirt and moved her palms around to caress the warm smooth skin of his back. His muscles tensed at the contact, his breath was sucked in; she inhaled sharply as she felt his hardness through their layers of clothing, an answering fluidness in her legs.

His eyes met hers; they had never been a darker blue. "Last chance," he said softly, meaning it.

Her last chance to run.

And suddenly she didn't want to run anymore, didn't want to evade or play it safe. She felt as if she had been waiting for this man—this moment—for a lifetime. He wasn't someone she could give up. She needed to be touched again, loved. She needed to be intimately known, accepted, appreciated. She needed to be with him. Yes, there were risks, problems that would have to be worked out. But there was also the here and now, and that she intended to enjoy. She'd been sensible for too much of her life, responsible and alone for too long. Now was her time, her time and his.

She rested her forehead against his chest. Their breaths were coming raggedly. Her hands tightened around him. Although her emotions were whirling, her thoughts were calm. "I don't want to leave here either," she said firmly, her mind made up. She looked up at him defiantly, almost daring him to try to convince her to do otherwise. She didn't want to go to dinner, didn't want to spend time in yet another restaurant, no matter how much candlelight or wine or music there was. "I just want to be with you." She looked up at him, her low soft voice ardently underscoring every word she said. "I want to be alone with you."

He stared at her raptly, making absolutely certain she knew what she was doing. Convinced of that, he gave a low groan. Drugged with need himself, he parted her lips with his tongue, his hands pressing her lower body sensuously into his. His open palm slid warmly and intimately down her lower spine, pressing her closer still. As he molded her to him, thigh to thigh, she felt the yearning pouring out of him with the force of a flooding river. He was intense, overwhelmingly ardent. She was warm and yielding—surrender, she thought dimly. It had never felt so sweet.

"Oh, God, Elyse, I want to make love to you."

He gave her no chance to respond, but kissed her again, his lips sweet and tender, then flaming with passion and desire. Elyse could barely breathe; she was helpless to do anything but feel, aching with a need only he could fill. She was limp with longing, as he released the back zipper on her dress and guided it over her shoulders, down past her hips. Conscious of his watching her and liking what he saw, she—who'd never undressed to deliberately entice—kicked off her heels and slowly, provocatively stepped out of the circle of silky fabric. His hot gaze drifted down her legs, roamed the silk-covered curves of her legs and the tiny triangle of blue silk and cream lace between her thighs. Expelling a stream of air, he murmured an appreciative comment. She blushed, feeling shamelessly pleased at his pleasure.

He smiled, telling her it was just the beginning.

Deliberately he moved toward her, his hands smoothing over her hips, dragging her closer, closer still, tracing the rounded curves of her hips, her slim waist, the womanly curves of her breasts. She moaned in frustration as he teased her nipples, then let his hand slip lower to explore the apex of her thighs. He wasn't going to stop. She saw it in his face. She felt a quicksilver flash of fear at the unknown. And then she felt calm. Intuitively she knew that when she was with him everything would be all right. Feeling like a sleepwalker, her eyes glazed with the slumberous lights of passion, she freed him of his shirt, trousers, letting her hands roam at will over his warm golden skin. The rest of his clothing fluttered to the floor beside her dress.

In no hurry he traced the swell of her breasts above the

near transparent navy lace of her bra. Through the fabric his thumbs and forefingers teased the nipples into tingling crowns. She moaned low in her throat, feeling increasingly abandoned and free as he tenderly cupped the swelling weight of her breasts from beneath. With his thumbs he brushed the fabric aside to worship her gently with his open mouth. Tremors chased through her body, her unaccustomed pliancy weakening her knees. She held her breath and clasped his head tightly, burying her fingers in his thick hair. No one had ever made her feel like this, no one. And she never wanted it to stop.

His mouth curved over hers again; he kissed her until desire trilled through her like an unstoppable song. Alternating his thumbs, he rubbed them across her lips. "God, you're beautiful," he said. "All over. Every inch of you. And so soft. Your skin…"

He was so strong. "I've wanted to touch you this way for weeks," she whispered.

"Every night I've thought about having you in my bed." He rained kisses over her throat and his arms tightened possessively around her. His voice dropped a notch. "I wondered what it would be like to hold you in my arms all night, to sleep with you next to me, my hand curled on your breast or draped between your thighs.…"

He slipped his hand around the back of her neck and drew her close for another kiss. His hunger was real and it beckoned her own. "I dreamed about you at night," he whispered softly, his mouth poised over hers. "Every night. And I'd wake up wanting you so badly."

"I dreamed about you, too." She leaned into him, until the tips of her breasts were buried in the thick, soft mat of his chest hair. "I couldn't wait to get home at the end of the day, to see you," she whispered. Her lips were wanting beneath his. She nestled against him, softness to hardness, loving the feel of him, wanting more. He made her feel safe, secure—treasured as never before. And still they kissed, the caresses flowing one into the next, until there was no ending, no beginning, only a sweet continuum. Their hands drifted lower. She felt his taut thighs and narrow hips. The more they touched, the more she felt like liquid inside.

He discovered her secrets, how she liked to be touched. She felt feverish and greedy. He was hers and hers alone. And she didn't want to be apart any longer. His control ebbing too, he brushed her hands aside and secured her tightly and commandingly against him. There was no more play, no more languid, sensual climb. Their urge was to join, to make their loving complete.

He followed her to the sofa and covered her with tender care. Stretched out length to length, gossamer softness met softness, heat melded into heat. Slowly he filled her, slowly she received him, gasping at the pressure and pleasure. His name on her lips, her breath caught in her throat, she twined her arms and legs around him and cloaked him with her softness. He responded with tenderness and protective strength. She gave him her heart and her soul. He gave her his.

The strength of their love rushing through her, she arched against him, asking for all he had to give, knowing that at last she had come home to love. He was equally demanding and possessive, taking and giving. Gradually their consciousness of all else faded, their past and present disappeared beneath the fierce sweet satisfaction of mutual need. She'd never felt such tenderness. She'd never dreamed of such love. And it was theirs, she thought joyously, holding him close, all theirs.

Chapter Eleven

"I'm glad you could get out to Los Angeles on such short notice," attorney Maureen Gleason commented as Elyse and Matt joined her for lunch in the swank Wilshire Boulevard eatery some two weeks later. "I really needed your help on the Andrews case and the background information you supplied was indispensable. Thanks. I really feel prepared to go to court now."

Matt lifted his hands as if to say no big deal. "What some people won't do for a free meal," he joked. They all laughed and then he continued amiably, "Besides I've been meaning to get out here anyway. The check the firm gave the family for Nick's memorial—well, it means a lot, to all of us." While he had met with former colleagues at Smith and Lowe, Elyse had attended a nursing seminar at UCLA.

Not that business alone was the reason they'd headed for the West Coast. She and Matt had both needed time alone together.

Two weeks had passed since they first made love. They'd managed to be together romantically twice since then. It hadn't been nearly enough for either of them.

"We wanted to help," Maureen continued sincerely and for several more moments the talk was of Nick's memorial. Following that they studied the menus. "I suppose you've heard Bob Osborne's out of jail," Maureen continued when the waiter had left with their orders.

"Yeah, I have," Matt's face darkened as he recounted. "I refused to have any part of his travesty of a book."

"So did everyone else at the firm," Maureen said, her mouth set grimly. She shook her head in obvious regret. "The worm's got a lot of nerve, you can credit him with that. We're still losing clients because of him."

"How he could have expected us all just to forget..." Matt's voice trailed off. His mouth was set grimly.

Elyse understood his pain, as did Maureen, apparently.

"You've heard the latest, haven't you?" Maureen asked in a sarcastically aggrieved tone. "That the book he's working on has turned into a kiss-and-tell story of epic proportions? *Oh, yeah.* He's taking us *all* to task. Apparently his own crimes weren't enough, now he's raking us all over the coals. He's supposedly going to tell what it's like to work in one of the biggest, most prestigious law firms on the West Coast. And he's not just stopping at his own division. He's covering everything from the real estate law group to divorce law and family practice, to the business management division and corporate law."

"Then he's setting himself up for slander," Matt said angrily. "Because if there's anything negative in his book about me, I'll sue."

"So will the rest of us. Although I've heard the names and dates have been changed to protect the innocent," Maureen said dryly.

For a moment Elyse was too stunned to do anything but stare at both Matt and Maureen wordlessly. How could she have been so wrong in her judgment about Bob Osborne? she wondered. There had been hints he wasn't exactly white knight material, but she had never once thought him capable of such personal treachery.

"How could we ever have trusted such an operator?" Matt wondered out loud. He followed his query with a muffled curse.

"He sure fooled all of us," Maureen admitted.

Matt nodded, linking gazes with both Maureen and Elyse. "Right up until the time he got caught."

"I guess you were right not to trust him," Elyse said finally, tossing in her two cents' worth. And she'd been wrong to take Matt to task about it. She looked at Maureen, explaining, "I felt sorry for Bob when he first got out of jail—"

Maureen frowned. "Well, no one out here did. But enough about Bob. Let's talk about your work. How was the nursing seminar over at UCLA?"

"Great. I'm now up to date on all the latest technology for pediatric ICUs."

"You like your work?"

"Yes, I do, very much."

Maureen turned to Matt. "So, pal, how's it going with you? How's the new practice working out?"

"Great." Matt stirred more sugar into his iced tea. "I'm still having a few slow days now and then, but by and large I have enough work to keep me busy."

Maureen grinned. "Coming from the firm here couldn't have hurt."

"It didn't." He paused to take a sip of his tea. "By the way, how's that malpractice case going? You still working on it?"

Elyse almost spilled her own drink. She chalked it up to nerves and the fact that anything even close to the subject of malpractice was enough to set her off these days, especially knowing the secret she was still keeping. Nick, after all, could still be sued for medical negligence himself. His reputation, his memorial could be ruined....

"Oh, yeah," Maureen continued, answering Matt's questions about the case. "Not that it will get to court anytime in the near future. It's already been delayed twice—the physician charged suffered a stroke right after you left L.A. It was a real mess. The guy apparently has some aphasia and problems with his memory—"

"Regarding the malpractice case?" Matt queried.

"Of course."

"You think it's an excuse?" Matt asked Maureen.

The other lawyer shrugged. "I don't know. Thus far his counsel, Bernie Caitlin—you know him—has avoided using the term brain damage, but it's possible some occurred. At any rate the defendant is no longer practicing medicine. And it doesn't look as if he ever will again. So—" Maureen spread her hands wide and sighed.

"But you're still planning to bring suit against him," Elyse said.

Maureen nodded. "The man was negligent. Somebody has to pay."

As Nick would have had to pay, Elyse thought. Cold chills swept through her. She suddenly had no appetite for lunch.

Matt surveyed Elyse thoughtfully. He knew she was upset. "Nick and I used to argue about the medical malpractice issue constantly," he remembered quietly, his intent gaze still on Elyse. "Because he was a surgeon, his premiums were outrageously high." Matt glanced at Maureen. "Nick felt we lawyers should stay out of it entirely."

"I'll bet," Maureen said.

"There was a lot of risk in his field," Elyse interjected, remembering how difficult her husband's work had been. How pressured. And that same pressure coupled with the commitment to help each and every patient who came to him had led to Nick's death.

"Nick was adamantly against malpractice suits of any kind," Matt recalled.

Elyse nodded, her pulse racing. Out loud, she shared the recollection. "He felt medicine was enough of a crap shoot as it was without adding the pressure of wondering constantly if you were going to be sued." She had to act composed. She couldn't give away what she knew!

Matt studied her openly. His look reminded Elyse of all they still had to discover about one another. They were lovers now, together whenever they had a chance, but there was also still a newness to their love, a sense of all they had yet to learn about one another, to understand and accept and discover. She wanted to be close to him. She didn't want him sharing the burden of Nick's guilt. She knew instinctively they would choose different courses of actions and that difference of opinion would separate them, perhaps, irrevocably.

"And you agree with Nick's view?" he asked quietly, still studying her with a mixture of a lawyer's powers of observation and his personal intuition where she was concerned. He always knew when she was upset. He seemed to have a sixth sense about it.

She swallowed hard, fighting for an outward ease she couldn't begin to feel. "I know how Nick felt." Because both Matt and Maureen were looking at her, she felt obliged to continue, "Sometimes nurses and doctors do all that we can and the patient still dies. And then sometimes patients who we don't think have a ghost of a chance will beat all the odds and live. People in the medical profession aren't as omnipotent as we're often perceived to be. People come to us, to the hospital expecting miracles. They expect modern medicine to have a cure for literally every disease, every trauma, and it simply isn't so. In many cases we're still as helpless as we were twenty years ago."

Maureen listened intently. "You don't think we should be suing this doctor?"

Elyse shrugged. "I don't know the case very well, of course, but I don't see the point in it if he's no longer practicing." Just like she couldn't see the point of suing Nick now that he was dead.

"Look, just because the doctor charged is out of the business of medicine now doesn't mean the family bringing suit against him isn't still suffering, too," Matt pointed out calmly. "In this particular case there's a man who is no longer able to work because he's been paralyzed. He has a wife and two college-age children. There's not nearly enough money for them to even provide decent nursing care

for this man, not to mention what his family is now going
through trying to make ends meet.'' He paused, letting his
words sink in.

Elyse knew full well what it was like to live on a fixed
income with children to support.

"You still don't like it, do you? The fact that we're suing
a retired physician," Maureen asked curiously.

"I can't help but wonder about his family," Elyse admitted, struggling to maintain an air that was as calm and
analytical and unguilty as Matt's and Maureen's. She picked
up her fork and speared a piece of lettuce. "They're going
to be put through an awful lot because of this and for what?
It's not as if this doctor could hurt anyone else now that
he's retired.''

"You're saying you could just overlook what this guy
did?" Maureen asked skeptically, "if it were someone in
your family who was now suffering a permanent disability
that needn't have happened?"

Elyse was silent. "I hate it when a doctor doesn't do his
or her job properly. But for you lawyers to step in...you
don't have complete medical backgrounds; you can't possibly understand the complicated decision making and di-
agnostic processes doctors go through. I just think the medical profession is better off policing their own.'' Aware she
was beginning to sound defensive—the memory of Nick's
situation was getting to her—Elyse fell silent once again.

"You think the medical profession does a good job of
that?" Matt asked, interested in her answer. Finished with
his salad, he pushed it away.

Elyse nodded, meeting his gaze equally. "Most of the
time.''

Except in Nick's case, she thought. Nick's mistake hadn't
been caught and a child had died. The plain fact of the
matter was that Nick could still be sued posthumously for
his mistake. Only now Nick wouldn't be here to defend
himself or explain. Everyone in the family would be hurt.

She had to keep his error a secret. Matt was bound to

report the mistake if he were cognizant of it. The boy's family might feel compelled to sue. And for what? All of them would be put through an enormous amount of pain, but no real good would be done, no one would be saved from further harm.

Nick's mistake was not a novel one. Doctors were already aware it could happen. Since Nick was dead, it wasn't as if he would repeat the mistake on another patient, Elyse reasoned calmly, sure she was doing the right thing by keeping quiet. And the little boy could not be brought back to life. No, all that would happen were Nick's mistake to be made public would be traumatic. At best, money would change hands, Nick's reputation would be ruined and both families would be forced to relive that little boy's death. Not only would she bear the guilt but Ronny Dilmore's family would have to live with it as well. They would have to live wondering what would have happened, if only *they'd* remembered to write down the stress ulcer on the presurgery forms. She didn't want to see them go through that kind of pain. She didn't want to live it herself.

The waiter appeared, bringing their entrees. Matt and Maureen, deep in conversation again about the firm's most interesting cases, barely seemed to notice her distracted air.

She resolved to put it out of her mind. It was really better if she just forgot....

"So, the two of you are staying on for the weekend?" Maureen asked genially, clearly interested in them as a couple.

Matt nodded, his careful expression revealing nothing of the depth of his feelings for Elyse. "Elyse has never had a chance to see much of California. I thought we'd drive down to Catalina tomorrow morning."

And there they would have two whole days and two whole nights alone, their first solid block of uninterrupted time.

"I'm envious," Maureen smiled, digging into her meal. "The only reprieve I'm likely to get this weekend is the father-son softball game at our church. Both my boys and Chet are playing.''

"Give them my best," Matt said.

Maureen smiled. "I will." She dabbed at her mouth with her napkin. "By the way, I meant to mention we found some old files of yours the other day. A secretary came across them when she was cleaning out some drawers. We thought you might like to have them."

Matt looked blank, so Maureen prodded his memory gently, "The ones on B.C. Benton."

She didn't have to say anything more. They all knew who B.C. Benton was—the director who'd worked on Holly's last film. The director responsible for her death.

"YOU'RE NOT GOING TO ASK ME about those files on B.C. Benton, are you?" Matt said, as they returned to their hotel in downtown L.A. after they'd concluded their lunch with Maureen.

Matt had looked anything but happy when reminded of the existence of the files. Although Elyse had been curious, the stressed look on his face had kept her from asking about the files directly. She knew that if he wanted her to know the contents he would tell her when he was able. "I didn't think it was any of my business," she hedged finally. As close as she felt to Matt, she also understood there were matters they needed to handle alone. She'd felt the B.C. Benton files fell into that category. Now suddenly, Matt needed to talk about it.

"I had him investigated after the accident that killed Holly."

"Why?" Elyse sat down on the edge of the bed, trying not to show how stunned she felt. She knew what a private person Matt was. He wouldn't have pursued Benton in such a manner unless he felt something needed to be unearthed.

He sat next to her and covered her hand with his own, then restlessly traced her palm with his fingers. "I don't know. I guess I was anxious to blame someone," he said quietly, his face looking haggard and tired. She was reminded of the bleak period he had experienced after Holly's death. She could feel the pain he'd been through and her heart went out to him.

"I sensed they weren't telling me everything, that there was some type of a cover-up going on."

"And was there?" Her voice was tense, mirroring the way she felt.

Slowly Matt lifted his head. He nodded reluctantly. "Unfortunately, yes, although it wasn't the kind I expected."

"I don't understand."

He paused, gritting his teeth and exhaled wearily. "There was a lot Holly hadn't told me about Benton. For starters," he paused and swallowed hard, "they were lovers several years before we met and married."

Elyse's throat went dry. She had the sudden image of a child who'd been invited to a party given by his peers. Feeling elated at having been included for the first time, he later realized the invitation had meant nothing, for at the party he is as much an outsider as before. The illusion that he had belonged, therefore, was both cruel and fleeting. As had been Matt's relationship with his wife. "She kept that from you deliberately?" Elyse managed finally, her throat aching from the effort to hold her voice steady. She could feel Matt's pain. More importantly still, she could understand why he'd never talked about this before—to anyone in the family as far as she knew. It would've been too humiliating too difficult. Hence, his silence after Holly's death....

In response to her question, he lifted his hands and spread them wide. "Maybe. I don't know. We didn't trade stories about our romantic pasts." They hadn't been children when they met. "But had I known she had a past with Benton, I don't think I would have been eager for her to work closely with him again."

"That's understandable." Elyse would have taken objection, too, in the same situation.

He smiled wanly at her show of support. "Anyway, back

to Benton. Even before they were lovers, he helped her get her start in films. I knew she regarded him as part-mentor, part-friend. I had no idea how deep her gratitude went or how attracted to her he still was.'' He paused and grimaced before continuing wanly. ''They slept together the night before the accident. Apparently she had regrets the next day and then had trouble keeping her mind on the work. When it came time to film the car scene, he tried to convince her not to do it. Originally he'd wanted her to try it—he thought it was important for the success of the film.''

''They why'd he change his mind?'' Elyse asked, aware Matt was gripping her hand tightly.

Matt shrugged. ''Apparently he felt she didn't have the mental concentration to be able to film the scene effectively; therefore, to have her even in the car during the chase scene would be an unnecessary physical risk.''

''She disagreed?''

''They had words—no one knows exactly what was said because almost as soon as it started they moved the fight into her motor home—but when she came out of her dressing room minutes later she got in the car.''

''And that's when the accident occurred.''

He nodded. ''During the second time they shot that particular scene. The police investigation proved it to be a fluke—the car accident during the chase scene was an accident, an unavoidable one—it was Holly's affair people were trying to cover up.''

''I'm sorry.'' She put her hand on his arm. She knew he never would have believed Holly capable of such a betrayal. Elyse could barely believe it, either, although she'd never really known Holly all that well. The few times Matt had brought his wife home to Texas she'd always seemed ''on-stage'' in a down-home, Southern sort of way. ''At the time, I always thought you and Holly had, well—if not a perfect marriage—then, a strong one,'' she observed quietly.

Matt nodded understandingly and continued in a voice thick with hurt, ''So did I. That was what was so hard about it later. If she'd been unhappy or dissatisfied for any reason...if she'd just told me, leveled with me, been honest with me, maybe we could have changed whatever was wrong. As it is, I'll never know what drove her to do such a thing.''

"Maybe it was just a lapse in judgment on her part," she offered, wanting to ease his pain. Although she couldn't understand anyone cheating on Matt, ever.

Matt turned to her, his expression tight. "Maybe. And maybe she wanted to hurt me, wanted me to find out. Why else would she have...? My God, it was such a public place. It's not as if she thought no one would find out. She knew people talked...if not for the accident—and the cover-up afterward," he paused grimly again, "word would have gotten back to Los Angeles." And to him.

"And then what?" Elyse asked quietly. "Would you have confronted her with what you knew?"

Matt nodded bleakly, brooding eyes turned to the distant wall. "Yeah." Silence. "She was my wife, after all."

"And then what?" Elyse asked gently, aware that her heart was beating very fast. "Would you have left her?"

He didn't turn toward Elyse, didn't move. "Maybe. Probably." He gestured helplessly. "I wouldn't have wanted to, but I'm not sure I could have trusted her again, either." Not after such a betrayal.

Clearly he was still reeling from the blow—not just to his ego, although that had been hurt, too, but his heart. "Why would she do such a thing?" Elyse asked in a hoarse whisper. She just couldn't understand any woman walking away from Matt, trying willfully to hurt him.

"That's just it. I've been over it and over it and I don't know. Was I not supportive enough? Was I too detached? I was very busy then, working on a number of cases." He shrugged and gestured helplessly, his eyes filling with tears. "Holly was always very impulsive. And she could be very destructive when she didn't get her own way. Maybe she just wanted my attention." Matt remembered she had asked him to visit the film set a few times. He'd never been able to do so. But was that reason enough to destroy a marriage? Or were there other flaws in his relationship with Holly, flaws he still didn't want to see? He knew from his law practice that there was a tendency to martyr those that died. Spouses were particularly vulnerable. "Maybe I never had her love at all," he sighed. "Maybe she was always just playing a role...."

"And maybe she was incapable of committing herself fully to any man," Elyse said, surprised the angry voice was her own. "Maybe she just wasn't cut out for marriage."

Matt sent her a look that was both cynical and grateful, then lapsed into silence once again. He swore softly. "The truth is my marriage to Holly is over. Maybe it was over long before she died. Maybe I just didn't want to admit that then. Maybe the affair was her way of telling me. She probably knew it would get back to me that I'd react angrily and predictably—"

"Demand a divorce."

"But cover up the indiscretion to protect my ego and image and then she'd be free—with no groveling on my part to try again or try harder, and no remorse on her part."

"That's a very cynical picture."

"Cynical, but true," he sighed. "I guess coming back here again, after knowing you, has opened my eyes to a lot of things."

Elyse was quiet. She was glad he'd shared so much with her. She felt she knew and understood him better now. "Do your parents know this?" she asked curiously.

He shook his head emphatically, his eyes trained on her face. "No. No one knows."

She stared at him in confusion, taking in the dark rumpled hair, the expensive suit, the aura of power and intelligence, his smoky-blue eyes, his sensuous mouth. Matt was close to his parents. They were understanding. Why hadn't he talked to them, talked to someone? Surely this must have been weighing on him for quite some time. Like Nick's secret had been weighing on her. "Why didn't you ever tell anyone?" she asked quietly. And why did she suddenly feel so torn? As if half of her wanted to run before she got in any deeper with him, as if half of her wanted only to get closer, to understand and know everything about him.

Matt shrugged. "What would have been the point? She was dead. I was already hurting enough as it was, rehashing it at that point wouldn't have served any purpose." On that he was firm.

"You were protecting your parents, Holly's family," she ascertained.

"As well as myself."

She thought about his dilemma, compared it to her own quandary. Abruptly she knew there was much she had to ask him. "If there had been anything amiss about the accident, any wrong-doing," she asked slowly, needing to know, "what then? Would you have come forward, reported it even if it meant the truth about Holly's infidelity would have been made public?"

"If there was the potential for someone else to get hurt again, yes, I would've," Matt said quietly. "But it was a freak accident. The chances of it happening again were one in a million."

Their situations had been different. "So you protected her."

"Yes," Matt nodded, patiently explaining, "her memory was all her family had left."

Elyse understood that. She stared at him in confusion. "Why are you telling me now?" Especially when he'd kept quiet about it for so long.

"Because I want us to be able to talk about everything and anything to each other," he said softly, honestly, drawing her close. His arms were warm and solid around her. "I want to know there's one person to whom I can always turn and I want to be there for you," he said softly, stroking her hair. "Not just now, but always..."

Elyse, achingly aware of the secrets she still kept, said nothing, merely snuggled closer into his embrace.

Matt's declaration stayed with Elyse all the following night and during their drive out to Catalina the next morning. She didn't want there to be any secrets between them, either. She wanted to tell Matt about Nick's mistake and her late discovery of it, but she was afraid. She knew, from her lunch with Maureen, and their mutual discussion, how Matt felt about malpractice in general and specifically the continuing responsibility for justice, whether a physician was still practicing or not. If she were to tell him now about Nick and Sears, he might understand, forgive her for keeping it from him. He might also feel compelled to see that justice was done and a lawsuit undertaken. Elyse didn't want that. Neither did she want to risk upsetting their current happiness with an argument about what they should or shouldn't do. She wanted to make the decision herself without help or interference or argument from anyone else. And especially not from Matt.

After all, the circumstances in Nick's case were different, from the one Maureen was handling, she reasoned securely. Smith and Lowe had to sue for the widow—she was financially hurting with two children to raise. Ronny Dilmore had not been supporting his family. His records had indicated he'd had excellent medical insurance that had paid for his care. And even if his family were to receive settlement money from the insurance company, it wouldn't ease his family's pain. In fact, it would most likely increase it.

She had to keep quiet, hope the memorial was made a joint one so Sears would also keep quiet. Then no one else would have to know. As for Matt, she would have to hope, if it ever came out, that he would understand why she'd wanted to cover up what had happened now that both parties were dead. After all Matt'd kept the scandal behind Holly's death quiet. She was just doing the same for Nick now.

And yet she knew he wouldn't approve. He'd argue that n B.C. Benton's case there'd been no evidence of work-

related negligence. The final lack of judgment and reckless-
ness had been all Holly's. In Nick's case there was evidence
of professional error.

If she told Matt, she wouldn't win. He would be forced
to act. People would be hurt. The stress would drive them
apart, like it or not. And she couldn't bear to lose Matt now
that she'd found him.

"YOU'VE BEEN AWFULLY QUIET," Matt observed late during
their last day on Catalina island. They were staying in a
charming old-style inn half a block from the beach. The
previous day they'd taken a ride around the gleaming blue
bay in a glass-bottomed boat, toured a beautiful cactus gar-
den and rented bikes for an early evening ride through the
charming seaside city of Avalon.

Sunday morning they'd breakfasted early, then walked
along the beach and later taken a tram to the Wrigley mansion. Late afternoon found them rambling down the main
street, sampling freshly made taffy and frozen bananas.

"I was just thinking how nice it's been to get away for
a while, just the two of us," Elyse confessed softly. Although she loved her children dearly and couldn't imagine
life without them, there were times when she wished she
didn't always have to be quite so responsible. Sometimes
she wished she could just go with her feelings, with what
was in her heart, without worrying about the effect of her
actions on her three daughters. And then there were Matt's
parents. They had given the two of them their blessing but
were they ready for this? Elyse thought not. She knew that
as modern as Abigail and Peter considered themselves, they
would feel uncomfortable with Matt and Elyse's physical
closeness, no matter how much they obviously cared for one
another.

"It has been good, hasn't it, getting away?" Matt said
turning her to face him.

"Yes, it has." The time spent in the sun had deepened
Matt's tan. His eyes were a bright blue. He looked healthy

and happy, more relaxed than she'd seen him in quite a while. She wanted him to continue to feel that way.

"You're worried about going home, aren't you?" he asked softly.

She nodded. "Yes, I guess I am. It won't quite be the same." She wouldn't be able to share a bed with Matt, to know the pleasure of waking in his arms, of loving him unrestrainedly.

The past few days they'd operated under an entirely different set of rules. With the exception of the people at his old law firm, no one in California had known her as Matt's former sister-in-law. Hence they hadn't had to worry about being seen together. Once in Catalina, they'd been able to kiss whenever they wanted. Just relax and be together. It would be hard going back to Dallas where, in addition to being sensitive to the feelings of her children and his parents, they also had to be wary of Nick's memorial and the effect any scandal or gossip would have upon it. The general public knew she and Matt were close again; they knew nothing of the romance, nor would they, until after August 15th, the date of Nick's memorial ceremony.

"If it weren't for the tongue-wagging our being together would cause," he said quietly, "I'd let everyone know about you now."

"I know that." She shared his reservations, felt his judgment was sound and in keeping with his usual sensitivity to the feelings of others.

"Think you can wait a few more months?" His smile was coaxing, soft.

She thought of the tenderness he had shown her, the compassion. She thought of short-term sacrifices for long-term gains. "Yes," she said, clasping both his hands tightly and looking up into his face. "I can wait a few more months. I can wait however long it takes." One way or another she and Matt would find a way to be together, not just for now but for always. And whatever they had to go through to achieve that would be worth it.

Well worth it.

"Oh, you can, can you?" Matt teased, drawing her into his arms and holding her so they were length to length. "Well, I can't." His voice dropped to a husky love-roughened timbre. "Most of the time I feel like even one more day apart is too much to bear."

"Only most of the time?" she demanded flirtatiously, placing her hands on his chest.

"Only most of the time," he affirmed, a sparkle in his blue eyes, an amused grin on his face. "The rest of the time I can't stay away from you for even a minute."

Elyse smoothed her hands thoughtfully over his chest, feeling the bunched muscles beneath her hands and frowned at him like a doctor puzzling over an elusive cure. "Hmm, that is a problem," she teased.

"Isn't it though?" he asked huskily, his palms inching down her back, joining together at the hip. At the intimate contact, sensation swept through her. His eyes narrowed tauntingly. "Got any ideas for a quick cure?" he asked lazily, his deep velvety voice reminding her of their sun-kissed days together, their passion-drenched nights, the fleeting time they had left, the memories left to make....

"Keep that up," she purred with a mischievous smile, curving her body into his and lifting her face to his for another long heartfelt kiss, "and I just might."

Chapter Twelve

Elyse and Matt returned to Dallas on Monday morning. Elyse returned to work at the hospital on Tuesday. For several days everything went smoothly. On Thursday, however, she detected a problem from the moment she arrived on the floor. One of the other nurses, a veteran of twenty years, was obviously in a stew about something. Curious, Elyse joined the huddle of nurses behind the desk. "What's up?" She poured herself a cup of coffee.

"New orders on a patient of Dr. Sears's," the veteran nurse growled. The two younger subordinates, just a couple of years out of nursing school, also looked upset.

"Mrs. Calivarci, the sixty-year-old woman brought in two days ago."

Elyse nodded. Although she was officially assigned to care for pediatric ICU patients, she worked closely with the adjacent ICU units as well, often lending a hand to other nurses when needed. They did the same for her. "I remember. She's been in a lot of pain, hasn't she?"

"A lot," the veteran nurse agreed. "So we asked Dr. Sears if he might up her medication dosage a bit—"

"And he wrote out orders for a dosage that would sedate a two-hundred-pound man!"

"You know Mrs. Calivarci doesn't weigh more than one hundred pounds."

"Add her age, to boot—what she's recently been through—"

"Elyse, I can't give her that shot. It's too much medication." Not fatal or even close to it, but certainly more than what she needed.

Elyse looked at the chart. They were right. There was a definite mistake in medication. "Have you talked to Dr. Sears?" she asked crisply. She knew that although Nick had concentrated on pediatric heart surgery, Lawrence had always taken on patients of all ages. To date, although she'd often known him to be difficult and high-strung, Sears had never been incompetent. The odds were he wouldn't accept news of his mistake graciously.

The three nurses exchanged wary glances. Finally one of the younger ones mumbled, "The last person that even questioned one of his orders was harassed so badly she finally quit."

"He made sure she was miserable."

"Elyse, I'm scared," the veteran nurse admitted. "I need this job and I don't do well under the kind of nonstop criticism and pressure Sears can dish out. At my age…well, I don't want anything negative on my record, and since Sears and I have never gotten along to begin with…"

Elyse knew what she had to do. The other nurses were afraid of him. Elyse also detested the man personally, but she wasn't averse to standing up to him in a medical matter. Maybe because she'd seen him outside of work for some time, not just as one of her superiors but simply as a man. A man with many flaws. "I'll handle it." A determined look on her face, she took custody of the chart. This wasn't going to be pleasant but it would be taken care of.

"What are we going to do about Mrs. Calivarci in the meantime?" one of the younger nurses asked.

"Give her the old dosage," the veteran nurse decided with a glance at Elyse.

Elyse concurred, "It may not be enough, but at least it won't dangerously overmedicate her."

While the other nurses gratefully went about finishing up their tasks, Elyse sought out Dr. Sears. She found him in the office finishing up some paperwork before heading off for a day of surgery.

"Any news about the memorial?" he asked as soon as Elyse shut the door behind her. Elyse looked at him with thinly veiled disgust.

She forced a smile. "Not yet. I'm hoping it will be resolved soon. The absent board members are due back any day now." She didn't want him part of Nick's memorial. She dreaded his slightest involvement in the project, but she also wanted him out of her life, and since bowing to his demands was the quickest, only sure way to get rid of him she really had no choice.

"You'll let me know?" Lawrence prodded with an ingratiating smile that sent chills up and down her spine.

"The minute I hear," she promised, forcing another too bright smile. She took a deep bolstering breath and took a seat in front of him. "Dr. Sears, we have a problem with Mrs. Calivarci." Briefly Elyse explained the patient's symptoms.

"You think she's overmedicated?" Dr. Sears's voice was silky, but his face was thundercloud dark. He drummed his pen restlessly on the surface of his desk, waiting for her answer.

Elyse hesitated. She wanted to handle this gracefully. What was important here was not the egos of the individuals involved but the care of the patient. She owed it to herself and Mrs. Calivarci to say what she thought as diplomatically as possible. Only then would the patient's needs be assured of being met. "Yes, I think she may be getting too much medication," Elyse said finally, handing the chart over for his perusal.

Sears glanced down at the chart. He found the mistake and scribbled in new orders. He handed the chart back to Elyse, his face impassive. "You know you're out of line here. You're a nurse, not a physician," he said tersely.

Elyse failed to see where acting in the best interest of a patient was out of line. She opened her mouth to defend herself and a nurse's right to aid in determining patient care.

He cut her off before she could get one word out. "Do it again and your name will be dirt with every physician in this hospital."

Elyse didn't think so; her professional reputation was simply too good to be trashed by Sears. He could, however, make her life very miserable. She stared at him silently, her teeth gritted, her limited patience with the man waning. She knew if she were smart, she would let him have the last word and just forget the whole lousy incident. Others had done it in the past. Maybe too many others. Suddenly she knew she wasn't going to cut and run. Not this time. If it meant going into battle with Sears, so be it. This situation—his bullying of the staff nurses—couldn't continue. Dr. Sears had pushed around too many nurses too many times; if it didn't stop, they could have a real crisis in patient care on their hands. She didn't want that for University Hospital.

Calmly and quietly she responded to his statement as professionally as possible. "I fail to see where acting in the best interest of a patient is out of line. Dr. Sears, it's my understanding a nurse not only has the right but the obligation to aid in patient care as best she or he is able. That's all I'm trying to do here, is make sure Mrs. Calivarci's needs are met."

That she dared speak to him at all, after the tongue-lashing he had just given her, infuriated him beyond measure. Knowing it was now or never, however, Elyse continued firmly, trying hard to be as diplomatic as possible and still have her say. "Whether you want to admit it or not, I did you a favor just now, coming to you first—"

"You think so, do you?" He stood, both hands planted firmly on his desk, his jaw jutted out pugnaciously. No waiting for her to respond, he commented icily, "You're also insubordinate and that can get you fired."

Elyse glared at him, not the least bit intimidated, but feel ing furious as hell. She'd just saved his neck, coming to him the way she had. Rather than admit that, though, the arrogant son of a gun would take them all to the guillotine with him. The man truly was a louse through and through, she thought. It wasn't enough that he'd betrayed Nick, tried to seduce her; now he was out to take her job away as well. Well, he wasn't going to get away with it.

Her temper ruling her, Elyse said silkily, "I suppose my insubordination *could* get me fired." And then before she could think, she delivered the coup de grace, "I suppose if the whole story about Mrs. Calivarci came out we could all be hurt." She spoke slowly, emphasizing her words.

Sears whitened, furious. There was a silence during which she realized she'd made a grievous mistake.

"Are you talking about Nick now, or me?" He leaned across the desk, malice in his eyes. "I think you're confusing us, Elyse. In fact I think you're confusing a lot of things. don't think you've been yourself since your husband died."

A chill went through her at the icy disregard in his tone. He would ruin her and Nick, too, and enjoy every miserable minute of it.

She forced herself to calm down, to try and reason with Sears one last time. She owed Nick that much. She had her daughters to think of. "Look, this is getting out of hand. We're both saying things we don't mean—"

"Are we? I wonder."

Silence.

Elyse took a deep, calming breath, assumed a fake smile on her face and tried again, "Doctors and nurses ought to be able to work together," she said quietly, trying on a more peaceful tact.

He made no concession to the validity of her statement. He arched his brows reprovingly, sent her a disdainful look. "You're a nurse, Elyse. You take orders and accept medical decisions, not give them."

If you back down now, he'll always have the upper hand

and he'll know it. He'll never stop harassing you. "I was just doing my job," Elyse repeated evenly. And she knew she would continue to do so in the future.

His mouth tightened into an unforgiving line. "You're a fool, you know that? You always were."

Too late, she realized she had pushed him too far by refusing to give him the mumbled apology he was clearly trying to extract from her. A surgeon's ego had no match. Because she had "humiliated" him, he was out for revenge now. He would take it any way he could get it.

Grabbing the chart, she turned and started slowly toward the exit, her heart pounding in her chest.

He swiftly circled around his desk, grabbed her arm and held her still, his fingers digging into her arm. "Whether you realize it or not, I could have you fired right now," he threatened. "I could spread the word about you so quickly and thoroughly you'd never be hired in any medical institution in this city again."

"I doubt that," she said coldly, remaining perfectly motionless.

"Try me." Slowly and in his own time, he let her go.

They stared at one another wordlessly, opponents measuring one another before the final match. Seeing the unveiled malice in his eyes, Elyse's first inclination was to shudder and run; her second was to simply hold her ground. He had bullied her enough in the past. It was enough that she had given in to his demands concerning the memorial in exchange for the preservation of Nick's secret. She wouldn't let him bully her at the hospital, too. It was time she put a stop to his bulldozing once and for all, to let him know that she wasn't afraid of him, not where her own reputation was concerned. There, if he insisted, she would fight him relentlessly. Not just for her sake but for the sakes of all the nurses under his tyrannical supervision.

Her hands tightened into fists at her sides. She sent him a contentious look that effectively kept him from touching her or advancing on her again. "Yes, you could report me to my supervisor and you could bad-mouth me to other doctors in Dallas," she asserted with icy triumph, feeling she was standing in the middle of a hurricane, ready to do battle. "But we both know you won't, because to do so would mean that the whole story would eventually come out. And that, Dr. Sears, would make you look bad." And that Dr. Sears would never allow...

"I'M GLAD YOU GOT THIS WEEKEND OFF, Mommy," Betsy said, two days later as she played with a beach ball in the swimming pool.

"So am I," Elyse admitted, getting up off the chaise where she'd been sunning herself and watching the girls. She walked over to the water's edge and slowly began immersing herself in the crystal clear water.

Since Sears had threatened her, she'd never known a moment's peace. He hadn't reported her, nor to her knowledge had he been careless again in his duties. But just the fact he was watching her, while waiting for the board's decision about the joint memorial, was enough to make her nervous. To make her wish she had never known the man.

"Hey! How's the water?" Matt asked the group, coming across the patio. Elyse looked up, shielding her eyes from the sun's glare. Matt had been out running errands all morning. Despite the day's heat, he looked fresh and handsome in khaki trousers and an open-throated blue shirt. Kicking off his boat shoes, he walked barefoot over to the water's edge and hunkered down beside Elyse. She was immediately aware of their nearness.

A cover-up hadn't been necessary when she'd walked out to the pool with the girls. Now she wished she'd worn one. Her violet and white print maillot was precious little protection against Matt's searing, all inclusive glance as his eyes touched her bare thighs and back, and the swell of her breasts above the V-neckline.

"The water's great...cool," Elyse managed finally, un-

able to tear her eyes from his or quell the riotous activity
of her suddenly racing pulse.

Betsy, Caroline and Nicole waded over to greet their uncle. The trio stopped at the edge of the pool and looked up
at him adoringly. "The water's neat. Are you going to come
swimming with us, too?" Nicole asked. Betsy and Caroline
pleaded for the same.

"I might." Matt lifted his glance to Elyse's. He gave her
another lazy, all-male smile. "What do you think?" he
asked huskily, his eyes lingering on the tousled dampness
of her hair and her sunkissed cheeks. "Is there room for
one more?"

Elyse grinned as a faint breeze whispered through her
hair.

"There's always room for you, Uncle Matt!" Caroline
shouted, impatient with her mother's uncommonly day-
dream like state.

Jogged into awareness of the others around them, Elyse
gestured toward her daughter. That was precisely what she'd
been about to say. "Saved by the gracious hostess on my
right."

Matt laughed and smiled. "I'll change and be right
down."

When he joined her minutes later, Elyse had just finished
swimming ten laps—two with each of her daughters, four
alone. Glancing up at him, her mouth went dry. Uncon-
scious of her yearning stare, he stood a moment next to the
umbrella table, stripping off his watch and draping his towel
over the back of a chair. He didn't flaunt his physique, yet
there was no denying his was breathtaking—all trim and
muscled, masculinely gilded with soft dark body hair. He
was wearing simple navy blue trunks. They were made of
a quick-drying cotton and they sported a drawstring waist
and reached to midthigh. Beneath and above, he was all
tanned, muscular, male.

He looked up at and caught her eye. She knew then he
was aware she'd been assessing him. He walked toward her

lazily, absolutely at ease. He then stepped down into the water beside her. "So, how are your half of the preparations for the anniversary party going?" he asked, leaning against the pool wall, the water up past his waist.

"Great. Yours?" Again, reaction to his nearness spread through her, more warming than the sun above them. She positioned herself beside him so she was looking out at the horizon rather than into his eyes.

She wanted to kiss him, hold him, express all the love for him she felt in her heart. And yet she couldn't, not yet, not in front of the girls. This constant holding back was killing her, and judging from the sudden tenseness in his tall frame, it was taxing him, too.

Matt's voice was low and slightly husky as he finished, "Everything's all set for next week."

"Oh, good." Elyse swallowed hard, trying hard not to give in to the intimate feelings that threatened to overwhelm her.

They were saved by the girls. The three of them approached, asking for more playmates. Matt was only too glad to comply. Elyse joined in. Forty-five minutes later, her children were pleasurably exhausted and more than ready to leave the pool. Elyse took them upstairs, helped them change into dry clothes, then made them stretch out on their beds for a rest period. Within minutes all three were sound asleep.

Knowing they were set for at least an hour's nap, she ventured back downstairs and found Matt in the kitchen. His hair was still damp but had been combed neatly around his face. He wore a T-shirt over his swim trunks. He was surrounded by the makings of his favorite barbecue sauce. "I thought we'd throw something on the grill for supper..." he said casually, adding a little Worcestershire sauce to the mixture, "maybe some spareribs. What are you smiling at?" He put down his measuring spoon and turned to face her.

She couldn't help grinning. "Do you realize how domestic you sound?" Hands on her hips, she approached him teasingly. In a couple of months he'd gone from a confirmed single man to man of the house.

His eyes roamed the floor-length terry cloth cover-up she'd put on over her suit. He shrugged, his eyes holding hers for an exceptionally long moment. "I'm getting used to planning meals for seven."

And she was getting used to having him around. Putting a hold on her swirling emotions, she forced a casual note into her voice as she corrected, "Five tonight. Your parents are in town for that bridge tournament."

A look of recognition crossed his face. "That's right. I forgot."

"Is this going to mess up your dinner plans?" she asked. When they'd moved in together as a family, they'd agreed to split cooking and cleaning chores, rotating them all so no one person would get stuck doing the same thing over and over again. Matt generally cooked on the weekends. Tonight was his night. She would do the dishes.

"Nope. We'll have some barbecue leftover, but it'll be good for lunch tomorrow."

Elyse smiled, looking forward to the leftover every bit as much as the meal. "I'll say. You're getting to be quite a chef."

He accepted the compliment, then chuckled, reminding her with his thinly veiled amusement of the disasters they'd endured on the way to domestic harmony. "Well, it's not so hard, really. All I have to do is remember not to serve any more icky bernaise sauce to the girls."

Elyse cringed, remembering his one major culinary mistake. Though normally cooperative, her children couldn't have been paid to eat what Matt had dished up his first night as chef; worse, he had sauced all the meat before bringing it to the table. Fortunately he'd had a sense of humor about the girls' disinclination toward anything the least bit gourmet in appearance. Fortunately the adults had all enjoyed the entire repast immensely, so it hadn't been a total waste,

Cathy Gillen Thacker 201

ust a learning experience for them all. She could see then
vhat a generous, understanding individual Matt really was.

"Children tend to like things plain, simple," she admitted
carefully.

He remembered all too well and was pleasantly unaf-
ected. She heaved a sigh of relief, glad Matt was so easy-
oing. The truth was he'd adapted to the father role in so
many ways. Initially he'd done so out of duty and compas-
ion, later it'd just become more and more comfortable, and
: seemed to her he was linked to them forever.

In many ways she felt they were already married. And
et there were also severe limitations in the way they were
ving. Their sexual relationship had been put on hold for
ne most part. Except for the rare times they were able to
neak away, they had to do without major physical contact.
ler sense of propriety wouldn't allow her to sleep with him
nere at the ranch; under the circumstances she knew she
ouldn't be comfortable. She just…didn't feel right about
. Not with everyone else living there, too.

But she missed him at night. Sleeping with him in Cali-
ornia had spoiled her, made her realize again the special
leasure of sharing her bed with a man, of waking to find
is strong body curled around hers. She wanted him all the
me, wanted to be free to hold him and kiss him and just
e with him as intimately as she wanted. Yet it was impos-
ble.

She didn't know how much longer she could go on the
ay they were, and she sensed he was beginning to get
stless, too.

He looked up from his cutting board, zeroed in on her
own. "Okay," he conceded, following the direction of her
ightly perturbed gaze, "I'll do the onions."

Her head lifted. She had a feeling he knew darn well her
ind had not been on the cooking chores. "Matt—"

"I don't want you looking sad." His words were low.
ithout warning, he slid his hands around her waist and
ld her close. For the moment she appreciated the silence

of the house, the fact they were alone. She rested her face against the solidness of his chest and laced her arms around his neck.

"You feel so good," he said softly, tightening his arms around her. "So right in my arms." He pressed a kiss on the exposed slope of her neck.

She listened to the steady thrumming of his heartbeat. "So do you." A sigh of contentment escaped her parted lips.

His hand moved in circles over her back, transmitting warmth through the terry cloth cover-up to the skin below. "Times like this I don't know what I ever did without you," he whispered, kissing her again.

She moved closer, until she was touching him completely from head to toe, her breasts nestled against the hardness of his chest, her thighs fitting solidly in the hard cradle of his thighs. She looked up at him, showing everything she felt. "I find myself wishing time would speed up." She wished that the memorial would be over and done with so she could go on with her life.

From the look on his face, Matt wished that, too. "But there are good things about the present," he said, his hand moving up to massage the muscles between her shoulder blades.

"Like what?" She tilted her head back even further to better see his face.

His smile was slow and sexy. His eyes glimmered with appreciative humor and good cheer. "Like...I'm learning how to cook a lot of different things."

She laughed softly, knowing that was true. At first he'd only known how to cook steak and eggs. Now he was turning into a gourmet chef who could do anything in the Betty Crocker cookbook. "Move over Craig Claiborne," she teased.

His hands slid down to her waist. "Your turn," he prompted softly.

"What?" She smoothed the material over his chest, low

ing the solid feel of him, the faint chlorine water and fresh-
air scent of his skin.

"Your turn to think of something good." His hands suddenly stilled. His eyes darkened, became more intent.

She tingled with the earthy vibrations flowing between
them. Her voice was a little breathless as she responded, "I
like living in a house full of people again, with adults to
talk to."

"And help pick up," he added genially, his hands caressing her shoulders, her collarbone, gently idling over the
slope of her neck to curve against either side of her face.

"I feel less alone." Suddenly her knees were trembling.
She was hot and weak all over, so vulnerable, so needy,
with so much to give.

He nodded slowly, his eyes never leaving hers. "Family's
important," he murmured softly, touching his lips to her
temple.

She sighed her reaction to his caresses. "Yes, they are."
They had promised not to do this, not to make love here,
under this roof. And they wouldn't, somehow she knew that
even now. But the temptation was very strong, and getting
more potent by the moment.

"Loving someone is important, too. Very important," he
said gently, bending to kiss her tenderly, to caress her lips
a dozen different ways. They were breathless when they
parted, shaking like trees being buffeted by strong winds.
"And I love you," he whispered gently, the look in his eyes
telling her it was true and wouldn't change.

Her arms tightened around him. "I love you, too," she
whispered, holding him close.

"So...?" He moved back, so they parted several inches.

"So what?" She stared at him in confusion, seeing the
sudden teasing light come into his eyes.

"So, what could be so bad that would make you frown
like that?" he kidded her gently, questioning her earlier rest-
lessness.

Suddenly she couldn't think of a thing. She would appre-

ciate what she had. "Nothing," she said softly, in response
"Nothing at all. The time for us to be together will come
We have only to believe that to make it happen."

FOR MATT the next two weeks passed in a haze of pleasure
and contentment. He spent every evening either at home
with family or out on an errand with Elyse. Sometimes the
children went with them, sometimes they didn't. Either way
it didn't seem to matter. They were together. They were a
family. He had someone he cared about deeply, someone in
his life who cared about him. He knew it would only get
better. His parents seemed to know it, too. For not only did
they approve of Elyse and Matt as a couple, they seemed
to constantly find opportunities that would allow them time
together.

Matt was grateful his parents were so understanding. It
made the prospect of their surprise anniversary party all the
more special, somehow. And, to his delight, his parents were
truly surprised at the gala he arranged, blinking and staring
in shock at the guests he had invited to their house the last
Sunday in July.

Their three grandchildren, who'd been let in on the secret
earlier in the day after their grandparents had gone to play
bridge, were also excited beyond belief. The moment after
Abigail and Peter walked in the door to a multivoiced cho
rus of "Surprise", Caroline ran forward to greet them
"Grandma! Grandpa! It's a party! For you!" she shouted
dancing up and down.

"An anniversary party," Matt said, walking forward to
hug both his parents. "Happy fiftieth!"

Abigail shook her head in disbelief at her son. "You
schemer!"

Matt grinned at Elyse. "Yep, that's us." They wanted to
make that day special for his parents and they had. While
more congratulations filled the entrance hall, Matt stood
back, watching Elyse interact with the guests. Her dark hair
swaying gently around her shoulders, her aquamarine eyes

bright and welcoming, she made sure everyone felt at home. Matt reflected on how relaxed she looked, how untroubled. In the months since he had been back in Texas, she had bloomed before his eyes. Going back to work had been a strain for her at first, but eventually she and her daughters both had adjusted to her new schedule. Now she came home from the hospital invigorated, renewed. And the girls liked hearing stories about her patients who got well and went on to complete recoveries.

She was no longer as anxious when it came to Nick's memorial, either. Part of that may have been due to the fact that donations were pouring in. Before, no one in the family had known how many lives Nick had touched, but they knew now. Patients' families had written, sent money, sent letters. All were touching examples of the miracles Nick had wrought.

For some reason, though, Elyse wasn't entirely comfortable with that, he realized. She didn't like seeing Nick cast in a savior role; whenever it happened she would either flinch or murmur some mild but practical rebuttal. "Nick was a man, not a saint," she'd say.

Matt had wondered before if Elyse had resented her husband's profession, the demands it had put on him, and the lack of time he'd subsequently been able to spend with his family. Now, he wondered again because it was clear something about Nick's profession, his former dedication, did bother her. But to his frustration she wouldn't talk about it or even admit such resentment existed on her part.

Fortunately she didn't seem to mind Matt's dedication to his work. On the nights he'd been late getting in from the city, she had never indicated even the slightest resentment. Rather, she'd been the first to offer to warm his dinner or get him something cold to drink. It couldn't have been just work-related absences that annoyed her. So what was it?

He couldn't figure her out.

He did know she loved him. He had only to look into her eyes when they were alone to see the feelings there. He felt the same. The only thing that bothered him now was his impatience. He resented the memorial because it was keeping him from being with the woman he loved. That made him feel guilty briefly, but then he'd realized Nick would have been the first to have understood. He never would've wanted Elyse to spend the rest of her life alone. He would have liked the idea of his children remaining very close to the rest of the family, and he would've understood that Matt's feelings toward Elyse were genuine. It was clear that Matt's feelings had developed only in Nick's absence and were in no way a reflection on what she had once shared with his brother. Yes, Nick would've understood, just as his parents did. He would have understood and accepted it. Matt could relax....

"So, what'd you think of the party tonight?" Elyse asked several hours later as they finished the last of the dishes together.

Matt was beginning to like the cozy domestic scenes, the time he spent with Elyse alone. Although he and Holly had cooked together, they'd never managed to feel so close when doing so. Nor had they possessed the teamwork he and Elyse seemed to share. He didn't even have to ask half the time; he could look at her and tell what she needed or wanted him to do, whether it was to help load the dishwasher or mop the floor, he just knew. And she, too, seemed to know what he needed, always being the first to offer to get his toolbox if the sink backed up, or the cabinet door in the laundry room came unhinged.

With a start he realized she was still waiting for his assessment of the party. "I thought it went very well," he admitted. "Mom and Dad had a good time." Their friends had all enjoyed themselves immensely.

"They were surprised, weren't they?"

"And touched." He washed several more crystal serving plates, rinsed them, then handed them over to Elyse to dry before he confided matter-of-factly, "You know, I envy them. Their lives haven't been perfect, their marriage far from it, but they've always muddled through the bad times and cherished and respected one another through the good." They hadn't turned to outside affairs or shut one another out, not even during the stressful aftermath of their eldest son's death.

"That's what you want? Fifty years?"

"Don't you?"

"Yeah. I guess I do. I always thought marriage should be forever."

"So did I."

They lapsed into silence again. *One of these days the memorial will be over, and I'll be free again,* Matt thought, rinsing another dish and putting it into the rack. *I can't wait.*

"ELYSE, WILL YOU HURRY UP?" Matt shouted impatiently from the bottom of the stairs, several nights later.

Elyse sprinted out of her room at the unusually madcap sound of his voice. Because the children had been whisked off for an outing in town with their grandparents, the house was unusually quiet. It wasn't like Matt to be so demanding, she thought. And for heaven's sake, why did he look so happy, like he had the whole world on a string?

Not wanting him to think she would come running anytime he called—she probably would but didn't want him to know that—Elyse took her good old time getting down the stairs.

As she sauntered down the last step, he made a loud show of clearing his throat. Though he was pretending to be totally out of patience, she knew that was far from the case. He would have waited for her all night long if necessary. And vice versa.

"I'm hurrying, I'm hurrying!" Elyse said as slowly and nonchalantly as possible. After rolling his eyes and casting a look at the heavens, he levered away from his place at the wall, his lazy gestures as exaggerated as her own. She started laughing. Hands on her hips, she demanded, "What's gotten into you, anyway?" She'd just gotten home from work fifteen minutes before, only to find out Matt had made plans for them that evening. Plans he'd told her nothing about.

Suddenly Matt was all business. He took her arm and guided her toward the front door. "I want to get into town before the stores close."

"What's so important we have to go tonight?" Elyse asked. They had milk, bread, plenty of staples in the pantry and freezer.

"Nothing," Matt grinned, opening the front door and ushering her outside onto the porch with a sweeping gesture of his arm. "I just want to buy champagne, and chocolates, and fresh flowers."

Elyse slowed to a halt beside him. Together they sauntered down the front steps to his car. "Where's the party?" she asked slowly.

He grinned mysteriously. "I don't know. Maybe you can help me find it."

"Matt!" Elyse cried, but her demand evoked no response. "Really, what are we going to do tonight?" she asked as soon as he'd slid behind the wheel.

He started the car, and took off. "Buy candy, and flowers, and champagne…"

He was as good as his word, trotting them into one store and then the next. To her growing frustration, he was also as mysterious as could be. Elyse went along with it for the better part of an hour, but finally she couldn't stand not knowing anymore. "Really, Matt, what's going on?" she asked as they left the last store.

Matt gave her a bland look before he pulled out into traffic. "I want you to have all your favorite things."

"Right." They had been over that. And she now had all her favorite things, barring nothing. She searched her mind. It would've been impossible to pinpoint their anniversary since they'd never really formally begun courting. Somehow their relationship had just evolved. So what were they celebrating? And why did he continue to look so darn happy?

"There's no specific occasion," Matt said, adeptly reading the question in her eyes. "I just want you to know how much I love you."

She felt the hint of a blush warm her cheeks. "I already know that." She reached over to touch his thigh. Though there was only a foot or so between them, she felt impossibly far away.

"I know you do," he answered quietly, covering her hand with his own.

"So?" She withdrew her hand, sat up straight and swept her hair into place.

"So I want to pamper you," he said, starting toward home. "And when we get home we'll…oh, shit." Without warning, all the color left his face. He was pale and dismayed.

Elyse felt her heartbeat accelerate. Her every muscle tightened with the prediction of doom. "What?"

Matt exhaled loudly. His mouth twisted into a deep frown. "I forgot about the Rowe contracts." In self-directed exasperation, he groaned and touched his forehead with the palm of his hand. Eyes still on the light flow of traffic in front of him, he shook his head as if he couldn't believe how forgetful he'd been.

She swore inwardly, once and then again. If ever a mood had just been broken… "They're important?" She tried but couldn't quite hide her disappointment. Whatever merry goose chase they had been on had been fun. She didn't want to see it cut short for benefit of work. It was too reminiscent of her life with Nick because the moment they'd sat down together or gone out to dinner, his beeper had always sounded. He'd had to rush to a phone, often the hospital as well. To have that experience repeated, even marginally… Much as she hated to admit it, she resented the interruption. And more than that, Matt's apparent lack of foresight.

But Matt was totally caught up in his own worries as he maneuvered the car around the freeway system and back into the northbound lanes. "They're coming in to sign to-morrow, and I haven't even read over them." He sent her a fretful look. "Mind if we stop by my office? It'll just take a minute, I promise."

He looked so distressed, how could she say no? Besides she knew how important his work was to him. "Sure." It'll just take a moment, she reassured herself silently, though her formerly ebullient mood was plummeting fast.

"Want to stay in the car?" he asked, pulling up in front of the high-rise. He seemed to sense her distaste for any-thing even remotely connected with his business at that mo-ment.

A dark parking lot, even in a locked car, was not her idea of fun. "No, I think I'll come up with you," she decided quietly.

The building was silent, deserted, except for the lone se-curity guards and a few people working in offices on other floors. Elyse couldn't help but remember the first of many times they'd made love in his office. But looking at his face she could tell lovemaking was the last thing on his mind. He was irritated with himself for forgetting about work, and spoiling the impromptu outing he had planned for them.

Oh well, she thought, maybe some other time. She was no stranger to work coming between her and her man. She had to be adult about this. Not that it really seemed to matter to Matt. He was so preoccupied she could have danced a jig and he wouldn't have noticed.

Once in his office, Matt turned on the overhead light next to the door. Elyse blinked against the sudden illumination and waited for her eyes to adjust. Unperturbed, Matt crossed to his desk and began rifling through the stacks of papers. He frowned deeply as he continued to search through them, lifting and riffling through stack after stack of yellow and blue legal briefs.

"Can't find them?" she asked finally, wishing she could do something to help. Anything would be better than con-tinuing to stand there totally unnoticed.

He shook his head negatively, looking grim. "Not a trace."

It was her turn to cast a glance skyward. "You sure are disorganized tonight," she remarked, sauntering over to join him.

He looked up, brows raised in arch disagreement. "I suppose you think you can do better," he volleyed back.

"Won't be difficult," she teased and was rewarded with a smile. With a capable air, she strode over to his desk. There were plenty of papers, contracts galore, but nothing resembling a "Rowe contract." She frowned and thought about suggesting that they check the files.

Without warning, she felt his hands on her shoulders. He turned her to face him and wordlessly pressed something into her hand—it was a small navy blue velvet box. She looked down at it, not sure she understood, not daring to hope, lest she be disappointed. Finally she found her voice. "What is this?" Her heart was racing.

He smiled broadly and suddenly she knew what he was going to say. "Why don't you open it and find out?" they repeated laughingly in unison. "Why did I know you were going to say that?" she asked nervously, fumbling with the lid, then let out a heartfelt gasp of pleasure and excitement.

Inside was a small diamond surrounded by tiny sapphire stones. It was breathtakingly beautiful. She had no words to thank him. Suddenly there were tears shimmering in her eyes.

His hand tightened over hers. "Marry me," he said softly, and then putting the box aside, he drew her more fully into his arms and held her close for long tender moments. Releasing her, he said, "I know it won't be easy. We've already been through a lot and we still have a lot to work out. But I promise you that if you say yes I'll do my very best to make you happy. Not just for now, but for always." He looked so vulnerable then, so serious and somehow simultaneously so strong. She knew he was all she had ever wanted in a mate, all she would ever want.

"Oh, Matt, I'm already happy just being with you. Of course I'll marry you," she replied shakily, holding him close as tears of happiness streamed down her face.

He lowered his head to hers and placed his lips across hers. They kissed for long moments. Unhurried, tender, the caress spoke of all they felt for each other, would continue to feel for all eternity.

"You had this all planned out, didn't you?" she asked, when at last she could draw a breath again.

He smiled tenderly, still studying the happiness he saw reflected on her face. "Right down to the ring," he confessed softly.

She grinned, appreciating his devilry. "Why all the running around?" Her eyes sparkled as they continued to survey his.

He smiled and shrugged. "Didn't want to make it too obvious what I was up to."

"You didn't."

He ran a caressing hand along her back and drew her near. "Besides, I thought you were due a few surprises."

They were standing so close their heartbeats seemed to blend. "This office of yours seems to inspire them," she teased, thinking again of the first breathlessly passionate time they made love. It was exactly what she wanted to do at that moment.

He seemed to read her mind and agree. "You inspire me," he admitted on a soft ragged note. He kissed her again, his lips lingering deliciously on the arch of her neck. "Want me to show you how much?"

Elyse smiled and nodded and gave herself up to him, and all the pleasure and love he had to give.

"YOU'RE SURE YOU DON'T MIND waiting to wear the ring, to make the announcement?" he asked en route home.

Still glowing from the closeness they'd shared, she cuddled next to him in the car. "No, it really wouldn't be right until after the memorial's officially under way."

He nodded. "And with the dedication ceremony only ten days off..." It made sense to wait.

"And since we won't be announcing our plans until after the Christmas holidays or marrying until late in the spring anyway, there'll be plenty of time to prepare." She was touched he'd been so anxious to make his commitment to her more definite, more real. It was a joy to finally know exactly where they were heading. She'd wanted to marry Matt for a long while. She'd just been almost afraid to hope, to even think about the possibility, for fear she would somehow jinx it. It was silly to be so superstitious, she knew, but where Matt was concerned, their lives and love were too precious to let anything mess it up.

"The delay will also give people a chance to adjust to the idea of us together as a couple," Matt said pragmatically. "Think the girls will mind?"

She looked at him with all the love she felt. She knew they would be delighted. "They love you, Matt."

"And I love them."

Elyse rested her head on his shoulder. She was so happy she wanted to shout it from the rooftops for all of the city to hear. He apparently felt the same way. He smiled over at her, then squeezed her hand and she squeezed his back. "We're going to have a great life together," she prophesied happily.

He nodded, his vision of their future firm. "The good times are all ahead of us," he said confidently.

Elyse relaxed blissfully. They just had to get through the next few months. She had to make sure it was a joint memorial, and then it would be all over. The nightmare of Nick's mistake and her knowledge of it would be vanquished from her life. She would be able to go on with Matt. With love. Forever...

Chapter Thirteen

"You look tired tonight," Matt observed as he and Elyse finished up the last of the dinner dishes.

"I am. It was a brutal day." Sears had been making her professional life hell during the past few weeks. Every time she turned around he was there, looking over her shoulder, expressing a mixture of "concern" and disapproval. All the nurses knew why Elyse was getting the treatment from Lawrence; it didn't make his silent ongoing harassment any easier to bear. In fact if Elyse hadn't decided to be so stubborn, she might have simply quit and looked for another job. She knew that if she did that, however, Sears would have won—again. And she was bound and determined to prevent that from happening.

"Anything in particular or everything?" he asked softly.

Elyse decided to tell him what she could. She needed to vent her feelings. "It goes back a few weeks. I had a run-in with a doctor at University." For ethical reasons, Elyse carefully avoided mentioning any specific names.

Matt's brow furrowed worriedly. "What kind of run-in?"

Done with her task, Elyse folded the dish towel and hung it on the rack. She poured herself another cup of coffee. Matt joined her at the table. "He wrote out an incorrect dosage on a medication order. I had to set things right, and I offended him in the meantime," she explained wearily. "Since then he's been very angry with me." Briefly she explained the harassment, how subtly it was being dealt out. "I'm beginning to feel the pressure."

"Can't you report the physician?"

"For what? Giving me dirty looks? Double-checking everything I do? Technically he has a right to do that."

Matt was silent. "Well, for what comfort it is, it sounds like you did the right thing."

"Yes." And that much, at least, she felt good about.

"What's going to happen to the doctor in question?" Matt asked after a moment. He took another sip of his coffee and stretched his long legs out underneath the kitchen table.

"Nothing."

"You didn't report it?" He looked aghast.

"No. I—it was a mistake. It happens." Not often, but it did occasionally happen. "Doctors are people, too."

"People who deal in lives," Matt corrected archly, showing no leniency at all.

Remembering Nick, a prickle of fear went down Elyse's spine.

"That's why we have the system of checks and balances," Elyse said quietly. "Yes, mistakes are sometimes made, but usually someone is there to catch and rectify them. Whether it's a nurse or a pharmacist or another physician, an intern." She leaned forward persuasively, clasping his hand. "Medicine is an imperfect science, Matt. For instance, lab tests don't always turn out. Sometimes a test will produce false results. And that can screw up a whole diagnosis."

"Which is why lab tests are often run twice."

"If there's any doubt at all or something doesn't click."

He was silent a moment.

"Nonetheless, don't you think you should report this doctor?"

Elyse pondered that a moment. She'd thought about it briefly. She shook her head. "I'm sure the doctor will be more careful in the future." What would Matt do if he realized the doctor in question was Lawrence Sears, she wondered. Would he insist Sears be punished—because he was Sears and had once made a pass at her?

"You seem very accepting of this." He disapproved of her attitude.

Elyse met his gaze. "Don't lawyers ever make mistakes?"

"Touché."

She shrugged, confiding further, "Doctors are human." And Sears was a first-class jerk. But he'd also saved many, many lives. One small mistake could not be allowed to cancel out all the good he had done, for who among them was perfect? Who among them had never had even a momentary lapse in job performance?

"In medicine there is no room for error," Matt pronounced grimly.

That was true, Elyse thought. Furthermore, no one would have agreed with that particular statement more than Nick himself. Yet the passionately devoted Nick had made a mistake, too. A ten-year-old boy had died because no one had known his complete medical history. And then Nick had become ill. And Nick had died. One mistake, yet because of it so much grief and guilt. Elyse wanted only to forget.

"Is that all that's bothering you?" Matt traced the veins on the back of her hand.

She stared down at his hand, enjoying his touch, thinking.

"I guess I'm just tired." She stood abruptly. Moving away from the table, she stretched the tired muscles in her shoulders and arms.

"Only two more days until the ground-breaking and initial dedication ceremony," Matt said, walking over to join her.

Two more days and the hospital board still hadn't told her of their decision. Elyse forced a smile. "I'm glad you're here for me. It means a lot, knowing I have you in my corner." In fact if she hadn't had Matt to cheer her up and pleasurably distract her, she didn't know how she would have endured the past few months.

He put his arms around her and hugged her close. "It means a lot to me, having you in mine."

IT WAS LATE when Elyse went out to her car the following evening after work. Aside from the fact that she'd had a very rough day and pulled some extra duty because two of the regular nurses were out sick, she'd also been given some very bad news.

A masculine voice sounded behind her. "Elyse, wait up!"

Elyse turned to see Sears striding toward her.

She muttered a profanity and hurriedly pushed the key into the lock. She just had the car door open when Sears reached her side. He took her keys before she could get them out of the lock, then calmly walked around to unlock the passenger side. Elyse could tell from the bittersweet stench of whiskey on his breath and his slightly uncoordinated gait that Sears had been drinking.

Better let him say what he has to and get it over with she thought. *He's obviously heard about the board's decision, too.*

With a sigh, she stepped into the car. Her only saving grace was that it was nearly dark. With any luck, no one would see them together. Or think anything about it if they did. After all Sears and Nick had once been partners; the dedication ceremony was tomorrow morning; it would be logical for them to talk.

"You've been avoiding me." He removed a flask from his pocket and surreptitiously took another drink.

"Can you blame me?" Her voice was harsh. She wanted nothing more than to get out of there, away from him.

Unexpectedly a look of contrition crossed his face. "I'm sorry I've been hassling you. I—realize I should have been grateful to you for coming to me with that mistake. Had the hospital review board learned about it...well, needless to say I'd have a mark on my record by now."

He's drunk, she thought. *Be careful.* "Lawrence, I have to get home. The girls are expecting me."

"You can take a few minutes. I want you to understand what's been going on with me lately. My wife and I are having trouble. She hit me with divorce papers this morning."

Elyse took a deep breath. Was that what this was about? He wanted sympathy for his personal troubles? "I'm sorry," she said haltingly at last, but Sears wasn't really even looking at her, merely staring out the windshield. "I need a friend, Elyse. I've been alone too much lately. I think you have been, too."

She stared at him warily, recognizing the cold-blooded proposition for what it was. *He's never given up the idea of sleeping with me.* Something in her went very cold. "No."

"Why not?" He turned toward her questioningly, seeing nothing remiss in his request. Rather, he acted as if he would be doing them both a favor, handling their sexual needs so neatly and easily, in such a matter-of-fact, no-strings way. But then he was relentless in his pursuit of women, never loving it more than when confronted with a woman who was a real challenge. And knowing her as he did, he probably had calculated that a direct approach would be most effective.

"We're both alone—" he continued, taking her hand in his, refusing to let it go. When she tried to yank her hand free, he merely tightened his grasp.

But they weren't both alone, Elyse thought. And even if she was, she would never stoop to even being friendly with him again! She didn't trust him for a minute! Furthermore, it galled her to realize that he thought she'd be open to casual liaison. Nonetheless, she knew she had to be careful about how she refused him. She'd already angered him once—professionally. Now he was drunk and not likely to be very rational....

"I'm sorry. I thought you knew," she said finally. "I am

seeing someone. In fact—" using her other hand as leverage, she forcibly pried her hand from beneath his, and took
a deep bolstering breath "—it's very serious. I'm planning
to be married." There. That ought to scare him off. Or at
least encourage him to leave her alone.

"Who's the lucky man?" Sears gave her a sharp look.

Too late she realized he was jealous! "I don't—"

"It's Matt Donovan, isn't it?" he accused, his jaw tightening. "I've seen the way he looks at you." Sears threw
back his head and laughed; it was a bitter, ugly sound.
"Like to keep it all in the family, don't you, Elyse?"

He was even more obnoxious when he drank. "Get out
of my car." She pushed open her door and stood on the
other side of it. He still had her keys but, by God, if he
didn't leave quietly she would make a scene. She'd go in
and get the security guard and whoever else it took....

He got out of the car and circled around toward her.
Reading her thoughts, Sears said quietly, "Think about
Nick, Elyse, and his reputation before you say another
word."

At that, her temper exploded. "Fine," she snapped back,
her voice as low and ugly as his. "And you think about
Mrs. Calivarci."

"Is that a threat, Elyse?"

She folded her arms across her waist. "You don't want
word of that mistake to get out."

"It'd be your word against mine." He looked unperturbed, as if the fact that he was a doctor and she a nurse
automatically made him superior.

"My word and the word of a whole slew of nurses,"
Elyse lost her temper again, adding, "all of whom you've
managed to either insult or alienate over the last few years."

Lawrence's eyes darkened. "Go ahead, Elyse," he dared
her. "Tell everything you know. I'll survive the scandal."

He stepped closer. "The question is will your family survive the scandal about Nick? And just what do you think
the public is going to be more interested in? My mistake?

Mrs. Calivarci's dosage was simply a little too high. I corrected it. Nick...Nick killed someone, an innocent little—''

"Shut up."

Having scored a temporary victory, Sears said roughly, "Get back in the car, Elyse."

When she complied, and he'd joined her, he smiled. "That's better. You and I—well, we're going to be friends, Elyse—"

She gave him a withering look. "When hell freezes over." She'd kill the miserable bastard first.

"If you don't help me out, give me whatever I need, then I'm going to be forced to go to Matt Donovan to tell him what and where I was the night before Nick died."

At Matt's name Elyse's protective instincts kicked into gear. Matt didn't need this. Not after what he'd already been through with Holly. Elyse made her voice as dispassionate as possible, "He already knows you came by that night, and why, and nothing happened."

Sears's eyes glittered dangerously, reminding Elyse how much he hated to be thwarted. "Then I'll set him straight. I'll tell him we slept together then and are still sleeping together now."

"That's a lie."

"True enough, but once the seeds of doubt are planted." He paused, smiling evilly and shrugged. "It worked before, it'll work again."

Elyse stared at him, stupefied. "What are you...?"

"Nick. I told Nick you were sleeping around on him, or so the gossip said. It was right after your second daughter was born, I think, or was it your third?"

Elyse felt like she was going to be sick. "Why would you do such a thing?" She stared at him in horror.

"Because he was on my back," Sears snarled vindictively. "He wanted me involved in the research. I had no interest in it. There was no real money to be made in that. It was a waste of time and damn dangerous, too."

"His research helped saved lives!"

"Yeah? Well, for a while it made mine miserable, so I gave him something else to think about. Which brings me to my next point, Elyse. I know about the hospital's decision not to make it a joint memorial. Fortunately for you, there's still time to change their minds."

She swore beneath her breath, not caring that he heard. "The memorial's tomorrow!" she pointed out icily.

His jaw twitched as his eyes fastened threateningly on hers. "Then do some fast talking or telephoning tonight."

"It won't do any good," she pointed out calmly, desperately trying to make him see reason.

"You're supposed to give a speech tomorrow at the ground-breaking ceremony, on Nick's behalf. Rewrite it. Include me in it. Tell everyone—especially the press—how much you'd like it to be a joint memorial. Tell everyone that's what Nick would've wanted, too. The hospital will have no choice but to bow to the pressure."

"I can't do that," Elyse said calmly. Matt would never understand, the hospital would be furious, questions would be raised by family, friends and co-workers. To anyone who knew her and Sears well, it wasn't a logical move.

"You don't have a choice," Sears said roughly. "Unless you want Matt to know about us—"

Bolstered by her love for Matt and his for her, she gave Sears a steady glance. "Tell Matt whatever you want. He'll never believe you." Particularly when Elyse told him it was sour grapes....

"Maybe not. But he will believe the news about the death of the little Dilmore boy. So will everyone else. I've got all the proof I need. I'll go to the press, Elyse. Anonymously, of course. And I'll give them the full story, with copies of records. Not only will the memorial never get off the ground but you'll never live the scandal down."

She stared at him, knowing with certainty he meant every malevolent word he said. "Why do you hate me so?"

"I don't hate you, Elyse. I desire you." He surveyed her trim form slowly before returning to her furious gaze. "I thought I'd made that perfectly clear. But since you can't or won't accommodate me, you'll have to make it up to me in another way. One that really counts. Only then will I ever leave you alone.''

"YOU WANT TO TELL ME what's going on?" Matt said quietly from the edge of the patio. It was nearly dawn and Elyse was sitting alone on a chaise lounge, her robe drawn tight around her. She hadn't slept all night. She'd been crying for part of that time. She was terrified of Sears and the events of the day ahead of her. The dedication ceremony, the ground-breaking...

"I'm not feeling well," she hedged, knowing at least that much of what she said was true.

"Do you want me to call a doctor?"

She shook her head firmly. "No—"

"You're sure I—"

"I'm sure. It's just nerves." She swallowed hard and looked straight ahead.

"It's the dedication ceremony this morning, isn't it?" He sat down in front of her.

She nodded, aware she was trembling inside from head to foot. "Matt, I don't think I can give that speech—" Even her voice sounded shaky.

He rubbed her shoulder reassuringly. "Sure you can. I know you haven't done a tremendous amount of public speaking but once you get started, it'll be easy. Besides no one expects you to be perfect."

That was just it, though. Someone did expect her to be perfect. Sears. And if she didn't come through for him, by putting pressure on the hospital to make it a joint memorial...she felt sick just thinking about Nick's mistake being made public. Not to mention the legal and moral ramifications of such a scandal....

If Nick were still alive...

But he wasn't. The mistake was over. Both patient and

doctor were now gone. It would serve no purpose to expose the truth.

"Elyse?"

Matt's voice stunned her into attention. She glanced up at him, aware she hadn't heard much of what he'd said.

"I'm sorry—"

"Is something else wrong? Something you haven't told me about?"

She shook her head vigorously, unable to meet his eyes. "No. I—I just don't want to go this morning, that's all. I don't think your parents should go, either." What if Sears made a scene? What if somehow the truth came out anyway? Elyse didn't think she could bear to see Abigail and Peter hurt, never mind publicly humiliated in front of all the press and Nick's former friends and colleagues. No, it was too much to bear. She had to protect them.

"Elyse, you're making too much of this." He sank down beside her on the chaise and took both her hands in his. His tone and his manner were reassuring. "You've got to relax. I'll help you get through it." He stressed every word.

She knew she hadn't gotten through to him in the slightest. "Matt—"

He cut her off before she could finish. "You're going, Elyse. You're making the speech." This was for his brother and he would allow no last minute jitters to get in the way. "That's final."

MATT SAT ON THE PODIUM several chairs away from Elyse. She was the second guest scheduled to speak. He was the fourth and would detail the fund-raising efforts that had been made to date.

His speech wasn't bothering him. Elyse's strange behavior this morning was. Come to think of it, she'd been on edge for several days before but especially moody and withdrawn the evening before. He'd attributed it initially to fatigue and nerves. Now he wasn't so sure. It seemed, somehow, to be much more than that, judging by the way she kept scanning the audience almost fearfully.

The whine of a public address system being turned on interrupted his thoughts. Matt looked up to see the hospital director step up to the podium. After a round of applause, he gave a brief introductory speech. Though Elyse should have been listening to the director, at least looking his way, she was staring out at the audience. Front and center stood a well-dressed Lawrence Sears. He was staring meaningfully at Elyse, Matt noticed. And whatever was transpiring between them was… Matt's jaw clenched in sudden fury as the realization hit. Was Sears upsetting Elyse? Was he behind her trembling hands, her wan look?

Matt had no chance to find out, for even before the speaker had finished, Elyse was up and out of her chair, moving down the platform, behind it, out of sight. Matt wanted to go after her. He couldn't. Maybe she was ill, he thought, concerned. And maybe, just maybe, Lawrence Sears had something to do with her malaise. If so, there was going to be hell to pay when he got hold of Sears; Matt would see to it.

When the applause died down, Matt stood and, gathering up Elyse's notes as well, prepared to speak on her behalf.

To Matt's relief, the rest of the ceremony went without a hitch. Elyse did not return. Matt couldn't help but notice that Sears looked as coldly furious as Elyse had been upset. Something *was* going on between the two of them; he could feel it.

Matt sought Sears out as soon as the reception began. "I want to talk to you," he said bluntly. Sears followed him to a deserted corner beneath a large shade tree. Matt continued, "What the hell is going on between you and Elyse?"

Sears didn't blink. "Why don't you ask her?" he suggested smoothly, lifting a glass of punch to his lips.

"I'm asking you." He stared at Sears until Sears looked away.

Sears's lip curled derisively. "Your brother was no saint,

Donovan. And your sister-in-law, she's pretty good at keeping secrets, too.''

It was all Matt could do not to grab him by the collar and string him up on the nearest branch. ''What the hell are you talking about?'' He moved another step closer. His hands were knotted into fists at his sides.

Sears sized up Matt. His eyes turned to obsidian. ''I'm not your messenger boy, Donovan,'' he said contemptuously. ''You want to know something? Ask Elyse.''

THANKFULLY the girls were still in nursery school and would be there until early that afternoon. The house was empty when Elyse returned. Pausing only long enough to put on a suit and bathing cap, she went down to the pool and began methodically swimming laps. She knew she had to get rid of some of her adrenaline. She had to calm down. Swimming seemed the best way and far healthier than gulping whiskey, which she was also tempted to do.

She never should have left the dedication. She knew that. But to stand up there with Sears watching her, threatening every second—she couldn't do it. She'd had to leave or be ill. And so, hands and knees shaking, she'd simply bolted. Once off the podium, she'd sought sanctuary in her car. And once in her car, the freeway had seemed a good idea. Then home. Now that she was here again, she didn't know how she was going to explain her absence to Peter, Abigail or Matt. Not to mention the press and the hospital staff. She had promised to help. She'd chickened out. Would they ever forgive her?

Reaching the end of the pool for the fifteenth time, Elyse stopped and grabbed for her towel. No sooner had she lashed the water from her eyes, than she saw Matt standing there in his suit and tie. He looked impossibly handsome yet more upset with her than she'd ever seen him. Her fingers tightened as she pulled off the bathing cap and shook her hair free.

Wordlessly Matt stepped toward her. His expression wa
steely and his eyes were haunted.

Elyse shivered, whether from the suddenly cool breez
blowing across her skin or his icy presence, she didn't know
He was furious with her and obviously hurt—as he ha
every right to be.

"I don't like being lied to, Elyse," Matt said calmly, to
calmly. "Or evaded."

She walked up the steps that led out of the pool, he
stomach churning with turbulent emotions. How much di
he know? How much had Sears told him? And what wa
she going to say? She only knew she wanted to buy hersel
time and that she still wanted to run away. Using the towe
to slough moisture from her arms and thighs and abdomen
she started silently for the robe she'd left on the chair. Mat
caught her arm before she could reach it and swung he
around to face him. "Enough games, Elyse! What the hel
is going on? Why did you leave like that?"

He was begging her to explain. She knew if she didn'
talk to him, confide in him, it was all over. Holly had kep
secrets from him; he wouldn't tolerate it from her. Elys
swallowed hard and lifted pleading eyes to his face. Sh
wanted to tell him everything and yet she knew he wouldn'
understand, that he wouldn't agree. "Don't ask me," sh
said softly, tears blurring her vision and stinging her eyes
"Please, just—" she swallowed the sob caught midway u
her throat "—let it go."

He stared at her, waiting. "Dammit, I have to ask! I hav
to know what the hell is going on!" Grabbing her othe
arm, he shook her slightly, his voice low and torture
"Sears is making innuendos right and left! About som
wrongdoing that involved Nick and you! I didn't believ
him." Matt's laugh was hollow. "I called the bloody bas
tard a liar." Matt's mouth twisted ruefully. "I thought h
had to be making it up." Recognition hit him swiftly an
it was followed by a hurt that went soul deep. "But I wa
wrong, wasn't I? You do know what he's talking about an

you've been part of this cover-up he's been talking about all along.'' He took a deep calming breath and made an effort to inject sanity into the scene. ''Just tell me what's been going on,'' he said tiredly, running his hands through his hair. ''Elyse, I have to know.'' His look said he loved her and trusted her and wanted to believe this all had a plausible explanation.

She knew then that it was only a matter of time before Sears kept his promise.

She sat down on the chaise. Matt remained in front of her, his hands hooked loosely around his waist. His was an aggressively gentle stance, a stance that said he was waiting to be convinced. Because if she couldn't do that...

''Sears knows what was bothering Nick before he died,'' Elyse related miserably. ''Nick didn't get a complete medical history on a patient of his, and the child died as a result of complications during surgery. I checked the records, it's all true. Nick obviously blamed himself. Before he got so caught up in doing research, he always double- and triple-checked all medical histories himself. This time the history was taken by a medical student. All the records were sent for. All came in with the exception of one. Apparently no one noticed it prior to surgery—''

''And because of that, the child died?'' Matt was shocked, disbelieving. She knew how he felt; she'd had much the same reaction initially.

Elyse nodded miserably. ''If the parents had noted it on the medical forms they filled out, that he'd had a previously treated ulcer, Nick would have been prepared for any complications. But they didn't—''

''Why? Why would they leave out something that vital?''

Elyse lifted her shoulders and let them drop. ''My guess is they were so concerned over his life-threatening heart condition, they completely forgot about the ulcer. Five years had elapsed. They'd moved around often, switching doctors as often as some people change shoes. He'd had other illnesses. A bout with scarlet fever, pneumonia—''

"How long have you known?" The tension suddenly drained from his shoulders. Matt sat down beside her and took her hand, understanding why she'd found the memorial praising Nick difficult, if not impossible, to sit through.

"Weeks."

Matt stared at her. Slowly he released his grip on her hand, the depth of his hurt evident on his face as he realized how deliberately she had shut him out.

Tears flooded her eyes again. She tried to put her arms around him but he moved away. She'd never meant to hurt him, only to protect him. "I couldn't tell you, Matt," she whispered desolately. "I knew if I did you'd feel compelled to go forward with the truth."

"And you don't?" He spoke numbly and shot her an incredulous glance before offering her his back.

She stared at the tense set of his shoulders, feeling equally confused and frightened. "What purpose would it serve except to ruin Nick's reputation?"

He had no answer for her. "Where does Sears come in to all this?" he asked, still looking stunned and confused, as if he felt sick inside. "And what's been going on between you?" his mouth was white around the edges.

Elyse shivered uncontrollably at the memory of all she had been through. "He's been blackmailing me." Elyse slipped on her robe, glad for the warmth. It seemed even the August sun wasn't hot enough, that she'd never feel warm again. "He wanted me to make sure it was a joint memorial," she said wearily.

At that, Matt uttered a string of particularly vile curses.

Ignoring his assessment of Sears's character, and wanting to get the truth-telling session over with, Elyse continued doggedly, "He asked me to go to the board on his behalf. To protect Nick's reputation, I did so privately. Unfortunately they refused. I found out last night. So did Sears. He was furious. He said either I made a public announcement today at the memorial saying that was what I'd wanted or he'd trash Nick's reputation."

Matt studied her quietly, his compassion at what she'd been through softening the lines of his face. A grave weariness settled over his features. "That's why you couldn't sleep last night?"

"I didn't want your parents hurt." She was silent, staring down at her hands. It occurred to her that she didn't know what had gone on at the memorial after she left. "Did he…?"

"Not that I know of, although he's obviously thinking about it," Matt said pensively, staring broodingly over at the shimmering blue surface of the pool. His mouth tightened angrily as he considered the options.

"Maybe he won't," Elyse said hopefully, getting up to pace the pool area. "Maybe, in the interest of self-preservation, he'll forget all about it." As vindictive as Sears was, he was also self-serving. He wouldn't do anything that would make himself look bad, and trashing his former partner would certainly hurt him to some degree! Yes, surely he would realize that, and if not, Elyse could point it out. If she hadn't been so upset, she would've thought of this before.

"Elyse, we've got to go forward with the truth," Matt said tiredly. "It's the only way to free the family of the threat of blackmail—"

"I want to wait, Matt. See what happens."

"Why?" He closed the distance between them. He looked angry and upset with her again. "So we can see what Sears's next demand is going to be? Wise up, Elyse. The man is not going to stop, not until he gets everything he wants—"

Part of her thought that, part of her didn't. "You don't know that—" she disagreed, her face flaming. "And until we do, I think we ought to wait."

"For how long? Until Nick's charged with criminal negligence or malpractice? The statute of limitations isn't up yet and won't be for four to five more years! Nick's insurers could still be sued and so could the hospital.…"

"Not if no one knows the truth," she interrupted bluntly.

He glared at her impatiently, his disillusionment evident. "Sears already knows the truth. You know the truth! I know the truth! How long do you think it's going to be before someone else stumbles onto the truth, if someone hasn't already?"

He had a point, but she wouldn't let his fear push them into doing something that was equally as pain inducing. "I still think we ought to wait."

With difficulty he maintained his composure. "And I think you're being stubborn, foolish and blind. Your efforts to protect Nick are probably going to be futile anyway."

"We won't know that until we try. Please, Matt, help me in this. Help me preserve Nick's good name. We can do it as long as we both stand together." As long as they didn't let the stress of the situation drive them apart.

He leaned forward and looked at her with an intensity that made her catch her breath. "Listen to me, Elyse. You've got to stop letting yourself be ruled by your emotions. I know you loved Nick; so did I. We all did. But you can't protect him now. Maybe you never could."

She stared at him. "You're going to go forward with what you know?" Dammit, she'd known this would happen if she got him involved!

Matt nodded solemnly. "I'll talk with the medical review board at the hospital as soon as I can set it up. One way or another, Elyse, the truth has to come out."

Did it? She didn't think so, but she also knew there was no stopping Matt now. He would do what he felt he had to do, as surely as she had followed the path that was right for her.

FOR THE REST OF THE DAY and into the next, Elyse thought about what Matt had said. When it came time for her to give Matt the proof, the specifics he needed, however, she couldn't do it. "I'm sorry, Matt, I can't help you."

His mouth compressed into a thin line. "Can't or won't?"

Was that jealousy she saw on his face...or simple anger that she wasn't as noble and fearless and thick-skinned as he seemed to be?

"I think you're reacting rashly," she said calmly, taking another breath. "Twenty-four hours have passed. We've heard not one word from Sears. There's been nothing in the press."

"Right. And you and I have been sitting on pins and needles the whole time. I agreed to give you twenty-four hours to adjust to the idea. Time's running out. I want those records, Elyse. I expect you to give them to me," he said gruffly.

Elyse hesitated. "And if I don't?" If she insisted on doing this her way? Then what?

Matt hesitated, too. "I hope it won't come to that."

Because if it did, it was all over....

"You'd desert me?" Elyse whispered, a sick, empty feeling welling up inside her. She stood absolutely still, unable, unwilling to accept the look of detachment she saw on his face. It reminded her of Nick, the times he'd shut her out so deliberately. Times they'd disagreed. She'd thought then she couldn't go through that again; she knew now it was true; she'd never survive. She needed a man who would stand by her through thick or thin, who wouldn't let stress drive them apart. She needed a man who would listen to *her* and take *her* needs into consideration, too.

Grimly Matt expelled a stream of air. "Dammit, stop being so naive," he said through clenched teeth. "We can't live our lives with this hanging over us. And there's only one way to rid ourselves of the threat of blackmail—"

"Now who's being naive?" she snapped angrily, her mouth twisting with derision. "You act like this will be a walk in the park! It won't! It'll be an ugly, muckraking mess!"

He held himself rigidly. "We can weather it." His pronouncement was firm.

Elyse had none of his faith. She watched his throat work,

the anguish in his eyes. "Can we?" she questioned quietly. "Look what just the initial stress has already done to us. We're barely speaking. We can't look at each other without wanting to quarrel." Her voice lowered a compelling notch. She had to make him see reason—she had to! "Now imagine dragging your parents into this, hurting them, too. I'm assuming we can keep the girls out of it for now, but with them going to nursery school and first grade...I don't know, Matt. It seems to me that sooner or later they'd be confronted with the truth, too."

He got to his feet, watching her with the old look that said he didn't much like her or trust himself to be around her. "You're probably right, they would be. Whether I go forward with this or not. Which leaves us with only one choice—"

"Not to go forward," she interrupted.

Emphatically he shook his head no. "To talk to the girls first—alone, gently. To let them know it was an honest mistake, one the medical authorities are going to try and look into so that it won't have to happen again."

And so they wouldn't have to live their lives with a cloud hanging over them. Part of Elyse wanted that, but part of her knew she couldn't endure a hell like that, especially not when it tore her from Matt as it was already doing. Panic tore at her throat—she knew she was losing him.

"Please, Matt, can't we just take a little more time before we act on this?" If he just had another week, she felt sure he would change his mind. Was that what he was afraid of? That he, too, might want to back down?

"No, Elyse, we can't take any more time. And if you can't see your way clear to help me on this—"

"Then what?" She asked, her voice low and brittle. His tone sounded suspiciously threatening. And she was dangerously close to tears. But tears wouldn't help. At this point, nothing would help.

He turned toward her. An unbearable weariness was etched on his face. "Then it's all over. I can't and won't

arry someone who insists on going through life with blind-
s on. Dammit, Elyse, when are you going to realize that
noring dangers doesn't make them nonexistent! Wishing
r something not to happen won't prevent a catastrophe!''

And he'd already lived with one woman who lived her
fe that way. He'd lost her because she had been naive and
npulsive, perhaps even open to emotional blackmail. Holly
id let Benton talk or manipulate her into his bed, into
ping whatever he wanted her to do—including the car
lase scene that had taken her life. Was Sears doing the
me to Elyse? Granted, she never would have slept with
m under any circumstances, but she had done as he had
ked when it came to Nick's memorial. She'd let him ma-
pulate her, and that had driven her apart from Matt.

So where did that leave them? What could she do?

Elyse was silent.

She'd never felt more far away from Matt. The twenty-
ur hours she had hoped would cool them both off and
low them to become close again had left them farther apart
an ever. And she knew that if it went into an investigation,
e stress would separate them farther. She couldn't bear
at again, living with a man she felt was virtually indiffer-
t to her. It hurt too much. "I want you to consider my
elings in this," she said tremulously at last. She wanted
em to figure out a way to shelve the past, to go on together
thout ever looking back again.

He looked at her bleakly, his own mind made up. "I
ve," he said warily.

"But it doesn't change anything?" Tears flooded her
es. She was hurt beyond measure that he would choose
; quest for justice over his love for her, that he could so
sily let go of all they had. Everything she had worked so
rd for during these past months seemed to be slipping
/ay.

"No, it doesn't." He was silent again, wanting her to
nd. "Does it for you?"

Slowly she shook her head.

His face hardened. He looked at her as if she were
convicted criminal. "I guess there's nothing left to say ther
is there?" Disillusionment edged his low tone.

Except maybe goodbye. Elyse took a deep breath, fightin
not to cry. "Not unless you change your mind." And the
both knew he wouldn't. She'd had her heart broken; sb
wouldn't humiliate herself by crying and groveling, too.

His eyes met hers, reminding her of all she was givin
up in walking away from him, in not agreeing to do thing
his way and his way alone. Moments ticked by, neither c
them moved. Neither of them spoke. They were at a stale
mate neither could break.

"It's over then," he said thickly, in a voice roughene
with regret.

Salty tears spilled down her cheeks. She trembled wit
the effort it took to hold back the sob in her throat. "Yes.

She could feel his anger and his hurt. A warning tensio
radiated through him. Unable to look at him directly any
more, she stared at his throat, where his Adam's apple wa
pulsing.

There was nothing left to say.

He was out the door before she could stop him. He wa
all she'd ever wanted. And she'd lost him.

Chapter Fourteen

Abigail and Peter Donovan sat together on the sofa, their faces pale, their hands tightly entwined. "You're sure of this?" Abigail asked at last in a trembling voice, tears streaming from her eyes. "That Nick was responsible for this child's death?"

Matt looked at Elyse, expecting her to give the medical expertise and explanation. She nodded reluctantly. "Had Nick taken a better history, been more thorough in his prep care, he would have been prepared and alert for any signs of internal bleeding in the abdominal area. Chances are, had he known, he could've saved the child."

"And Nick knew this before he died," Peter repeated slowly, looking crushed by the discovery.

Again Elyse nodded reluctantly. "I think so. I think that's the reason he became so ill himself...."

"But he didn't talk to you about it?" Abigail ascertained, making no effort to hide her tears.

Elyse shook her head reluctantly. "No. As far as I know, he didn't talk to anyone." She looked over at Matt. Though grim faced about the situation in general, he didn't seem at all affected by his parents' tears. Instead he was lost in silent ruminations of his own. How could he be so heartless, she wondered, enraged by both his distance and her previous wrong impression of him. He had to know how much worse this was going to get.

"When do you plan to go to the review board?" Pete asked, dabbing at his own eyes.

Matt's jaw hardened. He avoided looking deliberately a Elyse. "Tomorrow." It had taken him two weeks to fin the information Elyse had because she'd steadfastly refuse to give it to him. Nonetheless, he had found it. And thoug Sears had not followed through on any of his threats, Ma had felt compelled to go forward anyway with what h knew. His parents were first, the authorities next.

Matt was hurting them all, and Elyse couldn't forgive hir for that. For his part Matt could not forgive Elyse's stubbor conviction that it was better to turn a blind eye in this ir stance, forget the wrongs that had been done and hope tha Sears would stay quiet, if only in the interests of sel preservation.

Matt couldn't live with a weight hanging over his head ready to drop. Nor could Elyse live with Matt and the hear less way he was behaving, especially knowing all they ha once been to one another. They had been planning to ar nounce their engagement, marry and live happily ever afte Now they were barely speaking. The only reason she wa still living in his house was that she hadn't wanted to upse Peter and Abigail. But now that they knew the truth…

"You're angry with me?" Matt found her in the kitche after his parents, emotionally exhausted, had retired to the bedroom upstairs.

"Did you think I wouldn't be?" Elyse systematicall shredded lettuce into a bowl. She turned to face him, sti seething from the soul-destroying scene she had witnesse in the other room. "You just destroyed every memory o their son that they ever had. And now—now you want t go public with the truth! Even when there's no need!"

"There is a need," he said gruffly.

"Maybe for you. Not for the rest of us." She turne around and picked up the lettuce again. "What happens we find out Nick wasn't just responsible for the Dilmo boy's death but others as well! What then? How are yo going to live with that? How are my daughters going to live with that?''

His expression narrowed. ''You don't have much faith in Nick at all, do you? You never had—''

She bristled at his accusing tone. ''That's not true!''

''Isn't it? Then why are you so against this investigation?'' he asked her angrily. ''Unless you think they'll find more to incriminate him!''

Matt was right. She was afraid that it was possible they would discover more than they wanted to know in the course of an investigation into Nick's competence as a doctor. Elyse had never expected Nick to be careless, yet he had been—and all because he'd been so wrapped up in his research, so anxious to make strides in current surgical procedure. He'd wanted desperately to help others. Did that mean his mistake was excusable? She didn't know. He had worked unholy hours. Perhaps driven himself too far. Who was to say his carelessness hadn't happened just that once? And if it had, could she live with that? Could Abigail and Peter? Darn it, why was Matt pushing it so far? Why did he have to report it? Hadn't he seen how destructive his need for the truth was in this instance? Couldn't he see how much he'd hurt his parents? Didn't he care? Or was he too selfish, too blind? And if that was the case, did she really want him to be a part of her life at all? It was ironic that she'd finally found a man willing to share everything with her, and now she couldn't bear to be with him. ''I think it would be better for me to move out,'' she said quietly. ''I've been looking at apartments.''

For a moment he didn't react in the slightest. When he spoke, his face was impassive. ''What are you going to tell my parents?''

''That I want to be closer to the hospital.'' Finished with the lettuce, Elyse began slicing carrots.

''You don't think they'll see through that?'' He moved to lean against the counter so he could see her face. His arms were folded across his chest.

Aware that her hands were shaking and she was near tears herself, Elyse shrugged in resignation. "They might see through it." But what choice did she have? She couldn't stay on, not feeling as she did about Matt. Seeing him every day, knowing how angry they still were with one another, how much angrier they were bound to get, made her even more miserable.

"Elyse—" Abruptly he seemed to be beseeching her to forgive him.

Remembering what he had just put his parents through strengthened her resolve to be free of him, to prevent him from hurting her any more than he already had. "Now that I've sold the house I can afford live-in care for the children. I'll still have to work, but only part-time, at least for the next few years, until all the girls are in school full-time."

"Is it what you want?" he asked quietly. "Moving out?" It didn't seem to be his choice.

His handsome features blurring before her, Elyse looked down at her hands. They were still shaking. "No," she said, swallowing hard, "it isn't what I want, Matt. But it's best for both of us."

THERE WAS SIMPLY NO WAY she could have prepared herself for the chaos that followed Matt's revelation to the review board. Naturally the hospital tried to keep the matter quiet; nonetheless the press learned of it within forty-eight hours. Considerable community pressure was exerted to change the name of the hospital wing. Funds were quietly withdrawn and pledged elsewhere. What had promised to be one of the most publicized and successful fund-raising efforts in the history of the city became a financial and public relations fiasco overnight. The hospital, in an effort to cut its losses and save face while they could, denied any wrongdoing and put their plans for a new wing on temporary hold. The hospital then conducted its own in-depth investigation of Nick's performance in and out of the operating room. Savoring every bit of the malicious melee, scandal-hungry reporters swarmed both University Hospital and Matt's ranch house. Fortunately for her daughters' sake, Elyse had already moved into a furnished apartment with an unlisted phone, so she missed much of the initial unpleasantness. Determined to salvage their son's reputation and protect his memory until the bitter end, Peter and Abigail gave interviews, attesting to their son's fine intentions and noble nature. Matt spoke on his brother's behalf, too, though less idealistically than his parents. Though Elyse wanted to fault Matt for everything he said, she couldn't. With his usual lawyer's tact, Matt stuck to the truth, making no judgments, asking only that all information be gathered so they might fairly establish Nick's innocence or guilt.

Elyse had hoped all along that there would be only a single story in the newspaper. But as she'd feared, news was slow when the item broke, and after three days there was no letup in sight. Dr. Sears had started talking, too, disavowing and discrediting Nick at every turn.

Deciding to remove herself from the stressful situation, Elyse took her daughters and went to visit her parents in Galveston. For two weeks she walked on the beach, played with her girls, talked with her mother and father and completely avoided all the newspapers and television news. When she returned to Dallas—and work—the findings were in.

A private session for family members only was held in a hospital conference room.

The disclosure was brief and to the point. "We've looked in depth at all the cases Nick Donovan handled while he was here at University Hospital," the director began directly, facing the Donovan family. "We've found Nick to be not nearly as negligent as the rumors would imply. It's true, on several occasions, he used bad judgment, mostly in overestimating what he himself could do without an additional surgeon's help in the O.R., but he was not medically negligent in any other case. And as for the Dilmore boy, that may or may not have been avoidable. We've talked to his parents. They've assumed full responsibility for the omission on the medical history. They said Nick questioned them twice on the specifics of the child's health. At no time did they even remember the presence of the child's previous ulcer.''

Abigail and Peter breathed a sigh of relief. "Then we won't have to worry about a malpractice suit being lodged against Nick?"

"No. Nor is there any reason for any criminal charges to be filed. The damage to Nick's professional reputation, however, seems irreparable." The director lifted his gaze to Matt's. "The board has voted. It's unanimous, I'm afraid. We're going to have to rename and restructure the proposed hospital wing."

Abigail and Peter's shoulders slumped. Elyse knew how they felt.

"I'm sorry, Mr. and Mrs. Donovan, Matt and Elyse. But under the circumstances, Nick's memory is more a liability than anything else."

They all nodded their understanding. It would have been foolish to hope for anything else. Yet all were nonetheless disappointed.

The meeting concluded. They all rose. "Thank God that's over," Abigail said, dabbing at her eyes.

She and Peter both looked immeasurably relieved by the board's findings. Elyse knew how they felt; it was as if an enormous burden had been lifted from her, too. And all because of Matt. Only he had possessed the courage to insist upon the formal investigation that had cleared Nick's name.

No longer did she have to worry about Dr. Sears blackmailing her. She would still see him from time to time. They did work at the same hospital. But he no longer had any power over her, and that, too, was thanks to Matt.

Abigail and Peter chatted briefly with the board members then turned to Elyse and Matt simultaneously. "We're going to head on home," Peter confided to his son. "Tomorrow will be a big day, what with the press conference and all.'

"I'll see you later," Matt said bending to kiss his mother and give his father an affectionate clap on the shoulder. Elyse said her goodbyes and the Donovans departed along with most of the board. Elyse waited for her chance to speak to Matt alone. She got it when everyone else left.

When Matt started to step past her, Elyse moved to block his way. "Matt, I…we need to talk," she began awkwardly, wishing he were a bit more friendly or receptive to what she had to say. But then why should he be? her conscience argued She wasn't there for him or his family during most of the turmoil. Instead she'd taken her daughters and run away, even gone so far as to move out of his house. Why? Why had she felt it necessary to do so much to separate them?

"Why should we talk?" he said bluntly, resting his briefcase momentarily on the conference table beside him. "Haven't you said everything there was to say? Or are you going to chew me out about the loss of the memorial to Nick?"

Clearly he was disappointed about that, as was she.

For a moment she was silent. She still wasn't sure about the course of action he'd taken; if she'd had her way she would have avoided the issue altogether. And yet his actions had cleared Nick's name in many respects, ended the cloud of blackmail she'd labored under.

"No," she said quietly after a moment, meeting his gaze and reading the unending hurt in his eyes. "I'm not going to berate you for the loss of the memorial. All things considered, that's probably just and fair."

"Then what?" The muscles in his jaw twitched. He shifted restlessly from one foot to another.

For a moment she didn't think she could go on. She didn't want to confess her love for him—and if she were honest she would admit that was what she still felt, although she'd tried many times to erase the emotion—and have him throw back in her face. Yet she knew she had to tell him she still cared about him. He had to know.

"I just wanted to say I'm sorry about the way things

worked out. I know the past few weeks have been ver
difficult for you as well as your parents.'' And she hadn
been there for either of them, she realized guiltily.

''It was hard on you, too,'' he admitted gruffly after
moment.

Elyse nodded, knowing there was no sense in broodi
over what could not be changed. The ordeal was over. F
had done what he had felt he had to do. So had she. A
angry and hurt as she had been, she still respected him f
following through on his convictions. They had to go o
both of them. They had to find a way to make peace betwee
them; it was the only way either would ever have any re
olution.

Matt seemed to know that, too. For a moment he w
silent, refusing to pick up the olive branch she held out. Sl
knew he was still disappointed in her. But he was also
troubled by their newfound distance as she. He didn't li
being her adversary any more than she liked being his. Sl
met his compelling gaze. ''You don't hate me for what
did?'' he asked quietly.

She had at one time, there was no denying it. Sl
shrugged indifferently, realizing her feelings were still ve
mixed and probably always would be confused. She still fe
a certain loyalty toward Nick, she felt protective toward tl
Donovans, protective toward Matt—even though he didr
want her concern. She faced Matt honestly, knowing that
difficult as it was, certain things had to be said betwee
them, the air cleared. Only then would they be free to ¿
on, to have even any sort of friendship. She swallowed ha
and admitted in a voice laced with pain, ''If you hadr
come forward, we never would have known for sure wh
Nick had done or what he hadn't. I would have had to li
with that, as would you, and it would've torn us both apart
And that she had never wanted. *I only wanted you. A l*
together.

His eyes darkened. He shifted his briefcase from the tal
to the floor. ''It still tore us apart.''

Did he want a reconciliation? she wondered, aware of her
~art beating frantically in her chest. And if so, why didn't
~ give her some sign that he was as miserable without her
ow as she was without him? That he was sorry they'd let
~e stress of the situation take its toll on them? If only he
ould, it would be so easy for her to go to him, to tell him
l that was in her heart. "If it's possible, I'd like us to be
iends," she said finally, settling for what she could get at
~e moment.

Matt walked over to the window and stood looking down
the city street. He put his hands in his pockets. For long
oments he didn't say anything.

Whatever fleeting hope she'd had about a reconciliation
sappeared. She knew it was all over. He was just searching
·r the words to tell her so. Her shoulders slumped. It was
l she could do to hold back the tears that threatened to....
ot wanting him to see her fall apart, she turned to leave.

He stopped her before she reached the door. "Elyse—"
is voice was low, underscored with suppressed need, not
question but a command. "Don't go."

She turned toward him, afraid she hadn't heard right.

"I don't want to be friends," he said quietly. His eyes
:ld hers. "I don't think it's possible, either. After all that
~ had, or were to each other. To go back to a platonic
lationship..." His voice caught abruptly. He cleared his
roat.

The tears she'd been holding back spilled over her lashes
.d rolled down her cheeks. He stared at her wordlessly,
~ading the depth of her feelings for him on her face, dis-
vering what was true, what hadn't and would never
~ange, no matter how much they differed or disagreed. And
~en suddenly he was moving, crossing the conference room
·iskly, taking her into his arms.

"Dammit, Elyse," he swore emotionally, roughly.
)on't cry."

Her tears fell onto his jacket. She pressed her face into

his shoulder. "I can't help it. My life is such a mess now
Oh, Matt, I thought I was doing the right thing when I left."

He held her tighter. "I thought so, too." His low voic
was filled with regret.

"But I know now I made a terrible mistake." She dre
back to look at him, wiping away the tears away. "I shoul
have stayed, but I was so afraid of making things worse b
fighting with you—"

"So was I." She looked over at him, knowing she ha
heard something new in his voice just then…maybe a hi
of compromise.

They studied one another. "Maybe it was unrealistic
me to think that times of stress wouldn't create tension be
tween us," she whispered slowly. Maybe she'd wanted
second marriage that was perfect, flawless. She swallowe
hard. "What just happened with Nick, the memoria
would've upset any relationship." And yet Peter and Ab
gail had handled it well, sticking together, bolstering on
another's spirits throughout the ordeal.

Regret was etched on Matt's face. He sat back on th
edge of the conference table, guiding her down beside hir
He laced a comforting arm around her shoulders, holdi
her close against his side. "I've had time to think, too,"
said softly, baring his soul. "I realized when we were sitti
there this afternoon, listening to the hospital officials spea
that I should have respected your feelings more." He look
deep into her eyes and pinned her in place with a stea
look, wanting her to understand this much. "If it had be
anything else we were fighting about…anything less pe
sonal, less a moral issue, I would never have taken such
harsh stand or forced you to do the same." He swallowe
and went on, refusing to rehash their disagreement, adm
ting only, "I realized today that I handled it badly by a
tocratically deciding what should be done. This was a fami
matter. I should have let it be a group decision, given bo
you and my parents time to either adjust or disagree an

:onvince me to do otherwise. In any case we should have
vorked through the problem *together*.''

Elyse knew, however, that Matt would have had a very
lifficult time convincing her to do what he'd done. She
imply hadn't possessed the courage. Nor did she think,
ven in retrospect, she could have changed his views, or he
ers. They had to face the fact they wouldn't always agree;
t didn't mean the love and the caring they felt for one
nother stopped. Because if she were honest, she knew she
till loved him. Loved him deeply.

She stood and went toward him, taking his hand, drawing
im to his feet. ''You did the best you could,'' she mur-
hured softly, ''I know that.'' Her apology was in her eyes.

''And so did you,'' he assured her, his palm clasping and
ghtening over hers. Without warning Matt effortlessly
olded her back into his arms. He held her against him as
` he never wanted to let her go. Elyse leaned into him,
herishing his strength.

''But I can't help but think we could've done better,'' he
ontinued.

The hug—which had started out as simply friendly—was
eginning to feel like more than a platonic caress. Elyse
aught her breath, hope rising in her like a phoenix out of
ie ashes. She wanted to go back to where they had been
о very much. Trembling, she picked up the thread of the
onversation. ''Agreed to disagree, you mean?''

He nodded slowly, his hand stroking her hair, resting on
ie curve of her shoulder. His hand tightened on her pos-
essively; his voice was taut with suppressed emotion—and
egret. ''We should have just hung in there together,'' he
aid fiercely ''—and muddled through, no matter how hard
was.''

Elyse nodded, tears stinging her eyes. It was amazing how
uch clearer everything was in retrospect. She wanted a
econd chance. Was it possible? He'd said he didn't want
» be friends. This felt like a reconciliation, but he hadn't
aid.... Did she dare hope? Would she be a fool not to even

try? What did pride matter if they had even the slightest
hope of working things out?

Slowly she drew back to look at him. Her heart beat frantically.

"I've been trying like hell to forget you," he admitted
gruffly, a peculiar moistness shimmering in his blue eyes.

"I know," she whispered softly, the tears slipping silently
down her face.

"But nothing's working."

The knot in her throat tightened. "I know that, too," she
whispered hoarsely.

"I still love you, Elyse," he said softly, "and I've never
stopped."

"And I love you," she whispered back, hugging him
tightly. And she'd never stopped, not even for a moment.
He eased his lips over hers and kissed her gently at first,
then more passionately. When she felt his body filling with
renewed desire for her, she clasped his head with both hands
and raised it above hers. "Oh, Matt, you're everything to
me," she whispered emotionally, tears of happiness streaming down her face, "everything."

"And you're everything to me," he confessed.

She touched his cheek lovingly. "I want us to try again,"
she said softly. She knew now that the serenity she had
always searched for was tied up in one man, one love. It
was Matt for her, and no one else. And he loved her just as
deeply. Their commitment this time was real and irrevoca-
ble.

He lifted his head to look at her. Still holding her close,
he was unwilling to break the unity they had found. Softly
and solemnly he promised, "I want that, too." His voice
dropped another notch. "But this time we're going to do it
right. We're going to stay together through bad times and
good, no matter how much we disagree. If we fight like cats
and dogs, so be it. But no matter what, we'll get through—
together."

Elyse smiled and murmured her assent. She'd felt her life

was over when they'd parted; now she knew it just beginning and the possibilities for them were endless and wonderful. "You're right," she said tenderly, threading her hands through his hair. "As long as we're together we can handle anything, Matt. I know it." She knew her life would continue to have its share of challenges and problems, as would his, but with Matt by her side, they would truly be able to triumph over anything. Togetherness, yes, that was the key....

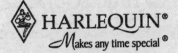

HARLEQUIN *Presents*

The world's bestselling romance series...
The series that brings you your favorite authors,
month after month:

Helen Bianchin...Emma Darcy
Lynne Graham...Penny Jordan
Miranda Lee...Sandra Marton
Anne Mather...Carole Mortimer
Susan Napier...Michelle Reid

and many more uniquely talented authors!

Wealthy, powerful, gorgeous men...
Women who have feelings just like your own...
The stories you love, set in exotic, glamorous locations...

HARLEQUIN *Presents*

Seduction and passion guaranteed!

HARLEQUIN®
INTRIGUE

WE'LL LEAVE YOU BREATHLESS!

If you've been looking for thrilling tales of
contemporary passion and sensuous love stories
with taut, edge-of-the-seat suspense—then
you'll love Harlequin Intrigue!

Every month, you'll meet four new heroes
who are guaranteed to make your spine tingle
and your pulse pound. With them you'll enter
into the exciting world of Harlequin Intrigue—
where your life is on the line
and so is your heart!

THAT'S INTRIGUE—
ROMANTIC SUSPENSE
AT ITS BEST!

HARLEQUIN®

Makes any time special ®

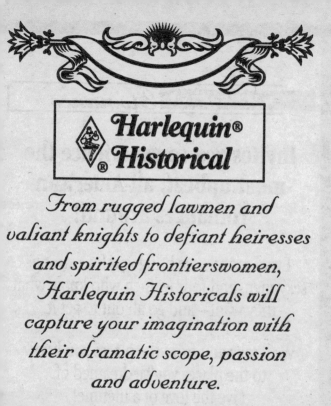

Harlequin® Historical

From rugged lawmen and valiant knights to defiant heiresses and spirited frontierswomen, Harlequin Historicals will capture your imagination with their dramatic scope, passion and adventure.

Harlequin Historicals... they're too good to miss!

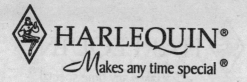

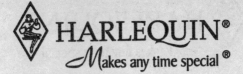

HARLEQUIN®
Makes any time special®

HARLEQUIN®
AMERICAN *Romance*
Upbeat,
All-American Romances

HARLEQUIN®
Duets™
Romantic Comedy

Harlequin® Historical
Historical,
Romantic Adventure

HARLEQUIN®
INTRIGUE
Romantic Suspense

Harlequin Romance®
Capturing the World
You Dream Of

HARLEQUIN® *Presents*
Seduction and passion
guaranteed

HARLEQUIN® *Super*ROMANCE®
Emotional,
Exciting, Unexpected

HARLEQUIN® *Temptation*
Sassy, Sexy, Seductive!